P9-CFJ-344

DORR TOWNSHIP LIBRARY (DOR)

THE STUNNING ADVENTURES OF
VLAD TALTOS

JHEREG

. . . in which your . . . . adventure, finds a faithful reptile companion.

"Engaging . . . good stuff!"   —*Publishers Weekly*

YENDI

. . . in which Vlad and his jhereg learn that a woman's love can scald a killer's blood.

"Fast-paced, action-packed!"   —*OtherRealms*

TECKLA

. . . in which two jhereg are better than one, especially during a revolution.

"Plenty of excitement!"   —*VOYA*

TALTOS

. . . in which Vlad and company walk on the wild side, the Path of the Dead.

"A breath of fresh chilly air."   —Ed Bryant, *Mile High Futures*

PHOENIX

. . . in which the Demon Goddess makes Vlad an offer he can't refuse.

"A fine, enjoyable novel . . . emotionally powerful . . . a wry sense of humor."   —*OtherRealms*

ATHYRA

. . . in which Vlad learns there are very few benefits for a retired assassin.

Continued . . .

DON'T MISS THESE OTHER NOVELS
BY STEVEN BRUST . . .

COWBOY FENG'S SPACE BAR AND GRILLE

"A great writer!"   —*OtherRealms*

"Flashes of brilliance . . . a good swift plot!"   —*Locus*

THE SUN, THE MOON, AND THE STARS

"Funny, smart and ambitious . . . A fresh, even daring approach to updating a folktale."   —*San Francisco Chronicle*

"Engaging . . . thoroughly refreshing!"   —*Publishers Weekly*

"An exciting example of how fantasy may be combined with modern themes and perceptions . . . dark and unpredictable."
—*Midwest Book Review*

"Brust stretches the boundaries of our field . . . stirs some unexpected emotions."   —*Denver Post*

"Highly experimental . . . It's my kind of book!"   —*Locus*

TO REIGN IN HELL

"Brust has let his imagination soar and created an engaging story with consummate skill and ability."   —*VOYA*

"Thoughtful and engaging . . . a well-wrought tale!"
                                        —*Minneapolis Star and Tribune*

"He tells a fantastically engaging story with consummate grace and genuine artistry."   —Roger Zelazny

BROKEDOWN PALACE

"Steven Brust has always been able to tell strongly paced, unforgettable stories. In *BROKEDOWN PALACE* he has found an authentic bardic voice to match the sweep of his tale."
                        —Jane Yolan, author of *Sister Light, Sister Dark*

"When I pick up one of Brust's books, I am never sure where I am going, but I am always glad to be along for the trip!"
                                        —Megan Lindholm, author of
                                        The Reindeer People and *Wolf's Brother*

Ace Books by Steven Brust

COWBOY FENG'S SPACE BAR AND GRILLE
THE SUN, THE MOON, AND THE STARS
TO REIGN IN HELL
BROKEDOWN PALACE

The Adventures of Vlad Taltos

JHEREG
YENDI
TECKLA
TALTOS
PHOENIX
ATHYRA

ATHYRA

STEVEN BRUST, PJF

DORR TOWNSHIP LIBRARY
1807-142nd AVE.
PO BOX 128
DORR, MI 49323

ACE BOOKS, NEW YORK

If you purchased this book without a cover, you should be aware that this book is stolen property. It was reported as "unsold and destroyed" to the publisher, and neither the author nor the publisher has received any payment for this "stripped book."

This book is an Ace original edition,
and has never been previously published.

ATHYRA

An Ace Book/published by arrangement with
the author

PRINTING HISTORY
Ace edition/April 1993

All rights reserved.
Copyright © 1993 by Steven Brust.
Cover art by Ciruelo Cabral.
This book may not be reproduced in whole or in part,
by mimeograph or any other means, without permission.
For information address: The Berkley Publishing Group,
200 Madison Avenue, New York, NY 10016.

ISBN: 0-441-03342-3

Ace Books are published by The Berkley Publishing Group,
200 Madison Avenue, New York, NY 10016.
The name "ACE" and the "A" logo
are trademarks belonging to Charter Communications, Inc.

PRINTED IN THE UNITED STATES OF AMERICA

10 9 8 7 6 5

For Martin, and it's about time

Acknowledgments

A whole bunch of people read early stages of this book and helped repair it. They are:

Susan Allison
Emma Bull
Pamela Dean
Kara Dalkey
Fred Levy Haskell
Will Shetterly
Terri Windling

As always, I'd like to humbly thank Adrian Charles Morgan, without whose work I wouldn't have a world that was nearly so much fun to write about.

Special thanks to Betsy Pucci and Sheri Portigal for supplying the facts on which I based certain portions of this book. If there are errors, blame me, not them, and, in any case, don't try this stuff at home.

PROLOGUE

WOMAN, GIRL, MAN, and boy sat together, like good companions, around a fire in the woods.

"Now that you're here," said the man, "explanations can wait until we've eaten."

"Very well," said the woman. "That smells very tasty."

"Thank you," said the man.

The boy said nothing.

The girl sniffed in disdain; the others paid no attention.

"What is it?" said the woman. "I don't recognize—"

"A bird. Should be done, soon."

"He killed it," said the girl, accusingly.

"Yes?" said the woman. "Shouldn't he have?"

"Killing is all he knows how to do."

The man didn't answer; he just turned the bird on the spit.

The boy said nothing.

"Can't you do something?" said the girl.

"You mean, teach him a skill?" said the woman. No one laughed.

"We were walking through the woods," said the girl. "Not that *I* wanted to be here—"

"You didn't?" said the woman, glancing sharply at the man. He ignored them. "He forced you to accompany him?" she said.

"Well, he didn't *force* me to, but I had to."

"Hmmm."

"And all of a sudden, I became afraid, and—"

"Afraid of what?"

"Of—well—of that place. I wanted to go a different way. But he wouldn't."

The woman glanced at the roasting bird, and nodded, recognizing it. "That's what they do," she said. "That's how they find prey, and how they frighten off predators. It's some sort of psychic ability to—"

"I don't care," said the girl.

"Time to eat," said the man.

"I started arguing with him, but he ignored me. He took out his knife and threw it into these bushes—"

"Yes," said the man. "And here it is."

"You could," said the woman, looking at him suddenly, "have just walked around it. They won't attack anything our size."

"Eat now," said the man. "We can resume the insults later."

The boy said nothing.

The woman said, "If you like. But I'm curious—"

The man shrugged. "I dislike things that play games with my mind," he said. "Besides, they're good to eat."

The boy, whose name was Savn, had remained silent the entire time.

But that was only to be expected, under the circumstances.

Chapter One

I will not marry a dung-foot peasant,
I will not marry a dung-foot peasant,
Life with him would not be pleasant.
Hi-dee hi-dee ho-la!
    Step on out and do not tarry,
    Step on back and do not tarry,
    Tell me tell me who you'll marry.
    Hi-dee hi-dee ho-la!

SAVN WAS THE first one to see him, and, come to that, the first to see the Harbingers, as well. The Harbingers behaved as Harbingers do: they went unrecognized until after the fact. When Savn saw them, his only remark was to his little sister, Polinice. He said, "Summer is almost over; the jhereg are already mating."

"What jhereg, Savn?" she said.

"Ahead there, on top of Tem's house."

"Oh. I see them. Maybe they're life-mates. Jhereg do that, you know."

"Like Easterners," said Savn, for no other reason than to show off his knowledge, because Polyi was now in her eighties and starting to think that maybe her brother didn't know everything, an attitude he hadn't yet come to terms with. Polyi didn't answer, and Savn took a last look at the jhereg, sitting on top of the house. The female was larger and becoming dark brown as summer gave way to autumn; the male was smaller and lighter in color. Savn guessed that in the spring the male would be green or grey, while the female would simply turn a lighter brown. He watched them for a moment as they sat there waiting for something to die.

They left the roof at that moment, circled Tem's house once, and flew off to the southeast.

Savn and Polyi, all unaware that Fate had sent an Omen circling above their heads, continued on to Tem's house and shared a large salad with Tem's own dressing, which somehow managed to make linseed oil tasty. Salad, along with bread and thin, salty soup, was almost the only food Tem was serving, now that the flax was being harvested, so it was just as well they liked it. It tasted rather better than the drying flax smelled, but Savn was no longer aware of the smell in any case. There was also cheese, but Tem hadn't really mastered cheeses yet, not the way old Shoe had. Tem was still young as Housemasters go; he'd barely reached his five hundredth year.

Polyi found a place where she could watch the room, and took a glass of soft wine mixed with water, while Savn had an ale. Polyi wasn't supposed to have wine, but Tem never told on her, and Savn certainly wouldn't. She looked around the room, and Savn caught her eyes returning to one place a few times, so he said, "He's too young for you, that one is."

She didn't blush; another indication that she was growing up. She just said, "Who asked you?"

Savn shrugged and let it go. It seemed like every girl in town was taken with Ori, which gave the lie to the notion that girls like boys who are strong. Ori was very fair, and as pretty as a girl, but what made him most attractive was that he never noticed the attention he got, making Savn think of Master Wag's story about the norska and the wolf.

Savn looked around the house to see if Firi was there, and was both disappointed and relieved not to see her; disappointed because she was certainly the prettiest girl in town, and relieved because whenever he even thought about speaking to her he felt he had no place to put his hands.

It was only during harvest that Savn was allowed to purchase a noon meal, because he had to work from early in the morning until it was time for him to go to Master Wag, and his parents had decided that he needed and deserved the sustenance. And because there was no good way to allow Savn to buy a lunch and deny one to his sister, who would be working at the harvest all day, they allowed her to accompany him to Tem's house on the condition that she return at once. After they had eaten, Polyi returned home while Savn continued on to Master Wag's. As he was walking away, he glanced up at the roof of Tem's house, but the jhereg had not returned.

The day at Master Wag's passed quickly and busily, with mixing herbs, receiving lessons, and keeping the Master's place tidy. The Master, who was stoop-shouldered and balding, and had eyes like a bird of prey, told Savn, for the fourth time, the story of the Badger in the Quagmire, and how he swapped places with the Clever Chreotha. Savn thought he might be ready to tell that one himself, but he didn't tell Master Wag this, because he might be wrong, and the Master had a way of mocking Savn for mistakes of overconfidence that left him red-faced for hours.

So he just listened, and absorbed, and washed the Master's clothes with water drawn from the Master's well, and cleaned out the empty ceramic pots, and helped fill them with ground or whole herbs, and looked at drawings of the lung and the heart, and stayed out of the way when a visitor came to the Master for physicking.

On the bad days, Savn found himself checking the time every half hour. On the good days, he was always surprised when the Master said, "Enough for now. Go on home." This was one of the good days. Savn took his leave, and set off. The afternoon was still bright beneath the orange-red sky.

The next thing to happen, which was really the first for our purposes, occurred as Savn was returning home. The Master lived under the shadow of Smallcliff along the Upper Brownclay River, which was half a league from the village, and of course that was where he gave Savn lessons; he was the Master, Savn only an apprentice.

About halfway between Smallcliff and the village was a place where a couple of trails came together in front of the

Curving Stone. Just past this was a flattened road leading
down to Lord Smallcliff's manor house, and it was just
there that Savn saw the stranger, who was bent over,
scraping at the road with some sort of tool.

The stranger looked up quickly, perhaps when he heard
Savn's footsteps, and cursed under his breath and looked
up at the sky, scowling, before looking more fully at the
lad. Only when the stranger straightened his back did Savn
realize that he was an Easterner. They stared at each other
for the space of a few heartbeats. Savn had never met an
Easterner before. The Easterner was slightly smaller than
Savn, but had that firm, settled look that comes with age;
it was very odd. Savn didn't know what to say. For that
matter, he didn't know if they spoke the same language.

"Good evening," said the Easterner at last, speaking like
a native, although a native of a place considerably south of
Smallcliff.

Savn gave him a good evening, too, and, not knowing
what to do next, waited. It was odd, looking at someone
who would grow old and die while you were still young.
He's probably younger than I am right now, thought Savn,
startled. The Easterner was wearing mostly green and was
dressed for traveling, with a light raincape over his shoulder and a pack on the road next to him. There was a very
fragile-looking sword at his hip, and in his hand was the
instrument he'd been digging with—a long, straight dagger. Savn was staring at it when he noticed that one of the
Easterner's hands had only four fingers. He wondered if
this was normal for them. At that moment, the stranger
said, "I hadn't expected anyone to be coming along this
road."

"Not many do," said Savn, speaking to him as if he
were human; that is, an equal. "My Master lives along this
road, and Lord Smallcliff's manor is down that one."

The stranger nodded. His eyes and hair were dark
brown, almost black, as was the thick hair that grew above
his lip, and if he were human one would have said he was
quite husky and very short, but this condition might,
thought Savn, be normal among Easterners. He was

slightly bowlegged, and he stood with his head a little forward from his shoulders, as if it hadn't been put on quite right and was liable to fall off at any moment. Also, there was something odd about his voice that the young man couldn't quite figure out.

Savn cleared his throat and said, "Did I, um, interrupt something?"

The other smiled, but it wasn't clear what sort of thought or emotion might have prompted that smile. "Are you familiar with witchcraft?" he said.

"Not very."

"It doesn't matter."

"I mean, I know that you, um, that it is practiced by—is that what you were doing?"

The stranger still wore his smile. "My name is Vlad," he said.

"I'm Savn."

He gave Savn a bow as to an equal. It didn't occur to Savn until later that he ought to have been offended by this. Then the one called Vlad said, "You are the first person I've met in this town. What is it called?"

"Smallcliff."

"Then there's a small cliff nearby?"

Savn nodded. "That way," he said, pointing back the way he'd come.

"That would make it a good name, then."

"You are from the south?"

"Yes. Does my speech give me away?"

Savn nodded. "Where in the south?"

"Oh, a number of places."

"Is it, um, polite to ask what your spell was intended to do? I don't know anything about witchcraft."

Vlad gave him a smile that was not unkind. "It's polite," he said, "as long as you don't insist that I answer."

"Oh." He wondered if he should consider this a refusal, and decided it would be safer to do so. It was hard to know what the Easterner's facial expressions meant, which was the first time Savn had realized how much he depended on these expressions to understand what people were saying. He said, "Are you going to be around here long?"

"I don't know. Perhaps. It depends on how it feels. I don't usually stay anywhere very long. But while we're on the subject, can you recommend an inn?"

Savn blinked at him. "I don't understand."

"A hostel?"

Savn shook his head, confused. "We're mostly pretty friendly here—"

"A place to spend the night?"

"Oh. Tem lets rooms to travelers."

"Good. Where?"

Savn hesitated, then said, "I'm going that way myself, if you would like to accompany me."

Vlad hesitated in his turn, then said, "Are you certain it would be no trouble?"

"None at all. I will be passing Tem's house in any case."

"Excellent. Then forward, Undauntra, lest fear snag our heels."

"What?"

"*The Tower and the Tree*, Act Two, Scene Four. Never mind. Lead the way."

As they set off along the Manor Road, Vlad said, "Where did you say you are off to?"

"I'm just coming home from my day with Master Wag. I'm his apprentice."

"Forgive my ignorance, but who is Master Wag?"

"He's our physicker," said Savn proudly. "There are only three in the whole country."

"A good thing to have. Does he serve Baron Smallcliff, too?"

"What? Oh, no," said Savn, shocked. It had never occurred to him that the Baron could fall ill or be injured. Although, now that Savn thought of it, it was certainly possible. He said, "His Lordship, well, I don't know what he does, but Master Wag is ours."

The Easterner nodded, as if this confirmed something he knew or had guessed.

"What do you do there?"

"Well, many things. Today I helped Master Wag in the preparation of a splint for Dame Sullen's arm, and reviewed the Nine Bracings of Limbs at the same time."

"Sounds interesting."

"And, of course, I learn to tell stories."

"Stories?"

"Of course."

"I don't understand."

Savn frowned, then said, "Don't all physickers tell stories?"

"Not where I'm from."

"The south?"

"A number of places."

"Oh. Well, you tell stories so the patient has something to keep his mind occupied while you physick him, do you see?"

"That makes sense. I've told a few stories myself."

"Have you? I love stories. Perhaps you could—"

"No, I don't think so. It was a special circumstance. Some fool kept paying me to tell him about my life; I never knew why. But the money was good. And he was able to convince me no one would hear about it."

"Is that what you do? Tell stories?"

The Easterner laughed slightly. "Not really, no. Lately I've just been wandering."

"To something, or away from something?"

Vlad shot him a quick glance. "An astute question. How old are you? No, never mind. What's the food like at this place you're taking me to?"

"Mostly salad this time of year. It's the harvest, you know."

"Oh, of course. I hadn't thought of that."

Vlad looked around as they walked. "I'm surprised," he remarked a little later, "that this has never been cleared for farming."

"Too wet on this side of the hill," said Savn. "The flax needs dry soil."

"Flax? Is that all you grow around here?"

"Almost. There's a little maize for the stock, but it doesn't really grow well in this soil. It's mostly flax."

"That accounts for it."

They reached the top of the hill and started down. Savn said, "Accounts for what?"

"The smell."

"Smell?"

"It must be flax oil."

"Oh. Linseed oil. I guess I must be used to it."

"That must have been what they served the last place I ate, too, half a day east of here."

"That would be Whiterock. I've been there twice."

Vlad nodded. "I didn't really notice the taste in the stew, but it made the salad interesting."

Savn thought he detected a hint of irony in the other's tone but he wasn't certain. "Some types of flax are used for cooking, some we use to make linen."

"Linen?"

"Yes."

"You cook with the same stuff you make clothes out of?"

"No, not the same. It's different."

"They probably made a mistake, then," said Vlad. "That would account for the salad."

Savn glanced back at him, but still wasn't certain if he were joking. "It's easy to tell the difference," he said. "When you make the seedblocks and leave them in the coolhouse in barrels, the true, *true* salad flax will melt—"

"Never mind," said Vlad. "I'm certain you can tell."

A pair of jhereg flew from a tree and were lost in the woods before them. Savn wondered if they might be the same pair he had seen earlier.

They came to the last hill before Tem's house. Savn said, "You never answered my question."

"Question?"

"Are you wandering to something, or away from something?"

"It's been so long, I'm not certain anymore."

"Oh. May I ask you something?"

"Certainly. I might not answer."

"If you don't tell stories, what do you *do*?"

"You mean, everyone must do something?"

"Well, yes."

"I'm not too bad a hunter."

"Oh."

"And I have a few pieces of gold, which I show around when I have to."

"You just show them around?"

"That's right."

"What does that do?"

"Makes people want to take them away from me."

"Well, yes, but—"

"And when they try, I end up with whatever they're carrying, which is usually enough for my humble needs."

Savn looked at him, again trying to decide if he were joking, but the Easterner's mouth was all but hidden beneath the black hair that grew above his lip.

Savn tore his eyes away, lest he be thought rude. "That's it below, sir," he said, wondering if he ought to say "sir" to an Easterner.

"Call me Vlad."

"All right. I hope the house is to your liking."

"I'm certain it will be fine," he said. "Spend a few weeks in the jungles and it's amazing how little it takes to feel like luxury. May I give you something?"

Savn frowned, taken by a sudden suspicion he couldn't explain. "What do you mean?"

"It is the custom of my people to give a gift to the first person we meet in a new land. It is supposed to bring luck. I don't know that I believe it, but I've taken to following the old customs anyway."

"What—?"

"Here." He reached into his pouch, found something, and held it out.

"What is it?" said Savn.

"A polished stone I picked up in my wanderings."

Savn stared at it, torn between fear and excitement. "Is it magical?"

"It's just a stone."

"Oh," said Savn. "It's a very nice green."

"Yes. Please keep it."

"Well, thank you," said Savn, still staring at it. It had been polished until it gleamed. Savn wondered how one might polish a stone, and why one would bother. He took it and put it into his pocket. "Maybe I'll see you again."

"Maybe you will," said Vlad, and entered the house. Savn wished he could go in with him, just to see the look on Tem's face when an Easterner walked through the door, but it was already dark and his family would be waiting for him, and Paener always got grumpy when he didn't get home to eat on time.

As Savn walked home, which was more than another league, he wondered about the Easterner—what he was doing here, whence he had come, whither he would go, and whether he was telling the truth about how he lived. Savn had no trouble believing that he hunted—(although how could he find game? Easterners couldn't be sorcerers, could they?), but the other was curious, as well as exciting. Savn found himself doubting it, and by the time he reached the twinkling light visible through the oiled window of home, he had convinced himself that the Easterner had been making it up.

At dinner that night Savn was silent and distracted, although neither Paener nor Maener noticed, being too tired to make small talk. His sister kept up a stream of chatter, and if she was aware of Savn's failure to contribute, she didn't say anything about it. The only time he was spoken to, when Mae asked him what he had learned that day from Master Wag, he just shrugged and muttered that he had been setting bones, after which his sister went off on another commentary about how stupid all the girls she knew were, and how annoying it was that she had to associate with them.

After dinner he helped with some of the work—the little that could be done by Paener's feeble light-spell. There was wood to be broken up into kindling (Paener and Maener chopped the big stuff—they said Savn wasn't old enough yet), there was clearing leftover feed from the kethna pens so scavengers wouldn't be attracted, and there was cleaning the tools for the next day's harvest.

When he was finished, he went out behind the small barn, sat down on one of the cutting stumps, and listened to the copperdove sing her night song from somewhere behind him. The copperdove would be leaving soon, going south until spring, taking with her the sparrow and the whiteback, the redbird and the daythief. But for the first time, Savn wondered where they went, and what it was like there. It must be too hot for them in the summer, or they'd remain there, but other than that, what was it like? Did any people live there? If so, what were *they* like? Was there a Savn who watched the birds and wondered what happened when they flew back north?

He had a sudden image of another Savn, a Savn naked to the waist and damp with sweat, staring back.

I could just go, he thought. *Not go back inside, not stop to get anything, just walk away. Find out where the copperdove goes, and who lives there, and what they're like. I could do it now.* But he knew he wouldn't. He'd stay here, and—

And what?

He suddenly thought of the jhereg he'd seen on Tem's roof. The flying reptiles were scavengers, just as, in another sense, were those of the House of the Jhereg. Savn had seen many of the animals, but none of the nobles of that House. What would it be like to encounter one?

Why am I suddenly thinking about these things?

And, *What is happening to me?* There was a sudden vertigo, so that he almost sat down, but he was afraid to move, for the instant was as wonderful as it was terrifying. He didn't want to breathe, yet he was keenly aware of doing so, of the air moving in and out of his lungs, and even filling his whole body, which was impossible. And in front of him was a great road with brick walls and a sky that was horribly black. The road went on forever, and he knew that up ahead somewhere were branches that could lead anywhere. And looming over them was the face of the Easterner he had just met, and somehow the Easterner was opening up some paths and closing others. His heart was filled with the joy of loss and the pain of opportunity.

With some part of his consciousness, he knew what was happening; some had called it Touching the Gods, and there were supposed to be Athyra mystics who spent their lives in this state. He had heard of such experiences from friends, but had never more than half-believed them. "It's like you're touching the whole world at once," said Coral. "It's like you can see all around yourself, and inside everything," said someone he couldn't remember. And it was all of these things, but that was only a small part of it.

What did it mean? Would it leave him changed? In what way? Who would he be when it was over?

And then it *was* over; gone as quickly as it had come. Around him the copperdove still sang, and the cricket harmonized. He took deep breaths and closed his eyes, trying to burn the experience into his memory so he'd be able to taste it again. What would Mae and Pae say? And Coral? Polyi wouldn't believe him, but that didn't matter. It didn't matter if anyone believed him. In fact, he wouldn't tell them; he wouldn't even tell Master Wag. This was his own, and he'd keep it that way, because he understood one thing—he could leave if he wanted to.

Although he'd never thought about it before, he understood it with every sense of his body; he had the choice of the life of a physicker in Smallcliff, or something unknown in the world outside. Which would he choose? And when?

He sat and wondered. Presently, the chill of early autumn made him shiver, and he went back inside.

Her name was Rocza, and sometimes she even answered to it.

As she flew upward, broke through the overcast, and began to breathe again, the sky turned blue—a full, livid, dancing blue, spotted with white and grey, as on the ground below were spots of other colors, and to her there was little to choose among them. The dots above were pushed about by the wind; those below by, no doubt, something much like the wind but perhaps more difficult to recognize.

She was not pushed by the wind, and neither did it carry her; rather, she slipped around it, and through it. It is said that sailors never mock the sea, yet she mocked the winds.

Her lover was calling to her from below, and it was that strange call, the call that in all the years she had never understood. It was not food, nor danger, nor muting, although it bore a similarity to all of these; it was another call entirely, a call that meant her lover wanted them to do something for the Provider. She didn't understand what bound her lover to the Provider, but bound he was, and he seemed to want it that way. It made no sense to her.

But she responded, because he had called, and because he always responded when she called. The concept of fair play did not enter her brain, yet something very much akin whispered through her thoughts as she spun, held her breath, and sliced back through the overcast, sneering at an updraft and a swirl that she did not need. Her lover waited, and his eyes gleamed in that secret way.

She saw the Provider before she scented him, but she wasn't aware of seeing, hearing, or smelling her lover; she simply knew where he was, and so they matched, and descended, and cupped the air together to land near the short, stubby, soft neck of the Provider, and await his wishes, to which they would give full attention and at least some consideration.

Chapter Two

I will not marry a serving man,
I will not marry a serving man,
All that work I could not stand.
Hi-dee hi-dee ho-la!
        Step on out . . .

THE NEXT DAY was Endweek, which Savn spent at home, making soap and using it up, as he wryly put it to himself, but he took a certain satisfaction in seeing that the windowsill and the kitchen jars sparkled in the blaze of the open stove, and the cast-iron pump over the sink gave off its dull gleam. As he cleaned, his thoughts kept returning to the experience of the night before; yet the more he thought of it, the more it slipped away from him. *Something* had certainly happened. Why didn't he feel different?

He gradually realized that he did—that, as he cleaned, he kept thinking, *This may be one of the last times I do this.* These thoughts both excited and frightened him, until he realized that he was becoming too distracted to do a good job, whereupon he did his best to put it entirely out of his mind and just concentrate on his work.

By the time he was finished, the entire cold-cellar had new ratkill and bugkill spells on it, the newer meal in the larder had been shuffled to the back, the new preserves in their pots had been stacked beneath the old, and everything was ready for the storebought they'd be returning with in the evening. His sister worked on the hearthroom, while Mae did the outside of the house and Pae cleaned the sleeping room and the loft.

His work was done by the fourteenth hour of the morning, and everyone else's within half an hour thereafter, so that shortly before noon they had a quick lunch of maize-bread and yellow pepper soup, after which they hitched Gleena and Ticky up to the wagon and set off for town. They always made the necessary stops in the same order, generally spiraling in toward Tem's house where they would have the one bought meal of the week, along with ale for Mae, Pae, and, lately, Savn, and beetwater for Polyi while they listened to the farmers argue about whether the slight dry spell would mean lower yields and poorer crops, or would, in fact, tend to make the flax hardier in the long run. Those of Savn's age would join in, listen, and occasionally make jokes calculated to make them appear clever to their elders or to those their own age of the desired sex, except for those who were apprenticed to trade, who would sit by themselves in a corner exchanging stories of what their Masters had put them through that week. Savn had his friends among this group.

The first two stops (the livery stable for the feed supplements, and the yarner for fresh bolts of linen) went as usual—they bought the feed supplements and didn't buy any linen, although Savn fingered a yarn-dyed pattern of sharply angled red and white lines against a dark green fabric, while Mae and Pae chatted with Threader about how His Lordship was staying in his manor house near Smallcliff, and Polyi looked bored. Savn knew without asking that the fabric would be too expensive to buy, and after a while they left, Mae complimenting Threader on the linen and saying they'd maybe buy something if His Lordship left them enough of the harvest.

They skipped the ceramics shop, which they often did, though as usual they drove by; Savn wasn't sure if it was from habit or just to wave at Pots, and he never thought to ask. By the time they pulled away from Hider's place, where they got a piece of leather for Gleena's girth-strap,

which was wearing out, it was past the third hour after
noon and they were in sight of both the dry goods store
and Tem's house.

There was a large crowd outside Tem's.

Mae, who was driving, stopped the cart and frowned.
"Should we see what it is?"

"They seem to be gathered around a cart," said Pae.

Mae stared for a moment longer, then clicked the team
closer.

"There's Master Wag," said Polyi, glancing at Savn as
if he would be able to provide an explanation.

They got a little closer, finally stopping some twenty
feet down the narrow street from the crowd and the cart.
Savn and Polyi stood up and craned their necks.

"It's a dead man," said Savn in an awed whisper.

"He's right," said Pae.

"Come along," said Mae. "We don't need to be here."

"But, Mae—" said Polyi.

"Hush now," said Pae. "Your mother is right. There's
nothing we can do for the poor fellow, anyway."

Polyi said, "Don't you want to know—"

"We'll hear everything later, no doubt," said Mae.
"More than we want to or need to, I'm sure. Now we need
to pick up some nails."

As they began to move, Master Wag's eyes fell on them
like a lance. "Wait a moment, Mae," said Savn. "Master
Wag—"

"I see him," said his mother, frowning. "He wants you
to go to him." She didn't sound happy.

Savn, for his part, felt both excited and nervous to suddenly discover himself the center of attention of everyone
gathered in the street, which seemed to be nearly everyone
who lived nearby.

Master Wag did not, however, leave him time to feel
much of anything. His deeply lined face was even more
grim than usual, and his protruding jaw was clenching at
regular intervals, which Savn had learned meant that he
was concentrating. The Master said, "It is time you

learned how to examine the remains of a dead man. Come along."

Savn swallowed and followed him to the horse-cart, with a roan gelding still standing patiently nearby, as if unaware that anything was wrong. On the wagon's bed was a body, on its back as if lying down to take a rest, head toward the back. The knees were bent quite naturally, both palms were open and facing up, the head—

"I know him!" said Savn. "It's Reins!"

Master Wag grunted as if to say, "I know that already." Then he said, "Among the sadder duties which befall us is the necessity to determine how someone came to die. We must discover this to learn, first, if he died by some disease that could be spread to others, and second, if he was killed by some person or animal against whom we must alert the people. Now, tell me what you see."

Before Savn could answer, however, the Master turned to the crowd and said, "Stand back, all of you! We have work to do here. Either go about your business, or stay well back. We'll tell you what we find."

One of the more interesting things about Master Wag was how his grating manner would instantly transform when he was in the presence of a patient. The corpse evidently did not qualify as a patient, however, and the Master scowled at those assembled around the wagon until they had all backed off several feet. Savn took a deep breath, proud that Master Wag had said, "We," and he had to fight down the urge to rub his hands together as if it were actually he who had "work to do." He hoped Firi was watching.

"Now, Savn," said the Master. "Tell me what you see."

"Well, I see Reins. I mean, his body."

"You aren't looking at him. Try again."

Savn became conscious once more that he was being watched, and he tried to ignore the feeling, with some success. He looked carefully at the way the hands lay, palms up, and the position of the feet and legs, sticking out at funny angles. No one would lie down like that on purpose. Both knees were slightly bent, and—

"You aren't looking at his face," said Master Wag. Savn gulped. He hadn't *wanted* to look at the face. The Master continued, "Look at the face first, always. What do you see?"

Savn made himself look. The eyes were lightly closed, and the mouth was set in a straight line. He said, "It just looks like Reins, Master."

"And what does that tell you?"

Savn tried to think, and at last he ventured, "That he died in his sleep?"

The Master grunted. "No, but that was a better guess than many you could have made. We don't know yet that he died in his sleep, although that is possible, but we know two important things. One is that he was not surprised by death, or else that he was so surprised he had no time to register shock, and, two, that he did not die in pain."

"Oh. Yes, I see."

"Good. What else?"

Savn looked again, and said, hesitantly, "There is blood by the back of his head."

"How much?"

"Very little."

"And how much do head wounds bleed?"

"A lot."

"So, what can you tell?"

"Uh, I don't know."

"Think! When will a head wound fail to bleed?"

"When . . . oh. He was dead before he hurt his head?"

"Exactly. Very good. And do you see blood anywhere else?"

"Ummm . . . no."

"Therefore?"

"He died, then fell backward, cutting open his head on the bottom of the cart, so very little blood escaped."

The Master grunted. "Not bad, but not quite right, either. Look at the bottom of the cart. Touch it." Savn did so. "Well?"

"It's wood."

"What kind of wood?"

Savn studied it and felt stupid. "I can't tell, Master. A fir tree of some kind."

"Is it hard or soft?"

"Oh, it's very soft."

"Therefore he must have struck it quite hard in order to cut his head open, yes?"

"Oh, that's true. But how?"

"How indeed? I have been informed that the horse came into town at a walk, with the body exactly as you see it. One explanation that would account for the facts would be if he were driving along, and he died suddenly, and, at the same time or shortly thereafter, the horse was startled, throwing the already dead body into the back, where it would fall just as you see it, and with enough force to break the skin over the skull, and perhaps the skull as well. If that were the case, what would you expect to see?"

Savn was actually beginning to enjoy this—to see it as a puzzle, rather than as the body of someone he had once known. He said, "A depression in the skull, and a matching one on the cart beneath his head."

"He would have had to hit very hard indeed to make a depression in the wood. But, yes, there should be one on the back of his head. And what else?"

"What else?"

"Yes. Think. Picture the scene as it may have happened."

Savn felt his eyes widen. "Oh!" He looked at the horse. "Yes," he said. "He has run hard."

"Excellent!" said the Master, smiling for the first time. "Now we can use our knowledge of Reins. What did he do?"

"Well, he used to be a driver, but since he left town I don't know."

"That is sufficient. Would Reins ever have driven a horse into a sweat?"

"Oh, no! Not unless he was desperate."

"Correct. So either he was in some great trouble, or he was not driving the horse. You will note that this fits well with our theory that death came to him suddenly and also

frightened the horse. Now, there is not enough evidence to
conclude that we are correct, but it is worthwhile to make
our version a tentative assumption while we look for more
information."

"I understand, Master."

"I see that you do. Excellent. Now touch the body."

"Touch it?"

"Yes."

"Master . . ."

"Do it!"

Savn swallowed, reached out and laid his hand lightly
on the arm nearest him, then drew back. Master Wag
snorted. "Touch the skin."

He touched Reins's hand with his forefinger, then pulled
away as if burned. "It's cold!" he said.

"Yes, bodies cool when dead. It would have been remarkable if it were not cold."

"But then—"

"Touch it again."

Savn did so. It was easier the second time. He said, "It
is very hard."

"Yes. This condition lasts several hours, then gradually
fades away. In this heat we may say that he has been dead
at least four or five hours, yet not more than half a day,
unless he died from the Cold Fever, which would leave
him in such a condition for much longer. If that had been
the cause of death, however, his features would exhibit
signs of the discomfort he felt before his death. Now, let
us move him."

"Move him? How?"

"Let's see his back."

"All right." Savn found that bile rose in his throat as he
took a grip on the body and turned it over.

"As we suspected," said the Master. "There is the small
bloodstain on the wood, and no depression, and you see
the blood on the back of his head."

"Yes, Master."

"The next step is to bring him back home, where we
may examine him thoroughly. We must look for marks and

abrasions on his body; we must test for sorcery, we must look at the contents of his stomach, his bowels, his kidneys, and his bladder; and test for diseases and poisons; and—" He stopped, looking at Savn closely, then smiled. "Never mind," he said. "I see that your Maener and Paener are still waiting for you. This will be sufficient for a lesson; we will give you some time to become used to the idea before it comes up again."

"Thank you, Master."

"Go on, go on. Tomorrow I will tell you what I learned. Or, rather, how I learned it. You will hear everything there is to hear tonight, no doubt, when you return to Tem's house, because the gossips will be full of the news. Oh, and clean your hands carefully and fully with dirt, and then water, for you have touched death, and death calls to his own."

This last remark was enough to bring back all the revulsion that Savn had first felt when laying hands on the corpse. He went down in the road and wiped his hands thoroughly and completely, including his forearms, and then went into Tem's house and begged water to wash them with.

When he emerged, he made his way slowly through the crowd that still stood around the wagon, but he was no longer the object of attention. He noticed Speaker standing a little bit away, frowning, and not far away was Lova, who Savn knew was Firi's friend, but he didn't see Firi. He returned to his own wagon while behind him Master Wag called for someone to drive him and the body back to his home.

"What is it?" asked Polyi as he climbed up next to her, among the supplies. "I mean, I know it's a body, but—"

"Hush," said Maener, and shook the reins.

Savn didn't say anything; he just watched the scene until they went around a corner and it was lost to sight. Polyi kept pestering him in spite of sharp words from Mae and Pae until they threatened to stop the wagon and thrash her, after which she went into a sulk.

"Never mind," said Pae. "We'll find out all about it

soon enough, I'm sure, and you shouldn't ask your brother to talk about his art."

Polyi didn't answer. Savn, for his part, understood her curiosity; he was wondering himself what Master Wag would discover, and it annoyed him that everyone in town would probably know before he did.

The rest of the errands took nearly four hours, during which time they learned nothing new, but were told several times that "Reins's body come into town from Wayfield." By the time the errands were over, Savn and Polyi were not only going mad with curiosity, but were certain they were dying of hunger as well. The cart had vanished from the street, but judging by the wagons in front and the loud voices from within, everyone for miles in any direction had heard that Reins had been brought into town, dead, and they were all curious about it, and had accordingly come to Tem's house to talk, listen, speculate, eat, drink, or engage in all of these at once.

The divisions were there, as always: most of the people were grouped in families, taking up the front half of the room, and beyond them were some of the apprenticed girls, and the apprenticed boys, and the old people were along the back. The only difference was that Savn had rarely, if ever, seen the place so full, even when Avin the Bard had come through. They would have found no place to sit had they not been seen at once by Haysmith, whose youngest daughter Pae had saved from wolves during the flood-year a generation ago. The two men never mentioned the incident because it would have been embarrassing to them both, but Haysmith was always looking out for Pae in order to perform small services for him. In this case, he caused a general shuffling on one of the benches, and room was made for Mae, Pae, and Polyi, where it looked as if there was no room to be found.

Savn stayed with them long enough to be included in the meal that Mae, with help from Haysmith's powerful lungs, ordered from Tem. Pae and Haysmith were speculating on whether some new disease had shown up, which launched them into a conversation about an epidemic that had cost a neighbor a son and a daughter many years before Savn had been born. When the food arrived, Savn took his ale, salad, and bread, and slipped away.

Across the room, he found his friend Coral, who was apprenticed to Master Wicker. Coral managed to make room for one more, and Savn sat down.

"I wondered when you'd arrive," said Coral. "Have you heard?"

"I haven't heard what Master Wag said about how he died."

"But you know who it was?"

"I was there while the Master was; he made it a lesson." Savn swallowed the saliva that had suddenly built up in his mouth. "It was Reins," he said, "who used to make deliveries from the Sharehouse."

"Right."

"I know he left town years ago, but I don't know where he went."

"He just went away somewhere. He came into some money or something."

"Oh, did he? I hadn't heard that."

"Well, it doesn't do him any good now."

"I guess not. What killed him?"

Coral shrugged. "No one knows. There wasn't a mark on him, they say."

"And the Master doesn't know, either? He was just going to look over the body when I had to go."

"No, he came in an hour ago and spoke with Tem, said he was as confused as anyone."

"Is he still here?" asked Savn, looking around.

"No, I guess he left right away. I didn't see him myself; I just got here a few minutes ago."

"Oh. Well, what about the b—what about Reins?"

"They've already taken him to the firepit," said Coral.

"Oh. I never heard who found him."

"From what I hear, no one; he was lying dead in the back of the cart, and the horse was just pulling the cart along the road all by itself, with no one driving at all."

Savn nodded. "And it stopped here?"

"I don't know if it stopped by itself or if Master Tem saw it coming down the road, or what."

"I wonder how he died," said Savn softly. "I wonder if we'll ever know."

"I don't know. But I'll tell you one thing—I'll give you clippings for candles that it isn't an accident that that Easterner with a sword walks into town the day before Reins shows up dead."

Savn stared. "Easterner?"

"What, you don't know about him?"

In fact, the appearance of the body had driven the strange wanderer right out of Savn's mind. He stuttered and said, "I guess I know who you mean."

"Well, there you are, then."

"You think the Easterner killed him?"

"I don't know if he killed him, but my Pae said he came from the east, and that's the same way Reins came from."

"He came from—" Savn stopped; he was about to say that he came from the south, but he changed his mind and said, "Of course he came from the east; he's an Easterner."

"Still—"

"What else do you know about him?"

"Precious little," said Coral. "Have you seen him?"

Savn hesitated, then said, "I've heard a few things."

Coral frowned at him, as if he'd noticed the hesitation, then said, "They say he came on a horse."

"A horse? I didn't see a horse. Or hear about one."

"That's what I heard. Maybe he hid it."

"Where would you hide a horse?"

"In the woods."

"Well, but *why* would you hide a horse?"

"How should I know. He's an Easterner; who knows how he thinks?"

"Well, just because he has a horse doesn't mean he had anything to do with—"

"What about the sword?"

"That's true, he does have a sword."

"There, you see?"

"But if Reins was stabbed to death, Master Wag would

have seen. So would I, for that matter. There wasn't any blood at all, except a little where his head hit the bed of the wagon, and that didn't happen until he was already dead."

"You can't know that."

"Master Wag can tell."

Coral looked doubtful.

"And there was no wound, anyway," repeated Savn.

"Well, okay, so he didn't kill him with the sword. Doesn't it mean anything that he carries one?"

"Well, maybe, but if you're traveling, you'd want to—"

"And, like I said, he did come from the east, and that's what everyone is saying."

"Everyone is saying that the Easterner killed him?"

"Well, do *you* think it's a coincidence?"

"I don't know," said Savn.

"Heh. If it is, I'll—" Savn didn't find out what Coral was prepared to do in case of a coincidence, because he broke off in mid-sentence, staring over Savn's shoulder toward the door. Savn turned, and at that moment all conversation in the room abruptly stopped.

Standing in the doorway was the Easterner, apparently quite at ease, wrapped in a cloak that was as grey as death.

Chapter Three

I will not marry a loudmouth Speaker,
I will not marry a loudmouth Speaker,
He'd get haughty and I'd get meeker.
Hi-dee hi-dee ho-la!
    Step on out . . .

HE STARED INSOLENTLY back at the room, his expression impossible to read, save that it seemed to Savn that there was perhaps a smile hidden by the black hair that grew above his lip and curled down around the corners of his mouth. After giving the room one long, thorough look, he stepped fully inside and slowly came up to the counter until he was facing Tem. He spoke in a voice that was not loud, yet carried very well. He said, "Do you have anything to drink here that doesn't taste like linseed oil?"

Tem looked at him, started to scowl, shifted nervously and glanced around the room. He cleared his throat, but didn't speak.

"I take it that means no?" said Vlad.

Someone near Savn whispered, very softly, "They should send for His Lordship." Savn wondered who "they" were.

Vlad leaned against the serving counter and folded his arms; Savn wondered if he were signaling a lack of hostility, or if the gesture meant something entirely different among Easterners. Vlad turned his head so that he was looking at Tem, and said, "Not far south of here is a cliff, overlooking a river. There were quite a few people at the river, bathing, swimming, washing clothes."

Tem clenched his jaw, then said, "What about it?"

"Nothing, really," said Vlad. "But if that's Smallcliff, it's pretty big."

"Smallcliff is to the north," said Tem. "We live *below* Smallcliff."

"Well, that would explain it, then," said Vlad. "But it is really a very pleasant view; one can see for miles. May I please have some water?"

Tem looked around at the forty or fifty people gathered in the house, and Savn wondered if he were waiting for someone to tell him what to do. At last he got a cup and poured fresh water into it from the jug below the counter.

"Thank you," said Vlad, and took a long draught.

"What are you doing here?" said Tem.

"Drinking water. If you want to know why, it's because everything else tastes like linseed oil." He drank again, then wiped his mouth on the back of his hand. Someone muttered something about, "If he doesn't like it here . . ." and someone else said something about "haughty as a lord."

Tem cleared his throat and opened his mouth, shut it again, then looked once more at his guests. Vlad, apparently oblivious to all of this, said, "While I was up there, I saw a corpse being brought along the road in a wagon. They came to a large, smoking hole in the ground, and people put the body into the hole and burned it. It seemed to be some kind of ceremony."

It seemed to Savn that everyone in the room somehow contrived to simultaneously gasp and fall silent. Tem scowled, and said, "What business is that of yours?"

"I got a good look at the body. The poor fellow looked familiar, though I'm not certain why."

Someone, evidently one of those who had brought Reins to the firepit, muttered, "I didn't see you there."

Vlad turned to him, smiled, and said, "Thank you very much."

Savn wanted to smile himself, but concealed his expression behind his hand when he saw that no one else seemed to think it was funny.

Tem said, "You knew him, did you?"

"I believe so. How did he happen to become dead?"

Tem leaned over the counter and said, "Maybe you could tell us."

Vlad looked at the Housemaster long and hard, then at the guests once more, and then suddenly he laughed, and Savn let out his breath, which he had been unaware of holding.

"So that's it," said Vlad. "I wondered why everyone was looking at me like I'd come walking into town with the three-day fever. You think I killed the fellow, and then just sort of decided to stay here and see what everyone said about it, and then maybe bring up the subject in case anyone missed it." He laughed again. "I don't really mind you thinking I'd murder someone, but I am not entirely pleased with what you seem to think of my intelligence.

"But, all right, what's the plan, my friends? Are you going to stone me to death? Beat me to death? Call your Baron to send in his soldiers?" He shook his head slowly. "What a peck of fools."

"Now, look," said Tem, whose face had become rather red. "No one said you did it; we're just wondering if you know—"

"I don't know," the Easterner said. Then added, "Yet."

"But you're going to?" said Tem.

"Very likely," he said. "I will, in any case, look into the matter."

Tem looked puzzled, as if the conversation had suddenly gone in a direction for which he couldn't account. "I don't understand," he said at last. "Why?"

The Easterner studied the backs of his hands. Savn looked at them, too, and decided that the missing finger was not natural, and he wondered how Vlad had lost it. "As I said," continued Vlad, "I think I knew him. I want to at least find out why he looks so familiar. May I please have some more water?" He dug a copper piece out of a pouch at his belt and put it on the counter, then nodded to

the room at large and made his way through the curtain in
the back of the room, presumably to return to the chamber
where he was staying.

Everyone watched him; no one spoke. The sound of his
footsteps echoed unnaturally loud, and Savn fancied that
he could even hear the rustle of fabric as Vlad pushed
aside the door-curtain, and a scraping sound from above as
a bird perched on the roof of the house.

The conversation in the room was stilted. Savn's friends
didn't say anything at all for a while. Savn looked around
the room in time to see Firi leaving with a couple of her
friends, which disappointed him. He thought about getting
up to talk to her, but realized that it would look like he
was chasing her. An older woman who was sitting behind
Savn muttered something about how the Speaker should
do something. A voice that Savn recognized as belonging
to old Dymon echoed Savn's own thought that perhaps in-
forming His Lordship that an Easterner had drunk a glass
of water at Tem's house might be considered an
overreaction. This started a heated argument about who
Tem should and shouldn't let stay under his roof. The argument ended when Dymon hooted with laughter and
walked out.

Savn noticed that the room was gradually emptying, and
he heard several people say they were going to talk to either Speaker or Bless, neither of whom was present, and
"see that something was done about this."

He was trying to figure out what "this" was when Mae
and Pae rose, collected Polyi, and approached him. Mae
said, "Come along, Savn, it's time for us to be going
home."

"Is it all right if I stay here for a while? I want to keep
talking to my friends."

His parents looked at each other, and perhaps couldn't
think of how to phrase a refusal, so they grunted permission. Polyi must have received some sort of rejection from
one of the boys, perhaps Ori, because she made no objection to being made to leave, but in fact hurried out to the

wagon while Savn was still saying goodbye to his parents and being told to be certain he was home by midnight.

In less than five minutes, the room was empty except for Tem, Savn, Coral, a couple of their friends, and a few old women who practically lived at Tem's house.

"Well," said Coral. "Isn't *he* the cheeky one?"

"Who?"

"Who do you think? The Easterner."

"Oh. Cheeky?" said Savn.

"Did you see how he looked at us?" said Coral.

"Yeah," said Lan, a large fellow who was soon to be officially apprenticed to Piper. "Like we were all grass and he was deciding if he ought to mow us."

"More like we were weeds, and not worth the trouble," said Tuk, who was Lan's older brother and was in his tenth year as Hider's apprentice. They were proud of the fact that both of them had "filled the bucket" and been apprenticed to trade.

"That's what I thought," said Coral.

"I don't know," said Savn. "I was just thinking, I sure wouldn't like to walk into a place and have everybody staring at me like that. It'd scare the blood out of my skin."

"Well, it didn't seem to disturb *him* any," said Lan.

"No," said Savn. "It didn't."

Tuk said, "We shouldn't talk about him. They say Easterners can hear anything you say about them."

"Do you believe that?" said Savn.

"It's what I've heard."

Lan nodded. "And they can turn your food bad when they want, even after you've eaten it."

"Why would he want to do that?"

"Why would he want to kill Reins?" said Coral.

"I don't think he did," said Savn.

"Why not?" said Tuk.

"Because he couldn't have," said Savn. "There weren't any marks on him."

"Maybe he's a wizard," said Lan.

"Easterners aren't wizards."

Coral frowned. "You can say what you want, I think he killed him."

"But why would he?" said Savn.

"How should I—" Coral broke off, looking around the room. "What was that?"

"It was on the roof, I think. Birds, probably."

"Yeah? Pretty big ones, then."

As if by unspoken agreement they ran to the window. Coral got there first, stuck his head out, and jerked it back in again just as fast.

"What is it?" said the others.

"A jhereg," said Coral, his eyes wide. "A big one."

"What was it doing?" said Savn.

"Just standing on the edge of the roof looking down at me."

"Huh?" said Savn. "Let me see."

"Welcome."

"Don't let its tongue touch you," said Tuk. "It's poisonous."

Savn looked out hesitantly, while Coral said, "Stand under it, but don't let it lick you."

"The gods!" said Savn, pulling his head in. "It *is* big. A female, I think. Who else wants to see?"

The others declined the honor, in spite of much urging by Savn and Coral, who, having already proven themselves, felt they wouldn't have to again. "Huh-uh," said Tuk. "They bite."

"And they spit poison," added Lan.

"They do not," said Savn. "They bite, but they don't spit, and they can't hurt you just by licking you." He was beginning to feel a bit proprietary toward them, having seen so many recently.

Meanwhile, Tem had noticed the disturbance. He came up behind them and said, "What's going on over here?"

"A jhereg," said Coral. "A big one."

"A jhereg? Where?"

"On your roof," said Savn.

"Right above the window," said Coral.

Tem glanced out, then pulled his head back in slowly,

filling the boys with equal measures of admiration and envy. "You're right," he said. "It's a bad omen."

"It is?" said Coral.

Tem nodded. He seemed about to speak further, but at that moment, preceded by a heavy thumping of boots, Vlad appeared once more.

"Good evening," he said. Savn decided that what was remarkable about his voice was that it was so normal, and it ought not to be. It should be either deep and husky to match his build, or high and fluty to match his size, yet he sounded completely human.

He sat down near where Savn and his friends had been seated and said, "I'd like a glass of wine, please."

Tem clenched his teeth like Master Wag, then said, "What sort of wine?"

"Any color, any district, any characteristics, just so long as it is wet."

The old women, who had been studiously ignoring the antics of Savn and his friends, arose as one and, with imperious glares first at the Easterner, then at Tem, stalked out. Vlad continued, "I like it better here with fewer people. The wine, if you please?"

Tem fetched him a cup of wine, which Vlad paid for. He drank some, then set the mug down and stared at it, turning it in a slow circle on the table. He appeared oblivious to the fact that Savn and his friends were staring at him.

After a short time, Coral, followed by the others, made his way back to the table. It seemed to Savn that Coral was walking gingerly, as if afraid to disturb the Easterner. When they were all seated, Vlad looked at them with an expression that was a mockery of innocence. He said, "So tell me, gentlemen, of this land. What is it like?"

The four boys looked at each other. How could one answer such a question?

Vlad said, "I mean, do bodies always show up out of nowhere, or is this a special occasion?"

Coral twitched as if stung; Savn almost smiled but caught himself in time. Tuk and Lan muttered something inaudible; then, with a look at Coral and Savn, they got up and left. Coral hesitated, stood up, looked at Savn, started to say something, then followed his friends out the door.

Vlad shook his head. "I seem to be driving away business today. I really don't mean to. I hope Goodman Tem isn't unhappy with me."

"Are you a wizard?" said Savn.

Vlad laughed. "What do you know about wizards?"

"Well, they live forever, and you can't hurt them because they keep their souls in magic boxes without any way inside, and they can make you do things you don't want to do, and—"

Vlad laughed again. "Well, then I'm certainly not a wizard."

Savn started to ask what was funny; then he caught sight of Vlad's maimed hand, and it occurred to him that a wizard wouldn't have allowed that to happen.

After an uncomfortable silence, Savn said, "Why did you say that?"

"Say what?"

"About . . . bodies."

"Oh. I wanted to know."

"It was cruel."

"Was it? In fact, I meant the question. It surprises me to walk into a place like this and find that a body has followed me in. It makes me uncomfortable. It makes me curious."

"There have been others who noticed it, too."

"I'm not surprised. And whispers about me, no doubt."

"Well, yes."

"What exactly killed him?"

"No one knows."

"Oh?"

"There was no mark on him, at any rate, and my friends told me that Master Wag was puzzled."

"Is Master Wag good at this sort of thing?"

"Oh, yes. He could tell if he died from disease, or if someone beat him, or if someone cast a spell on him, or anything. And he just doesn't know yet."

"Hmmm. It's a shame."

Savn nodded. "Poor Reins. He was a nice man."

"Reins?"

"That was his name."

"An odd name."

"It wasn't his birth name; he was just called that because he drove."

"Drove? A coach?"

"No, no; he made deliveries and such."

"Really. That starts to bring something back."

"Bring something back?"

"As I said, I think I recognize him. I wonder if I could be near . . . who is lord of these lands?"

"His Lordship, the Baron."

"Has he a name?"

"Baron Smallcliff."

"And you don't know his given name?"

"I've heard it, but I can't think of it at the moment."

"How about his father's name? Or rather, the name of whoever the old Baron was?"

Savn shook his head.

Vlad said, "Does the name 'Loraan' sound familiar?"

"That's it!"

Vlad chuckled softly. "That is almost amusing."

"What is?"

"Nothing, nothing. And was Reins the man who used to make deliveries to Loraan?"

"Well, Reins drove everywhere. He made deliveries for, well, for just about everyone."

"But did his duties take him to the Baron's keep?"

"Well, I guess they must have."

Vlad nodded. "I thought so."

"Hmmm?"

"I used to know him. Only very briefly I'm afraid, but still—"

Savn shook his head. "I've never seen you around here before."

"It wasn't quite around here; it was at Loraan's keep rather than his manor house. The keep, if I recall the landscape correctly, must be on the other side of the Brownclay."

"Yes, that's right."

"And I didn't spend much time there, either." Vlad smiled as he said this, as if enjoying a private joke. Then he said, "Who is Baron now?"

"Who? Why, the Baron is the Baron, same as always."

"But after the old Baron died, did his son inherit?"

"Oh. I guess so. That was before I was born."

The Easterner's eyes widened, which seemed to mean the same thing in an Easterner that it did in a human. "Didn't the old Baron die just a few years ago?"

"Oh, no. He's been there for years and years."

"You mean Loraan is the Baron *now*?"

"Of course. Who else? I thought that's what you meant."

"My, my, my." Vlad tapped the edge of his wine cup against the table. After a moment he said, "If he died, are you certain you'd know?"

"Huh? Of course I'd know. I mean, people see him, don't they? Even if he doesn't appear around here often, there's still deliveries, and messengers, and—"

"I see. Well, this is all very interesting."

"What is?"

"I had thought him dead some years ago."

"He isn't dead at all," said Savn. "In fact, he just came to stay at his manor house, a league or so from town, near the place I first saw you."

"Indeed?"

"Yes."

"And that isn't his son?"

"He isn't married," said Savn.

"How unfortunate for him," said Vlad. "Have you ever actually seen him?"

"Certainly. Twice, in fact. He came through here with his retainers, in a big coach, with silver everywhere, and six horses, and a big Athyra embossed in—"

"Were either of these times recent?"

Savn started to speak, stopped, and considered. "What do you mean 'recent'?"

Vlad laughed. "Well taken. Within, say, the last five years?"

"Oh. No."

The Easterner took another sip of his wine, set the cup down, closed his eyes, and, after a long moment, said, "There is a high cliff over the Lower Brownclay. In fact, there is a valley that was probably cut by the river."

"Yes, there is."

"Are there caves, Savn?"

He blinked. "Many, all along the walls of the cliff. How did you know?"

"I knew about the valley because I saw it, earlier today, and the river. As for the caves, I didn't know; I guessed. But now that I do know, I would venture a further guess that there is water to be found in those caves."

"There's water in at least one of them; I've heard it trickling."

Vlad nodded. "It makes sense."

"*What* makes sense, Vlad?"

"Loraan was—excuse me—is a wizard, and one who has studied necromancy. It would make sense that he lived near a place where Dark Water flows."

"Dark Water? What is that?"

"Water that has never seen the light of day."

"Oh. But what does that have to do with—what was his name?"

"Loraan. Baron Smallcliff. Such water is useful in the practice of necromancy. When stagnant and contained, it can be used to weaken and repel the undead, but when flowing free they can use it to prolong their life. It's a bittersweet tapestry of life itself," he added, in what Savn thought was an ironic tone of voice.

"I don't understand."

"Never mind. Would it matter to you if you were to discover that your lord is undead?"

"*What?*"

"I'll take that as a yes. Good. That may matter, later."

"Vlad, I don't understand—"

"Don't worry about it; that isn't the important thing."

"You seem to be talking in riddles."

"No, just thinking aloud. The important thing isn't how he survived; the important thing is what he knows. Aye, what he knows, and what he's doing about it."

Savn struggled to make sense of this, and at last said, "What he knows about what?"

Vlad shook his head. "There are such things as coincidence, but I don't believe one can go that far." Savn started to say something, but Vlad raised his hand. "Think of it this way, my friend: many years ago, a man helped me to pull a nasty joke on your Baron. Now, on the very day I come walking through his fief, the man who helped me turns up mysteriously dead right in front of me. And the victim of this little prank moves to his manor house, which happens to be just outside the village I'm passing through. Would you believe that this could happen by accident?"

The implications of everything Vlad was saying were too many and far-reaching, but Savn was able to understand enough to say, "No."

"I wouldn't, either. And I don't."

"But what does it mean?"

"I'm not certain," Vlad said. "Perhaps it was foolish of me to come this way, but I didn't realize exactly where I was, and, in any case, I thought Loraan was . . . I thought it would be safe. Speaking of safe, I guess what it means is that I'm not, very."

Savn said, "You're leaving, then?" He was surprised to discover how disappointed he was at the thought.

"Leaving? No. It's probably too late for that. And besides, this fellow, Reins, helped me, and if that had anything to do with his death, that means I have matters to attend to."

Savn struggled with this, and at last said, "What matters?"

But Vlad had fallen silent again; he stared off into space, as if taken by a sudden thought. He sat that way for nearly a minute, and from time to time his lips seemed to move. At last he grunted and nodded faintly.

Savn repeated his question. "What matters will you have to attend to?"

"Eh?" said Vlad. "Oh. Nothing important."

Savn waited. Vlad leaned back in his chair, his eyes open but focused on the ceiling. Twice the corner of his mouth twitched as if he were smiling; once he shuddered as if something frightened him. Savn wondered what he was thinking about. He was about to ask, when Vlad's head suddenly snapped down and he was looking directly at Savn.

"The other day, you started to ask me about witchcraft."

"Well, yes," said Savn. "Why—"

"How would you like to learn?"

"Learn? You mean, how to, uh—"

"We call it casting spells, just like sorcerers do. Are you interested?"

"I'd never thought about it before."

"Well, think about it."

"Why would you want to teach me?"

"There are reasons."

"I don't know."

"Frankly, I'm surprised at your hesitation. It would be useful to me if someone knew certain spells. It doesn't have to be you; I just thought you'd want to. I could find someone else. Perhaps one of those young men—"

"All right."

Vlad didn't smile; he just nodded slightly and said, "Good."

"When should we begin?"

"Now would be fine," said the Easterner, and rose to his feet. "Come with me."

She flew above and ahead of her mate, in long, wide, overlapping circles just below the overcast. He was content to follow, because her eyesight was keener.

In fact, she knew exactly what she was looking for, and could have gone directly there, but it was a fine, warm day for this late in the year, and she was in no hurry to carry out the Provider's wishes. There was time for that; there had been no sense of urgency in the dim echo she had picked up, so why not enjoy the day?

Above her, a lazy falcon broke through the overcast, saw her, and haughtily ignored her. She didn't mind; they had nothing to argue about until the falcon made a strike; then they could play the old game of You're-quicker-going-down-but-I'm-faster-going-up. She'd played that game several times, and usually won. She had lost once to a cagey old goshawk, and she still carried the scar above her right wing, but it no longer bothered her.

She came into sight of a large structure of man, and her mate, who saw it at the same time, joined her, and they circled it once together. She thought that, in perhaps a few days, she'd be ready to mate again, but it was so hard to find a nest while traveling all the time.

Her mate sent her messages of impatience. She gave the psychic equivalent of a sigh and circled down to attend to business.

Chapter Four

I will not marry a magic seer,
I will not marry a magic seer,
He'd know how to keep me here.
Hi-dee hi-dee ho-la!
    Step on out . . .

SAVN HAD THOUGHT they would be going into Vlad's room, but instead the Easterner led them out onto the street. There was still some light, but it was gradually fading, the overcast becoming more red than orange, and accenting the scarlet highlights on the bricks of Shoe's old house across the way. There were a few people walking past, but they seemed intent on business of their own; the excitement of a few short hours before had evaporated like a puddle of water on a dry day. And those who were out seemed, as far as Savn could tell, intent on ignoring the Easterner.

Savn wondered why he wasn't more excited about the idea of learning Eastern magic, and came to the conclusion that it was because he didn't really believe it would happen. *Well, then,* he asked himself, *why not? Because,* came the answer, *I don't know this Easterner, and I don't understand why he would wish to teach me anything.*

"Where are we going?" he said aloud.

"To a place of power."

"What's that?"

"A location where it is easier to stand outside and inside of yourself and the other."

Savn tried to figure out which question to ask first. At last he said, "The other?"

"The person or thing you wish to change. Witchcraft—magic—is a way of changing things. To change you must understand, and the best way to understand is to attempt change."

"I don't "

"The illusion of understanding is a product of distance and perspective. True understanding requires involvement."

"Oh," said Savn, putting it away for a later time to either think about or not.

They were walking slowly toward the few remaining buildings on the west side of the village; Savn consciously held back the urge to run. Now they were entirely alone, save for voices from the livery stable, where Feeder was saying, "So I told him I'd never seen a kethna with a wooden leg, and how did it happen that . . ." Savn wondered who he was talking to. Soon they were walking along the Manor Road west of town. Savn said, "What makes a place of power?"

"Any number of things. Sometimes it has to do with the terrain, sometimes with things that have happened there or people who have lived there; sometimes you don't know why it is, you just feel it."

"So we're going to keep walking until you feel it?" Savn discovered that he didn't really like the idea of walking all night until they came to a place that "felt right" to the Easterner.

"Unless you know a place that is likely to be a place of power."

"How would I know that?"

"Do you know of any place where people were sacrificed?"

Savn shuddered. "No, there isn't anything like that."

"Good. I'm not certain we want to face that in any

event. Well, is there any powerful sorcerer who lives nearby?"

"No. Well, you said that Lord Smallcliff is."

"Oh, yes, I did, didn't I? But it would be difficult to reach the place where he works, which I assume to be on the other side of the river, at his keep."

"Not at his manor?"

"Probably not. Of course, that's only a guess; but we can hardly go to his manor either, can we?"

"I guess not. But someplace he worked would be a place of power?"

"Almost certainly."

"Well, but what about the water he used?"

"The water? Oh, yes, the Dark Water. What about it?"

"Well, if he found water in the caves—"

"The caves? Of course, the caves! Where are they?"

"Not far. It's about half a league to Bigcliff, and then halfway down the slip and along the path."

"Can you find it in this light?"

"Of course."

"Then lead the way."

Savn at once abandoned the road in order to cut directly toward the hills above Bigcliff, finding his way by memory and feel in the growing darkness. "Be careful along here," he said as they negotiated the slip that cut through the hill. "The gravel is loose, and if you fall you can hurt yourself."

"Yes."

They came to the narrow but level path toward the caves, and the going became easier. Savn said, "Remember when you told me about how you encourage bandits to attack you?"

"Yes."

"Were you, uh, were you jesting with me?"

"Not entirely," said Vlad. "In point of fact, I've only done that once or twice, so I suppose I was exaggerating a bit."

"Oh."

"What makes you ask?"

"I was just wondering if that was why you carry a sword."

"I carry a sword in case someone tries to hurt me."

"Yes, but I mean, was that the idea? Is that why you do it, so these bandits—"

"No, I carried it long before that."

"But then why—"

"As I said, in case someone tries to hurt me."

"Did that ever happen? I mean, before?"

"Someone trying to hurt me? Yes."

"What did you do?"

"Sometimes I fought. Sometimes I ran."

"Have you ever . . . I mean—"

"I'm still alive; that ought to tell you something."

"Oh. Is that how—I mean, your hand . . ."

Vlad glanced down at his left hand, as if he'd forgotten he had one. "Oh, yes. If someone is swinging a sword at you, and you are unarmed, it is possible to deflect the blade with your hand by keeping your palm exactly parallel with the flat of the blade. Your timing has to be perfect. Also, you ought to remember to keep your pinkie out of the way."

Savn winced in sympathy and decided not to ask for more details. A little later, he ventured, "Isn't the sword annoying to carry?"

"No. In any case, I used to carry a great deal more."

"More what?"

"More steel."

"Why?"

"I was living in a more dangerous place."

"Where was that?"

"Adrilankha."

"You've been there?"

"Yes, indeed. I've lived most of my life there."

"I'd like to see Adrilankha."

"I hope you do."

"What's it like?"

"It's what you make of it. It is a thousand cities. It is a place where there are more noblemen than Teckla, it seems. It is a place of ease, luxury, and sudden violence, depending on where you are and who you are. It is a place of wishes fulfilled, and of permanent longing. It is like everywhere else, I think."

They began climbing up toward the caves. "Did you like it there?"

"Yes."

"Why did you leave?"

"Some people wanted to kill me."

Savn stopped, turned, and tried to look at Vlad's face to see if he was joking, but it was too dark to be certain. It was, in fact, almost too dark to walk safely. Vlad stopped behind him, waiting. There was a flapping sound overhead. Savn couldn't tell what sort of bird it was, but it sounded big. "We should get to the caves," he said after a moment.

"Lead on."

Savn did so. They came up the rise toward the first one, which was shallow and led nowhere interesting, so he ignored it. He said, "Have you really killed people?"

"Yes."

"Was there really someone in Adrilankha who wanted to kill you?"

"Yes."

"That must be scary."

"Only if they find me."

"Are they still looking for you?"

"Oh, yes."

"Do you think they'll find you?"

"I hope not."

"What did you do?"

"I left."

"No, I mean, why do they want to kill you?"

"I annoyed some business associates."

"What kind of business were you in?"

"One thing and another."

"Oh."

"I hear water from below."

"The river flats. That's where the people from Brownclay and Bigcliff go to bathe and wash clothes."

"Ah, yes. I was there earlier; I hadn't realized we were in the same place. This must be Bigcliff, then."

"Yes."

"You say you know a cave that has water in it?"

"One of the deep ones. That's where I'm taking us."

"Very good. It sounds like just what we're looking for."

"What will we do there?"

"You'll see."

"Okay. This is it. It goes way back, and down, and the further down you go, the wetter the walls get, and I remember once we heard water trickling below us, though we didn't actually find it."

"Excellent. Let's see what it looks like."

The immediate area filled with a soft, yellow light, displaying the weed-covered rocks. Savn said, "Was that witchcraft?"

"No, sorcery."

"Oh. My Paener could have done that, then."

"Yes. Let's go in."

The entrance to the cave was narrow and low, so that it would have been difficult to find even in the daylight if Savn had not known where it was. He pointed it out to Vlad, who bent over and caused his sorcerous light to fill the entrance. This was followed by the sounds of small animals, disturbed from their rest, who scurried off to find hiding places.

"Best not to know what they are," said Vlad.

"I agree," said Savn, and led the way into the cave.

At once it opened up, and in the sourceless, hazy light it appeared rather bigger than Savn remembered. He was very aware of the sound of their soft boots, and even the sound of his own breathing.

"Can you make light with witchcraft?"

"I don't know," said Vlad. "I've never tried. It's easier to bring torches. Which way?"

"Are you sure you want to go deeper, Vlad?"

"Yes."

"This way, then."

The pale light moved with them, growing brighter in small spaces, then more dim as they entered larger ones.

After a while, Savn said, "Do you want to go all the way down to the water?"

"If we can. It is certain to be a place of power."

"Why?"

"Because Lord Smallcliff used it. Even if it weren't before, it would be when he was done. He's like that."

"This is as far as I've ever gone."

"Bide, then."

Savn waited, listening to the flapping of bat wings, while Vlad's eyes narrowed, then widened slightly as he shook his head, and at last he moved his lips as if uttering an incantation. "All right," he said at last. "It's safe. If we climb over this ledge, crawl that way about forty feet, and drop down, we'll fall about five feet and land on a flat surface."

"How do you know?"

"That's what you've come here to learn, isn't it?"

"Was that witchcraft?"

"Yes and no. Without the Art, I couldn't have done it."

"And you're certain—"

"Yes."

Savn hesitated a moment, but Vlad, without waiting, went over the indicated ledge, actually a narrow slit in the rock wall which was barely large enough for them, and began creeping along it. Savn became aware that he'd been hearing the gurgling of water for some few minutes. He followed the Easterner; then, at the same place Vlad did, he hung over the edge and let go, landing easily. The sound of trickling water was louder as he landed. The yellow light grew until it faintly illuminated a large cavern, with a dark, narrow stream, perhaps four feet wide, making its leisurely way back into the hill.

"Is this the place?" said Savn, hearing his words come back to him. "Or should we go further in?"

"What do you think?" said Vlad.

"I don't know."

"Can you feel anything?"

"What do you mean?"

"Open yourself up to sensation. Do you feel power?"

Savn closed his eyes, and tried to feel something happening. There was a slight chill on his skin, and a soft whisper of wind against his ears, but that was all. "No," he said. "But I don't really know what I'm supposed to be feeling."

"Let's try it here, then. Sit down on that rock. Take my cloak and fold it up behind your head so you can lean back."

Savn did these things. "Now what?"

"Relax."

He tried to settle back into the unusual position, with only some success.

"Can you feel your scalp? The top of your head? No, I don't mean touch it. Put your hands back in your lap. Now, can you feel the top of your head? Think of your scalp relaxing. Imagine each hair on your head relaxing. Your temples, your ears, your forehead, your eyes, your cheeks, your jaw. One at a time, try to relax each of these muscles. Now the back of your neck. Feel your head sink into the cloak, pretend you are falling into the wall behind you. . . ."

Sometime later, Vlad said, "How do you feel?"

Savn realized that a great deal of time had passed, but he didn't know how much, nor what had occurred during that time. "I feel good," he said, surprised to discover it. "Like I'm, I don't know, alive."

"Good. You took to it well."

"You mean I'm a witch now?"

"No, that was only the first step, to prepare your mind for the journey."

"It feels great."

"I know."

"What do we do next?"

"Next, we get you home. It's late."

"Is it?" Savn reached for the time and blanched. "The gods! I had no idea—"

"Don't worry about it."

"Mae and Pae—"

"I'll speak to them."

"But they—" He bit off his words. He'd been about to say they wouldn't listen to an Easterner, then realized there was no polite way to say it. In any case, Vlad would find out for himself soon enough.

The Easterner did not appear to notice. He made a sign for Savn to approach, and when he was there, he clenched his fist, screwed his face up, and Savn found himself once more in Smallcliff, on the north side of town, barely able to make out his surroundings in the faint yellow radiance that Vlad continued to produce.

"You teleported us!" he cried.

"I know you live out somewhere in this direction, and this is the only place I knew well enough to—"

"But you teleported us!"

"Well, yes. You said you were late. I hope you don't mind."

"No, no, but I don't know anyone who is good enough to do that."

"It isn't all that difficult."

"You're a sorcerer."

"Well, yes, among other things."

Savn stared at him, his eyes wide, until he realized that he was being rude. Vlad just smiled back at him, then said, "Come. I don't know where you live, so we're going to have to walk the rest of the way."

Stunned, Savn set off along the deserted road. He said, "How do you teleport? I've heard of it—"

"It isn't that hard; you just have to be certain you know exactly where you're going. The tricky part is not getting sick afterwards, and for that there is witchcraft."

"But how do you know where you'll end up?"

"You have to remember it very well—perfectly, in fact. It's the remembering that allows the journey to take place."

"What if you can't remember it that well?"

"Then you're in trouble."

"But—"

"Sometimes you can prepare a place to teleport to. It limits you, but it's good if you're in a hurry."

"Can you teach me all this?"

"Maybe. We'll see. Where is your house?"

"On the other side of this hill, but we should take the road around, because the flax here hasn't been harvested yet."

"Very well."

Vlad seemed to have no trouble finding the road up to the house, though whether this was because Easterners had better night vision, or because of his magical powers, or for some other reason entirely, Savn didn't know and couldn't decide on a good way to ask, so he ended by saying nothing, and they spoke no more until they stood before the one-room house, with its single door held on with straps, and two windows covered with oiled paper. There was a pale yellow light from the lamps and the stove.

"Nice place," said Vlad.

"Thank you," said Savn, who had been thinking how small and plain it must look to someone who had lived in Adrilankha.

They had, evidently, been seen, because just before they reached the door it flew open so hard that Savn thought it would tear off its leather hinges, and there were Mae and Pae, silhouetted in the soft glow of the stove. They stood almost motionless, and while Savn couldn't see the expressions on their faces, his imagination had no trouble supplying Mae's wide-eyed anger and Pae's annoyed confusion.

As they stepped forward, Mae said, "Who are you?" which puzzled Savn for a moment, until he realized to whom she was speaking.

"Vlad. You saw me earlier today, at Tem's house."

"*You.* What have you been doing with my son?"

"Teaching him," said Vlad.

"Teaching him?" said Pae. "And what is it you think you'll be teaching my boy?"

Vlad answered in a soft, gentle voice, much different

than Savn had ever heard him use before. "I've been
teaching him to hear the voices of the stones," he said,
"and to see prophecy in the movement of the clouds. To
catch the wind in his hand and to bring forth gems from
the dunes of the desert. To freeze air and to burn water. To
live, to breathe, to walk, to sample the joy on each road,
and the sorrow at each turning. I'm sorry if I've kept him
out too late. I shall be more careful in the future. No doubt
I will see you again. I bid you all a good evening."

Mae and Pae stood there against the light, watching the
Easterner's back as his grey cloak faded into the night.
Then Pae said, "In all my life, I never—"

"Hush now," said Mae. "Let's get this one to bed."

Savn wasn't sure what Vlad had done, but they didn't
say a word more about the hour, or about what he'd been
doing. He went over to his corner under the loft, spread
his furs out, and climbed in underneath them without saying another word.

That night, he dreamed of the cave, which, upon waking, he did not find surprising. In the dream, the cave was
filled with smoke, which, at least as he remembered it,
kept changing color, and a jhereg kept flying out of it and
speaking in Vlad's voice, saying, "Wait here," and, "You
will feel well-rested, alert, and strong," and other things
which he didn't remember.

The dream must have had some effect, however, for
when he did wake up he felt refreshed and ready. As he
prepared for the day he realized with some annoyance that
he would have to spend several hours harvesting, and then
several more with Master Wag, before he had the chance
to find Vlad again and, he hoped, continue where they had
left off.

He forgot his annoyance, however, after the morning
harvest, when he arrived at the Master's, because the Master was in one of his touchy moods, and Savn had to concentrate on not giving him an excuse for a tongue-lashing.
He spent most of the day listening to an oft-repeated rant
to the effect that no one dies without a reason, so Reins
couldn't have, either. Apparently Master Wag had been un-

able to find this reason, and was consequently upset with himself, Savn, Reins, and the entire world. The only time he seemed pleasant was while scratching Curry's left arm with the thorn of the blister plant to treat his fever, and even then Savn knew he was in a foul temper, because he simply did it, without giving Savn the lecture that usually accompanied treatment.

After the fifth rant on the subject of causeless death, Savn ventured, "Could it have been sorcery?"

"Of course it could have been sorcery, idiot. But sorcery *does* something, and whatever it did would leave traces."

"Oh. What about witchcraft?"

"Eh?"

"Could a witch—"

"What do you know about witchcraft?"

"Nothing," said Savn honestly. "That's why I don't know if—"

"If a witch can do anything at all beyond fooling the gullible, which I doubt, then whatever he did would leave traces, too."

"Oh."

Master Wag started to say more, then scowled and retreated into the cellar, where he kept his herbs, splints, knives, and other supplies, and where, presumably, he kept the pieces of Rein's skin, bone, and hair that he had preserved in order to determine what had happened. Savn felt queasy considering this.

He looked around for something to do in order to take his mind off it, but he'd already cleaned everything in sight, and memorized the Tale of the Man Who Ate Fire so well that the Master had been unable to do anything but grunt upon hearing Savn's recitation.

He sat down next to the window, realized it was too cold, discovered that he still had at least another hour before he could go home, and put some more wood onto the fire. It crackled pleasantly. He walked around the room, looking over the Master's collection of books, including *On the Number of the Parts of the Body*, *Knitting of Bones*, *The Sorcerer's Art and the Healing of the Self*, *The*

Remembered Tales of Calduh, and the others which the Master had consulted from time to time in healing patients or instructing Savn. One book that he had never seen the Master consult was called *The Book of the Seven Wizards*, a thick, leather-bound volume with the title in gold lettering on the spine. He took it down, went over by the fire, and let it fall open.

It had been written in a neat, even hand, as if the scribe, probably a Lyorn, had attempted to remove all traces of his own personality. The pages were rather thicker than the leaves of many books, and in good condition. It occurred to Savn that Master Wag probably knew a spell to preserve books, so this one could be of any age. At the top of the page, he read: "On the Nature of Secrets."

He wondered if it were some sort of sign that it had fallen open in that spot—if, in fact, there were some sort of secret to be discovered. Probably not, he decided.

The book told him:

> Be aware of power in hidden places, and be aware of that which is apparent, for secrets may lie open to view and yet be concealed. All of the Seven Wizards know of secrets, and each, in his own way, speaks of them, calls to them, and reveals them to those who search diligently and honestly.

Diligently and honestly? he thought. Well, that could be said of everything. What about thoroughly? He turned his eyes back to the book and read:

> She Who Is Small finds the secrets of the present in the past; that when the past is known, it is the power of the mage to find Truth in Mystery; that thus is the latter transformed into the former.

It seemed to Savn that he knew very little of the past, and that there must be many secrets indeed that he could discover if he turned to history. He wondered how Master

Wag would feel if he asked for a history book. Not today, in any case.

He turned back to the book and read:

> She Who Is Tall says that the secret is in the song, and opens only to one who dares to sing. It is said that when she sings, the secret is plain to all who listen, but that it is hidden again when the song is past, and few are those who are blessed to hear the echoes of Truth in the Silence that follows.

Well, he liked music well enough, and he liked singing, but there was probably some sort of mystical and powerful meaning in the passage, which he didn't understand. He shrugged.

The next paragraph read:

> She Whose Hair Is Red wraps the secret ever tighter in skeins of words, so that it vanishes as if it never were, and in these layers of words the secret emerges, shining, so that it is hidden to those who look, yet revealed to those who take joy in the unfolding patterns and sounds of words.

There was certainly some mystical and powerful significance to this, and he certainly didn't understand it. He tried to visualize something being wrapped up in words, but all he got was an image of the black lettering from the book, removed from the page, attaching itself to some undefined thing and smothering it.

He read:

> He Whose Eyes Are Green knows where the secret lies, for his eyes pierce every shadowy place; yet he no sooner finds the secret than he buries it anew. But it is said that in the burying the secret has changed, while that which was hidden walks the land ever after, waiting but for one to recognize it, and offer it refuge.

That didn't make any sense at all. If he knew where the
secrets were, why did he want to hide them? And who
were these wizards, anyway?

The book went on:

> He Whose Hair Is Dark laughs at secrets, for his
> pleasure is in the search, not the discovery—and the
> paths he follows in this search stem from whim, not
> from plan. Some say that in this way he reveals as
> many as another.

That almost made sense. Savn could imagine how it
might be more fun to look for something than to actually
find it. He wondered if there was something he was looking for, or something he *should* look for. The secret to
Reins's death? But he could hardly expect to find that if
Master Wag couldn't.

He continued reading:

> Of the Gentle One it is said that she sets down the
> order and method of all things, and that, in this way,
> all hidden things may be found. To her, each detail is
> a signpost, and when each is placed in its own posi-
> tion, the outline of the secret will be laid bare for any
> who will look.

Well, that was certainly possible, thought Savn. But
what do you do when you don't know anything?

There was one more passage on the page:

> The Master of Rhyme still searches for the Way of
> the Wizards, for to him, this is the greatest Secret of all.
> Yet, as he searches, he lets fall Truths for all of those
> who come after, and in this he sees no miracle, for
> what is plain to one is a Secret to the next. He is often
> praised for this, but it is meaningless to him, for who
> among Men will rejoice in finding Truth that he has
> never thought hidden?

Savn frowned. That, too, almost made sense. It was as if you could see something, and maybe someone else couldn't, but to you it wasn't anything to get excited about, because it was right there all the time.

It occurred to him to wonder if there were things right in front of him that *he* couldn't see. He was pondering this when Master Wag returned and said, "What are you reading?"

Savn showed him the book. The Master snorted. "There's nothing in there you need, at least not yet. Why don't you go home?"

Savn didn't need to be given this suggestion twice. He put the book on the shelf, said farewell, and dashed out the door before the Master could change his mind.

He raced to Tem's house, expecting to see Vlad either lounging outside or in the common room, but the Easterner was not in evidence. As he stood there, wondering whether he dared to ask Tem which room Vlad was in, his sister walked through the door, accompanied by two of her friends, which caused him, for reasons he couldn't quite specify, to abandon this plan.

She came up to him at once and pulled him into a corner. "What happened to you last night?"

"What do you mean?"

"You were gone forever. Mae and Pae were going crazy. I finally went to bed, and when I got up this morning and asked if you'd shown up, they looked at me like they didn't know what I was talking about and said that you were already up and out."

"Well, I was."

"That's not the point, chag-brain."

"Don't call me chag-brain."

"Where *were* you?"

"Exploring the caves."

"At *night*?"

"Sure. Why not?"

"But why were you so late?"

"I lost track of time."

She frowned at him, clearly unsatisfied with the answer,

but uncertain how to find out more. "Well, then," she said, "don't you think Mae and Pae were acting a little strange, the way they were so worried at first, and then—"

"Oh, you know how they get. Look, I'll talk to you later, all right? I have to go."

"Go where? Savn, stop it. Don't you dare go running off like that! Savn . . ."

Her voice followed him out the door, but he paid no attention. The only place he could think of to find Vlad was back at the caves, so he set off for them at once. He followed the Manor road for the first mile, then cut across to the slip. As he was about to start down it, however, he saw, some distance away, a grey-clad figure standing on the cliff itself. He broke into a run, and at about the same moment he became convinced that it was indeed Vlad, the Easterner turned and waved to him, as if he'd known he was there.

When he reached him, he said nothing, only stopped to recover his breath. Vlad stood, staring out at the river flats so far below them, dotted with people bathing, washing clothes, or just talking. Savn tried to view the scene as if it were new; the river rushing in from the right, turning sharply around the Black Rocks, foaming white, then suddenly widening into the flats, brown against tan, then narrowing gradually once more as it cut down into the plains and began turning south, toward the sea, many impossible hundreds of miles away.

"It's beautiful, isn't it?" said Savn.

"Is it?" said Vlad, without turning his head.

"Don't you think so?"

"Maybe. Nature usually doesn't excite me very much. I'm impressed by what man makes of his world, not what we started with."

"Oh." Savn considered. "I guess I'm just the opposite."

"Yes."

"Does it matter?"

Vlad looked at him, and something like amusement glittered for a moment in his eyes. Then he turned back to watching the river. "Yes and no," he said. "A couple of years ago I met a philosopher who told me that those like me build, while those like you take more pleasure in life."

"Aren't there those who like both?"

"Yes. According to this lady, they become artists."

"Oh. Do you enjoy life?"

"Me? Yes, but I'm naturally lucky."

"Oh." Savn thought back to what the Easterner told him the night before. "You must be, to still be alive with people trying to kill you."

"Oh, no. That isn't luck. I'm alive because I'm good enough to survive."

"Then what do you mean?"

"I'm lucky that, living the way I do, with people trying to kill me, I can still take pleasure in life. Not everyone can, and I think if you can't, there isn't much you can do about it."

"Oh. I've never met a philosopher."

"I hope you do some day; they're always worth talking to."

"Pae says such things are a waste of time."

"Your Pae, I'm sorry to say, is wrong."

"Why?"

"Because everything is worth examining, and if you don't examine your view of the world, you are still subject to it, and you find yourself doing things that—never mind."

"I think I understand."

"Do you? Good." After a moment he said, as if to himself, "I learned a lot from that lady. I was sorry I had to kill her."

Savn looked at him, but the Easterner didn't seem to be joking. They continued watching the River Flats and said nothing more for a while.

Chapter Five

I will not marry a blessing priest,
I will not marry a blessing priest,
In his devotions I'd be least.
Hi-dee hi-dee ho-la!
     Step on out . . .

THEY WERE CLOSE enough so that Savn could identify some of the people below, more by how they dressed and moved than by their features. There were a few whose names he knew, but he knew none of the people well, and for the first time he wondered why that was. Smallcliff was closer to Bigcliff than to either Whiterock or Notthereyet, but those were the places he had visited, and from a little traveling and from his work with Master Wag, he knew a few people who lived in each of those villages; but the dwellers below were strangers, even those he could identify and had spoken with.

Mae and Pae hardly ever mentioned them at all, except for an occasional reference Pae made to its being filthy to bathe in the same place that you wash your clothes. Yet when those from below came to visit Master Wag, they seemed pleasant enough, and Savn didn't see any difference.

Odd, though, that he'd never thought about it before. Next to him, Vlad was watching them with single-minded concentration that reminded Savn of something he'd seen once, long ago, but couldn't quite remember. He felt something akin to fear as he made the comparison, however.

"Vlad?" said Savn at last.

"Yes?"

"Those people are . . . never mind."

"They are what?"

Savn haltingly tried to tell the Easterner what he'd been thinking about them, but he couldn't seem to find the right words, so eventually he shrugged and fell silent.

Vlad said, "Are they also vassals of Baron Smallcliff?"

"Yes. He's also the Baron of Bigcliff."

Vlad nodded. "What else?"

"I don't know. I know that someone else is lord over in Whitcrock, though. A Dzurlord. We hear stories about him."

"Oh? What kind of stories?"

"Not very nice ones. You have to work his fields two days of the week, even in the bad years when it takes everything to keep your own going, and he doesn't care how hard that makes it for you, or even if you starve, and sometimes he does things that, well, I don't really know about because they say I'm too young to know about them, but they're pretty awful. His tax collectors can beat you whenever they want, and you can't do anything about it. And his soldiers will kill you if you get in their way, and when the Speaker tried to complain to the Empire they had him killed, and things like that."

"Things like that don't happen here?"

"Well, the tax collectors can be pretty mean sometimes, but not that bad. We're lucky here."

"I suppose so."

They fell silent again. Vlad continued staring down at the River Flats. Eventually Savn said, "Vlad, if you aren't enjoying nature, what *are* you doing?"

"Watching the people."

"They're odd," said Savn.

"So you said. But you didn't tell me in what way they're odd."

Savn opened his mouth and shut it. He didn't want to

pass on what Mae and Pae said about them, because he
was sure Vlad would just think he was being small-
minded. He finally said, "They talk funny."

Vlad glanced at him. "Funny? How?"

"Well, there used to be a tribe of Serioli who lived
down there. They only moved away a few hundred years
ago, and until then they lived right next to the people from
Bigcliff, and they'd talk all the time, and—"

"And the people from Bigcliff use Serioli words?"

"Not when they talk to us. But it's, that, well, they put
their words together different than we do."

"Can you understand them?"

"Oh, sure. But it sounds strange."

"Hmmm," said Vlad.

"What are you watching them for?"

"I'm not certain. A way to do something I have to do."

"Why do you always talk that way?"

Vlad spared him a quick glance, which Savn could not
read, then said, "It comes from spending time in the company of philosophers and Athyra."

"Oh."

"And having secrets."

"Oh."

A strange feeling came over Savn, as if he and Vlad had
achieved some sort of understanding—it seemed that if he
asked the Easterner a question, he might get an answer.
However, he realized, he wasn't certain what, of all the
things he wondered about, he ought to ask. Finally he said,
"Have you really spent a great deal of time around Athyra
nobles?"

"Not exactly, but I knew a Hawklord once who was
very similar. And a drummer, for that matter."

"Oh. Did you kill them, too?"

Vlad's head snapped up; then he chuckled slightly.
"No," he said, then added, "On the other hand, it came
pretty close with both of them."

"Why were they like Athyra?"

"What do you know of the House?"

"Well, His Lordship is one."

"Yes. That's what brought it to mind. You see, it is a matter of the philosophical and the practical; the mystical and the mundane."

"I don't understand."

"I know that," said Vlad, still staring out at the River Flats.

"Would you explain?"

"I'm not certain I can," said Vlad. He glanced at Savn, then back out over the cliff. "There are many who are contemptuous of the intellectual process. But those who aren't afraid of it sometimes discover that the further you go from the ordinary, day-to-day world, the more understanding you can achieve of it; and the more you understand of the world, the more you can act, instead of being acted upon. That," he added, almost as an afterthought, "is exactly what witchcraft is about."

"But you said before you ought to get involved, and now you're saying you should stand apart."

"Got me," said Vlad, smiling.

Savn waited for him to continue. After a moment Vlad seated himself on the cliff.

"Not stand apart in actions," he said. "I mean, don't be afraid to form general conclusions, to try to find the laws that operate in the actions of history, and to— "

"I don't understand."

Vlad sighed. "You should try not to get me started."

"But, about the Athyra . . ."

"Yes. There are two types of Athyra. Some are mystics, who attempt to explore the nature of the world by looking within themselves, and some are explorers, who look upon the world as a problem to be solved, and thus reduce other people to either distractions or pieces of a puzzle, and treat them accordingly."

Savn considered this, and said, "The explorers sound dangerous."

"They are. Not nearly as dangerous as the mystics, however."

"Why is that?"

"Because explorers at least believe that others are real,

if unimportant. To a mystic, that which dwells inside is the only reality."

"I see."

"Baron Smallcliff is a mystic."

"Oh."

Vlad stood abruptly, and Savn had an instant's fear that he was going to throw himself off the cliff. Instead he took a breath and said, "He's the worst kind of mystic. He can only see people as . . ." His voice trailed off. He looked at Savn, then looked away. For a moment, Savn thought he had detected such anger hidden in the Easterner that it would make one of Speaker's rages seem like the pouting of a child.

In an effort to distract Vlad, Savn said, "What are you?"

It seemed to work, for Vlad chuckled slightly. "You mean am I a mystic or an explorer? I have been searching for the answer to that question for several years now. I haven't found it, but I know that other people are real, and that is something."

"I guess."

"There was a time I didn't know that."

Savn wasn't certain how to respond to this, so he said nothing.

After a moment, Vlad added, "And I listen to philosophers."

"When you don't kill them," said Savn.

This time the Easterner laughed. "Even when I do, I still listen to them."

"I understand," said Savn.

Vlad looked at him suddenly. "Yes, I think that you do."

"You sound surprised."

"Sorry," said Vlad. "You are, I don't know, better educated than most of us from the city would have thought."

"Oh. Well, I learned my ciphers and history and everything because I filled the bucket when I was twenty, so they—"

"Filled the bucket?"

"Don't they have that in the city?"

"I don't know. I've never heard of it, at any rate."

"Oh. Well, I hardly remember doing it. I mean, I was pretty young at the time. But they give you a bucket—"

"Who is 'they'?"

"Mae and Pae and Speaker and Bless."

"I see. Go on."

"They give you a bucket, and tell you to go out into the woods, and when you come back, they see what's in the bucket and decide whether you should be trained for apprenticeship."

"And you had filled yours?"

"Oh, that's just a term that means they said yes. I mean, if you come back with water, then Bless will try you out as a priest, and if you come back with sticks, then, well, I don't really know how they tell, but they decide, and when I came back they decided I should be apprenticed to Master Wag."

"Oh. What did you come back with?"

"An injured daythief."

"Oh. That would account for it, I suppose. Still, I can't help wondering how much of that is chance."

"What do you mean?"

"How often a child picks up the first thing he sees, and ends up being a cobbler when he'd be better off as a weaver."

"That doesn't happen," Savn explained.

Vlad looked at him. "It doesn't?"

"No," said Savn, feeling vaguely annoyed.

"How do you know?"

"Because . . . it just doesn't."

"Because that's what you've always been told?"

Savn felt himself flushing, although he wasn't certain why. "No, because that's what the test is for."

Vlad continued studying him. "Do you always just accept everything you've been told, without questioning it?"

"That's a rude question," said Savn without thinking about it.

Vlad seemed startled. "You're right," he said. "I'm sorry."

"Some things," said Savn, "you just know."

Vlad frowned, and took a step away from the cliff. He clasped his hands behind his back and cocked his head slightly. "Do you?" he asked. "When you 'just know' something, Savn, that means it's so locked into your head that you operate as if it were true, even when you find out it isn't." He knelt down so that he was facing Savn directly. "That isn't necessarily a good idea."

"I don't understand."

"You're so convinced that your Baron Smallcliff is invincible and perfect that you'd stand there and let him kill you rather than raising a finger to defend yourself."

"That's different."

"Is it?"

"You're changing the subject. There are things that you know way deep down. You know they're true, just because they have to be."

"Do they?"

"Well, yes. I mean, how do you know that we're really here? You just know."

"I know some philosophers who would disagree with you," said Vlad.

"The ones you killed?"

Vlad laughed. "Well taken," he said. He stood and walked over to the cliff again, and stared out once more. Savn wondered what he was trying to find. "But sometimes," continued the Easterner, "when it's time to do something, it matters whether you know why you're doing it."

"What do you mean?"

Vlad frowned, which seemed to be his usual expression when he was trying to think of how to say something. "Sometimes you might get so mad that you hit someone, or so frightened you run, but you don't really know why. Sometimes you know why you should do something, but it's all in your head. You don't really feel it, so you have trouble making yourself do it."

Savn nodded. "I know what you mean. It's like when I've been out late and Maener asks what I've been doing and I know I should tell her, but I don't."

"Right. It isn't always easy to act on what's in your head instead of what's in your heart. And it isn't always right to. The whole trick to knowing what to do is deciding when to make yourself listen to your head, and when it's okay to just follow your feelings."

"So, how do you do it?"

Vlad shook his head. "I've been trying to figure that one out myself for the last few years, and I haven't managed. But I can tell you that it works best when you understand why you feel a certain way, and to do that, sometimes you have to take things you know and question them. That's one of the good things Athyra and philosophers do."

"I see what you're getting at," said Savn slowly.

Vlad looked at him once more. "Yes? And?"

"Some things you just know."

Vlad seemed about to say something, but evidently decided to let the matter drop. They fell silent, and Vlad went back to scanning the area below them.

After a while the Easterner said, "Who's that lady wearing the green hat, talking to everyone in sight?"

"I don't know her name, but she's their priestess."

"Of?"

"What do you mean, 'of'? Oh, I see. Of Trout."

"Hmmm. No help there."

"No help for what?"

"Never mind. Do you, also, worship Trout?"

"Worship?"

"I mean, who do you pray to?"

"Pray?"

"Who is your god?"

"Bless seems to be on good terms with Naro, the Lady Who Sleeps, so that's who he usually asks things of."

Vlad nodded, then pointed once more. "Who is that fellow walking down toward the water?"

"I don't remember his name. He makes soap and sells it."

"Where does he sell it?"

"Just there, along the river. Most of them make their

own, I think, the same as we do, so he doesn't get much business except from those who are washing clothes and didn't bring enough."

"There's nowhere else he sells it?"

"No, not that I'm aware of. Why?"

"It doesn't matter."

"We don't wash at the river; we have wells."

"You wash in your wells?"

"No, no, we—"

"I was kidding."

"Oh. We go to the river to swim sometimes, but only upstream of them. You can't swim in the Upper Brownclay; it's too cold and fast."

"Who's that, just going beneath the scatterbush?"

"There? That's Fird. He came in to see Master Wag once with some sort of awful rash on his hand, and Master Wag rubbed it with rose leaves and it went away."

"What is he doing?"

"Selling fruit."

"Fruit? You have fruit around here?"

"Fird brings it in from upriver. We don't have very much. It's expensive. We get mangoes, though, and ti'iks, and oranges, and—"

"Doesn't Tem sell them?"

"He can't afford it. Fird is the only one."

"I'll have to meet him."

"He's by the river just about every day. We could go down if you want to."

"Not just yet. Where else does he sell this fruit?"

"Just here. And at the castle, I think."

"Really? He serves Smallcliff?"

"No, just those who serve His Lordship."

"That's interesting."

"Is it? At first that's all he did—bring in fruits and vegetables to feed His Lordship's staff, but then he found that if he went down to the river everyone wanted to buy something, so now, I think, he has more customers on the beach than in the servants, although I don't know if that matters—"

"His name, you say, is Fird?"

"Yes."

"Very well."

Vlad watched a little longer, then grunted and turned away from the cliff.

"Are we going to the caves again?" said Savn.

"No, I was thinking of going back to Tem's, for a glass of wine."

"Oh."

As they walked back along the slip, it seemed to Savn that the feeling had passed—that something which had been open within the strange man who walked next to him had shut again. *Well*, he thought. *Now that it's too late, I wonder what I should have asked him.*

As they reached the top of the hill and found the road once more, he said, "Uh, Vlad?"

"Yes?"

"Did you, um, *do* something to Mae and Pae last night?"

Vlad frowned. "Do something? You mean, cast a spell of some sort? What makes you think so? Are they acting strange?"

"No, it's just that I don't understand why they weren't angry with me for staying out so late."

"Oh. I took responsibility for it, that's all."

"I see," said Savn. He wasn't convinced, but then, he had trouble believing that the Easterner had really put a spell on them to begin with. Because he didn't want to leave that question hanging between them, he said, "What are your parents like?"

"They're dead," said Vlad.

"Oh. I'm sorry." He thought for a moment of what it would be like to be without Mae and Pae, then decided not to dwell on the thought. He said, "Are they the ones who taught you?"

"No, my grandfather did that."

"Is he—?"

"No, he's still with us. Or, at any rate, he was a few

years ago. He's an old man, but witches, like sorcerers, tend to live a long time."

They came to the widening of the road that wagons used when they had to turn around, which was located just west of where the road began its twisting way into town. The forest still rose high on either side of them.

Savn said, "Were you going to show me some more witchcraft today?"

Vlad seemed to shrug without actually moving his shoulders. "What would you like to learn?"

"Well, I mean, I don't know. I'd like to learn to do something interesting."

"That's one approach."

They walked back along the road, passing the place where Savn had first seen Vlad, and started up the gentle slope that lead to the last hill before town.

"What do you mean?" said Savn.

"The Art can be approached from several directions. One is learning to do interesting things, another is the search for knowledge, yet another, the search for understanding, or wisdom, if you prefer, although it isn't really the same—"

"That's what you were talking about before, isn't it? I mean, about witchcraft, and understanding."

"Yes."

"But isn't knowledge the same as understanding?"

"No."

Savn waited for the Easterner to explain, but he didn't. Instead he added, "And yet another way is the search for power."

"Which way did you go?"

"Like you. I wanted to learn to do interesting things. I sort of had to."

"Why?"

"It's a long story."

"Oh. Well, what about me?"

"You should think about which direction you want to take."

"I know already."

"Oh? Tell me."

"Like I said, I want to do interesting things."

"Hmmm."

"Like you."

"Why is that?"

"To impress girls."

Vlad looked at him, and Savn had the feeling that the Easterner was, somehow, seeing him for the first time. After a moment, a smile came to Vlad's mouth and he said softly, "Well, why not? Let's step off the road a ways. Forests and jungles always feel right for this sort of thing."

"What about a place of power?"

Vlad chuckled. "Unnecessary—for this stage."

"All right. I suppose I'll understand eventually."

"Yes, chances are you will, but we won't worry about that for now."

"Here?"

"A little further, I think. I don't want to be distracted by the sounds of horses and wagons."

Savn followed him around thick trees, over low shrubs, and under hanging boughs until he seemed to find what he was looking for, whereupon he grunted, settled down against the wide base of a sugar maple, and said, "Get comfortable."

"I'm comfortable," said Savn, seating himself. Then, realizing that he wasn't, really, adjusted himself as best he could. He began to feel excitement, but he shook his shoulders back and waited, trying to remember the relaxed state he'd been in before. Vlad looked at him carefully, smiling just a little beneath the hair that grew about his lip.

"What is it?" asked Savn.

"Nothing, nothing. What do you know of psychic communication?"

"Well, I know people who can do it, a little. And I know that sorcerers can do it."

"Have you ever tried?"

"*Me*? Well, no."

"Why not?"

"Well, I, uh, I have no reason to think I can."

"Everyone can. You just have to be shown how."

"You mean, read minds?"

"Not exactly. It's more like speaking without making a sound. It is possible to read minds, but that is far, far more difficult, and even then you might be caught at it." Vlad paused, and seemed to be remembering something, to judge by the distant look in his eyes and the half-smile on his face. "Many people become annoyed if you attempt to penetrate their thoughts."

"I would think so," said Savn.

Vlad nodded, then reached for a chain that hung around his neck, hesitated, licked his lips, and removed it. On the end was a simple setting which held what appeared to be a piece of black rock.

"What is—?"

"Don't ask," said Vlad. At the same time, there was a sudden flapping sound overhead, as if two or three very large birds had been disturbed. Savn jumped, startled, but Vlad shook his head, as if to say that it was nothing to worry about.

"Remember how we relaxed before?" he said. "Well, we're going to do it again, only this time the experience will be rather different."

"In what way?"

"You'll see. There will be a disorientation in time, but that is nothing to worry about."

"All right."

Once more he closed his eyes and allowed Vlad's voice to lead him through each muscle in his body, letting the tension leave, letting it flow down, down, into the ground below him, until he felt the now-familiar sensation of floating, as if he were no longer part of his body—as if he stood apart from it, distant and unconcerned. Then Vlad said, "You are feeling very warm, and light—as if you are nothing but a bubble of air, and you can go anywhere. Yes. Think of yourself as an air bubble that moves where you will. You are surrounded by nothing, and you are empty.

Feel that you can move however you please. You are relaxed and confident."

Yes, Savn agreed. *I will feel that way. I choose to, and
so I do. Isn't that remarkable?*

"Now," said Vlad, "picture yourself, a bubble of noth-
ingness, floating down through the ground, down through
layers of stone, meshing with it, and, with each layer, you
will fall more deeply asleep."

Yes, I will picture that; I will do that, he thought, and it
seemed as if his body were far away.

"Now very slowly, open your eyes, and look at me, but
do not rise up. Look at me, and imagine that I am there
with you—we are together, two bubbles of air beneath the
earth. With the eyes of your body, you see me holding a
small piece of fabric. Now you imagine yourself a wind,
and you brush against the fabric. There, you see how it
flutters? Touch it again, and again. Don't push; will it to
happen. Do you feel the texture of the cloth, smooth,
slightly cold, the veins of weave distinct beneath the fin-
gertips of your mind? Once more, a little push. Yes, that
was you, you felt it.

"Now we, as two bubbles of air, will touch. Do you
now hear my words, as if they were echoed, once spoken
aloud, once whispered softly? One coming just ahead of
the other, as if you were aware of the time it takes for the
sound to pass your ears, because you are now aware of
that time, and you choose to ignore it, so these sounds,
both my voice, both identical, come together; they are
strong, reinforcing each other. And now *you hear only the
whisper, and without making a sound, whisper back to me
with only your thoughts—you form words, and you give
them to me, as if you were placing a feather in my hand,
but your mouth and tongue do not move. Tell me, in this
way, that you can hear me.*"

"*I can hear you,*" Savn said, feeling awe, but a distant,
vague sort of awe, the reverse of a dream, as if it were
normal and nothing special, but he knew, somewhere, that
it would be remarkable when he awoke.

"*And I can hear you,*" said Vlad. "*You will remember*

that feeling, of touching my mind with yours, and you will always be able to call it back."

"Yes," said Savn. *"I will remember it."*

"Now, you begin to rise back through the ground, and with each layer, you begin to awake. You are coming back, closer and closer; you feel your limbs again, and know them as part of you, and you hear my real voice in your real ears, and with this sound, you awake, remembering everything that has happened, feeling rested, alert, and confident."

Savn blinked, and felt as if he were opening his eyes, although they had been open. He said, "I feel . . . funny. How much time has passed?"

"About half an hour."

"Half an hour?" Savn took a moment to see if this was true, then said, "Did I really move that piece of cloth?"

"You moved it," said Vlad.

Savn shook his head, but found no words to say.

"How do you feel?" said Vlad.

"Fine. A little tired, I guess."

"It'll pass. You'll have some trouble sleeping tonight. I'd suggest a great deal of physical exertion."

"All right. I'll run all the way home."

"Good idea."

They stood up. Vlad picked up his pendant and put it around his neck again. They walked slowly back to the road and started in toward town again. Savn couldn't find anything to say, and he was too lost in wonder and confusion to try very hard. He shook his head. Even now, he seemed more aware of the breeze against his throat, of the sharp outline of the trees against the twilit sky, and the sounds of the birds coming from all around him. They had always been there—why had he chosen not to hear them, and why was he hearing them now?

Such were his thoughts until he realized that they were walking through the town, and, in fact, had arrived in front of Tem's house. They stopped, and he said, "When will I see you again?"

"I'm not certain, my friend. Perhaps tomorrow."

"All right."

He did, indeed, run all the way home, relishing the way the air flowed through his lungs, the pounding of his feet along the road, the darkening sky, and the breeze, just getting chilly, biting at his face.

He made it on time for the evening meal, which prevented Mae and Pae from questioning him. Polyi, as usual, chattered throughout the meal, but Savn, who wasn't really listening, caught a few pointed remarks about himself. Fortunately, Mae and Pae didn't pick up on them.

That night, Savn fell asleep at once and while he slept, he dreamed that he stood in the street in front of Tem's house, while Lova stood in the middle of a faceless crowd and looked at him adoringly as he made the ground open and close, and made fire fall from the sky. When he awoke, he remembered the dream, and remarked to himself, "That's odd. I hadn't even known I liked her."

What now?

She flew down toward the little structure where the Provider dwelt, knowing that her mate was already there. And, even as she cupped the air to light on the roof, and was reaching with her feet for a grip on the soft wood, he took to the air once more, passing directly in front of her.

She hissed, and followed.

A soft one? Her mate was thinking about a soft one. But how to tell one from the others?

She tried to understand what her mate was asking of her. She understood something about fruit, or the smells of fruit, but when she tried to find out what sort of fruit, her mate became agitated.

At last, she understood what her mate wanted, and thought, if it must be, it must be. And at least it was flying.

Now up, out, upon the currents, treading them, through the overcast, careful not to breathe. Then up higher, higher, and, for the sheer pleasure of it, diving, falling like a stone past the cliff, to catch the air and drift, and glide.

*Something like a laugh came from her thoughts, and
echoed from her mate.*

*He found the one they were to watch, and she followed
the path he indicated. Yes, that was the one. So be it. A
long, dull time would follow, she thought.*

She hoped she would be able to stay awake.

Chapter Six

I will not marry a cursing wizard,
I will not marry a cursing wizard,
I'd ask for snow and get a blizzard.
Hi-dee hi-dee ho-la!
　　　Step on out . . .

AFTER BREAKING HIS fast, Savn went outside. He looked at
the stubble that covered almost every field in sight, his
view interrupted only by the bins and the outbuildings.
The soil looked lumpy and harsh, and somehow more
brown than it had in the spring, though he had been told
that was just his imagination.

It seemed such a short time ago that he had come out
here and seen the little flowers everywhere, most of them
blue, a few areas of pink or white. But now it looked almost like a wasteland, save for the long, narrow strip that
ran next to the road, where the densely packed flax stood
as high as his waist. It was here that he and his sister
would be working today. Mae and Pae had already finished the chores and were out among the flax plants,
working from the west, and Polyi was holding the small
reaper and waiting for him.

It was a fresh, cool day, and the air felt dry and clean.
It was a good day to work; he hated the early part of the
harvest most, because everything seemed twice as hard
when it was hot. Rain was almost as bad, but it didn't feel
like rain today, and there was no greying of the orange-red

sky, so perhaps they'd continue to be lucky with the weather.

He took a couple of the long cloth bags from under the porch, shook them and turned them inside out, then nodded to his sister.

"We're almost done," she said.

"I know. Today, or maybe tomorrow."

Polyi, hands on her hips and scythe leaning against her side, twisted in place a couple of times, as if to loosen muscles that were already tired. Savn rolled his shoulders and put his lyorn-skin gloves on. His hands would be hot and sweaty in half an hour, but blisters, as he well knew, would be worse.

He said, "Let's get to it." They headed out to the last field.

Savn collected the plants into sacks while his sister went ahead of him with the reaper. They fell into the rhythm easily—which was important. If they didn't, Savn would have had to pick the plants up off the ground, which was hard on his back and took much longer. But by now they knew each other, so that as Polyi swung the tool for each cut, the plant would fall neatly into Savn's gloved hand, and then he would take a half-step backward in order to miss the back sweep. He didn't have to watch either his hands or the plants—only his sister, to be certain that if for any reason the rhythm changed he would be able to avoid the sharp blade. He knew well what could happen if he looked away at the wrong time—he had helped Master Wag patch up three people this harvest.

It was boring drudge-work, but also easy and satisfying now that they had the system worked out, and he could hear the steady *shhhick, shhhick* as Mae and Pae worked from the other end. Soon—probably tomorrow, he decided, they would meet, and that would be the end of the harvest for this year. Then Mae and Pae would prepare the ground for the winter, and next year they would start all over again, and the next year, and the next, until the day Savn would begin earning money as a physicker himself, either in Smallcliff or elsewhere. Then there would be a few lean years before he could afford to send enough money back to pay for the work he could not do, but after that Mae and Pae would be able to hire someone, and after that he could begin saving, until he had so much money that he'd be able to travel, and—

When did I decide I wanted to travel? he asked himself.

Well, he wasn't sure he did want to, come to that, but he remembered when he had begun thinking about it—it was while he was standing outside his house, and the night had seemed to speak to him of distant places. He remembered his own question of Vlad, which had seemed to impress the Easterner: are you running to something or away from something? If he, Savn, were to leave, would he be leaving his family, or searching for more? Would he be deserting his home, or would he be setting out to find adventure and fortune? Had the Easterner inspired all of these thoughts? Was the Easterner somehow responsible for the experience he'd had on that strange, wonderful evening? *I don't care what they say, I'll bet he didn't kill Reins.*

They finished the row and began on the next, and so the morning passed. When it was nearly noon, their rhythm was broken by Pae, who whistled through his fingers to signal that Savn and Polyi were finished for the day.

As they walked back to the house, Polyi said, "Do you think they'll finish without us?"

Savn looked back at what remained to be done and said, "I hope it doesn't rain tomorrow."

Polyi nodded. "Me, too. Shall we go to Tem's house today?"

"Sure."

"You didn't wait for me yesterday, you know."

"I didn't? That's right, I didn't. I guess I was thinking about other things."

"Such as what?"

"I don't know. Things. Anyway, today we'll go there."

Savn bathed, and as he'd promised, waited for his sister, and the two of them set off for Tem's house. They spoke little as they walked, although it seemed to Savn that a couple of times Polyi started to say or ask something, then thought better of it. Eventually she started singing "Dung-Foot Peasant," and, after a verse or two, Savn joined in, changing pronouns as appropriate. He hadn't heard it in some time, and laughed at a few of the verses that had been added since he was his sister's age. He also sang her a few verses that had apparently been forgotten, and he was pleased that she liked them.

When they reached Tem's house, Vlad was not in evidence, but there was the usual noon crowd, and Savn noticed that he was receiving some odd looks from many of them. Polyi noticed it, too.

"Do you see that?" she said. "The way they look at you? They're wondering why you've been spending so much time with that Easterner."

Savn quickly looked around, but no one was looking at him just at the moment. "Are they really?" he said.

"Yes."

"Hmmm." He shrugged. "Let them wonder, then."

"Well, what *are* you doing?"

"I'm learning things."

"Like what?"

"Like, um, like how to catch gems in the wind—no, I mean, catch water in, uh—oh, never mind. I'm learning stuff."

Polyi frowned, but couldn't seem to think of anything to say, which was perfectly all right with Savn. He quickly finished his salad, said goodbye to his sister, and headed off to Master Wag.

On the way, it occurred to him that the sharpness of sensation that he'd felt the evening before was gone. He wondered if it was something that would return as he became more adept in this strange art he had begun to study.

The Master was in better spirits today, puttering around his small house (which had seemed much larger a year before, when Savn had begun studying with him) scattering bits of history with explanations of both the general and the particular. Savn wondered if he had solved the problem of Rein's death, but decided that, if so, the Master would speak of it in his own time, and if not, he had best not bring the subject up.

And in fact, Master Wag made no mention of it during the entire day, most of which Savn spent cleaning up the Master's house and listening to the Master's stories and lectures—a pastime Savn rather enjoyed, even though once Master Wag began to speak he soon lost track of his audience and went far beyond Savn's knowledge and understanding.

He's quite a bit like Vlad, he thought, then wondered why the notion disturbed him.

Toward the end of the day, the Master had him recite the questions, conclusions, and appropriate cures for various sorts of stomach ailments, and seemed quite pleased with Savn's answers, although, actually, Savn left out stabbing pains in the side, and the questions that would lead to a dose of pomegranate seeds to ease an attack of kidney stones.

Master Wag was standing in front of Savn, who was seated on the stool with his back to the hearth; there was a low fire which was just on the edge of being too warm. As the Master finished his explanation, he said, "So, what have you been thinking about, Savn?"

"Master?"

"You've had something on your mind all day. What is it?"

Savn frowned. He hadn't, in point of fact, realized that he *had* been thinking about something. "I don't know," he said.

"Is it our friend Reins?" the Master prompted.

"Maybe."

"Well, it's nothing for you to worry about, in any case. I still don't know what he died of, but I haven't quit looking, either."

Savn didn't say anything.

Master Wag stared at him with his intense gaze, as if he were looking around inside of Savn's skull. "What is it?" he said.

"How do you know what to believe?" said Savn, who was surprised to hear himself ask the question.

Master Wag sat down opposite Savn and leaned back. "That is quite a question," he said. "Care to tell me what it springs from?"

Savn found that, on the one hand, he couldn't dissemble when the Master was staring at him so, but on the other hand, he wasn't certain of the answer. At last he said, "I've been wondering. Some people say one thing, others say another—"

"Who's been saying what, about what?"

"Well, my friends think that the Easterner had something to do with Reins's death, and he says—"

"Rubbish," said Master Wag, but in a tone that was not unkind. "Your friends know nothing, and the Easterner is not to be believed.

"On the other hand," Wag continued, "that doesn't answer your question. The way to tell what is true is simply to keep your eyes and ears open, and to use your head. That's all there is to it."

Savn nodded, although he felt as if his question hadn't really been answered. But then, was Master Wag really the person to answer the question at all? He knew about helping people who were ill, but what need did he have to wonder about what truth was? He could ask Bless, but Bless would only tell him to trust the gods, and Speaker would tell him to trust what Speaker himself said.

But then, he wondered, what need did he, Savn, have to think about any of this, either? To this there was no answer, but it didn't help. He discovered that he wanted very badly to talk to Vlad again, although he wondered if trusting the Easterner too much would be a mistake.

He said, "Thank you, Master. Is there anything else?"

"No, no. Run on home now. And don't worry so much."

"I won't, Master."

He stepped out into the warm autumn afternoon and immediately began running back toward town, wishing he could teleport. *That would be best,* he thought. *All this time I spend getting from place to place, I could just* be *there.* He wondered if he could convince Vlad to show him how that was done. Probably not, he decided. Most likely it was too difficult, in any case.

Soon enough he was there, and, almost to his surprise, he found Vlad right away, sitting in Tem's house drinking wine and watching the door, as if he was waiting for Savn, and the smile he gave seemed to confirm this. There were three or four familiar faces as well, but no one Savn felt the need to speak to.

He sat down with the Easterner and gave him a good day, which Vlad returned, and offered to buy him a glass of ale. Savn accepted. Vlad signaled Tem, and Savn couldn't help but notice the glance the Housemaster gave him as he set the ale down. He wondered if he should be annoyed, and concluded that he didn't really care.

When Tem had returned to his place behind the counter, Savn said, "I've been thinking about our lesson all day. Can you show me some more?"

"Certainly," said Vlad. "But are you sure you want to be seen with me so much?"

"Why not?"

"Didn't you notice the looks you've been getting?"

"I guess I have," said Savn. "I noticed it earlier today, too, when I was here with my sister. But why?"

"Because you're with me."

"Why do they care about that?"

"Either because I'm an Easterner or because they still think I had something to do with the death of Reins."

"Oh. But you didn't, did you?"

"I've been wondering about that," said Vlad.

Savn stared at him. "What do you mean?"

"Well, I didn't kill him," said Vlad. "But that doesn't mean I had nothing to do with his death."

"I don't understand."

"As I said before, I doubt it's coincidence."

"I wish," said Savn slowly, "Master Wag could have learned what killed him."

"Your Master has failed?"

Savn considered the Master's words about not having given up, and he said, "Yes. He doesn't know."

"Then I do."

Savn felt his eyes growing wide. "What?"

"I know what killed him."

"How could you?"

"Because Master Wag failed. That is all the information I need."

"But, well, what was it?"

"Sorcery."

Savn shook his head. "Master Wag said that sorcery leaves traces."

"Certainly, if used in a simple, straightforward way, such as causing the heart to stop, or inducing a hemorrhage, or in a way that leaves a visible wound."

"But, then, what happened to him?"

"Do you know what necromancy is?"

"Well, not exactly."

"Necromancy, in its most basic form, is simply the magic of death—those particular forces that are released when a living thing passes from existence. There are those who study ways to cheat death, ways to extend or simulate life, attempting to erase the difference between life and death. And some study the soul, that which exists after the death of the body, and where it goes, which leads to the study of other worlds, of places that cannot normally be reached and those beings who live there, such as gods and demons, and the forces that operate between worlds, places where life meets unlife, where reality is whim, and Truth dances to the drum of desire, where—"

"I don't understand."

"Oh, sorry. I was rambling. The point is, a skilled necromancer would be able to simply send a soul into limbo, without doing anything that would actually kill the person."

"And the person would just die?"

"Usually."

"Usually? What happens the rest of the time?"

"I don't want to talk about it. It doesn't matter in this case, anyway. A necromancer could achieve the effect you saw in Reins."

"What about the horse?"

"What about it?"

"Well, it bolted, as if it were afraid of something."

"That doesn't surprise me. Animals are often very sensitive to magic. Especially the dumber beasts." There was something odd in the way he said that, as if he were sharing a joke with himself.

Savn thought all of this over, and said, "But who—?"

"Loraan, of course. I mean, Baron Smallcliff. He is a necromancer. Moreover, he is undead himself, which proves that he is a skilled necromancer, if I hadn't known it before."

"Undead? You want me to believe His Lordship is a vampire?"

"A vampire? Hmmm. Maybe. Do you know of any cases of mysterious death, blood drained, all that?"

"No. If something like that happened around here, I'd have heard of it."

"So perhaps he is not a vampire. Although that proves nothing. Sethra is a vampire, but she still eats and drinks, and requires very little blood."

"Who?"

"An old friend."

"I think I've heard of her," said Savn. "Although I can't remember from where."

"Doubtless just someone with the same name."

"I suppose. But do you really know a vampire?"

"An odd one. Never mind. Still, I wonder what he is—"

"What other sorts of undead are there?"

"I'm not an expert on the subject. Perhaps dear Lord Smallcliff will let me use his library to look it up."

"But then you could just ask him."

"I wasn't serious," said Vlad.

"Oh. I can't believe His Lordship is undead."

"Why not?"

"Well, because, uh, I just can't."

"I understand," said Vlad. "All your life there are people you just assume you can trust, yet you don't really know them. Then, out of nowhere, someone walks up to you and asks you to believe that one of them is some kind of monster. I wouldn't believe it either. At least, not without a lot more proof than you've seen."

Savn stared at him, not certain what to say. He seemed to be talking to himself, and, once more, Savn felt the undercurrent of hatred in the Easterner's voice.

"That's how they do it, that's how they get away with everything, because it's so much easier just to go along with what you're told than to look at—" He caught himself, as if aware that he had left his listener far behind.

For a moment he seemed to be thinking about trying to explain; then he shrugged. "Believe it or not, as you will. What I want to know is what the son of—uh, what the fellow has planned. The coincidence, as I said, is too great. He can't just kill me the way he killed Reins, so—"

"Huh? He wants to kill you?"

"He does indeed. But I'm protected rather better than Reins was."

"Oh. But why would he want to kill you at all?"

"He has reasons."

Savn thought about this. "So, what is he going to do?" he asked.

"I wish," said Vlad, "that I had some means of figuring that out. There's probably no point in running once things have gone this far. Besides, I owe him, for Reins."

"You owe him? You said something about that before. What do you mean?"

Vlad shrugged. "I was mostly talking to myself. But I just wish I knew what he was planning."

"Can't witchcraft tell you?"

"It's not very useful for seeing the future."

"That's too bad."

"Maybe."

"So what *are* you going to do?"

"Try to find out," said Vlad. "I have other ways. Sometimes they even work."

He stared off into the distance, as if he were communing with things unseen.

Chapter Seven

I will not marry a poor musician,
I will not marry a poor musician,
He'd be playing and I'd be wishin'.
Hi-dee hi-dee ho-la!
        Step on out . . .

VLAD TOYED WITH his salad but ate little, either because he didn't like the taste or because he was thinking of other things. Savn ate his own salad with, if no great delight, at least considerable appetite.

Savn felt Vlad watching him, which made him slightly nervous as he squeezed an expensive piece of lemon over the cheese and vegetables, put another handful of salad into his mouth, and wiped his hand on his shirt. The Easterner sighed. "I know a place," he said, "where one could eat every day for half a year and never taste the same dish twice. Where the servers are discreet and efficient; you never noticed them, but there is always a full plate in front of you and wine in your glass. Where the room is quiet and serene and tasteful, calling the diner's attention to the delight of the tongue. Where the appetizer is fresh, enticing and excites the senses like the first touches of love. Where the fruit is sweet and plump, or tart and crisp, and complements the cheese as the salad complements the bread—with reverence and solemn joy. Where there is a choice of wine to suit the most diverse taste, yet each has been selected with care, and tenderness. Where each meat

is treated with the honor it deserves, and is allowed to un-
fold its own flavor in the natural juices the gods gave it,
with touches of savory, ginger, or tarragon added to direct
the attention of the palate to the hidden joys which are
unique to that particular cut. Do you know what I am saying? A place where the mushroom and the onion dance
with the wine and the peppers in sauces that fire the palate, and the sweet at the end of the meal is the encore to
a symphony of the heart. Where—"

"You don't much like the food here, do you?" said
Savn.

"—there is quiet and ease, with only that conversation
that flows like the wine from the bottle, easy and natural,
and all else, save the sounds of dining, is the silence that
food requires for—"

"There isn't any music? I thought the best taverns had
music."

Vlad sighed and returned from his reverie. "No, there is
no music. I don't like music when I eat. Although," he
added, "I must admit that, here, music would be a welcome distraction."

"Well, you are likely to get your wish. There will probably be someone arriving today or tomorrow. There hasn't
been a minstrel in several days, and there are usually one
or two a week. Besides, harvest is almost over, and they
always show up around the end of harvest."

"Indeed?" said Vlad, sounding suddenly interested. "A
minstrel? Good."

"Why?"

"I like minstrels," said Vlad.

"You mean you like to listen to them, or they are the
sort of people you like?"

"Both, actually."

"You've known minstrels, then?"

"Several."

"I didn't know they had them in the big cities."

"Just about anything you can find outside the city you
can find in it as well."

"Really?"

"Yes." Vlad looked thoughtful for a moment, then added, "Although there are exceptions."

Savn returned to his salad, while waiting for Vlad to continue. When the Easterner did not do so, Savn swallowed and said, "What are the exceptions?"

"What? Oh. Peace and quiet, for example," said Vlad. "You don't know how pleasant these things are unless you've gone most of your life without them. Do you know, when I left the city I had trouble sleeping for quite a while, just because I wasn't used to the silence."

"That seems odd."

"Yes, it seems odd to me, too."

"When did you leave?"

"Shortly after the Uprising."

"What uprising?"

Vlad granted him another indecipherable look, this one a quick frown. He said, "There was some trouble in the city with the Easterners and the Teckla."

"Oh," said Savn. "Yes. I heard something about that. Didn't some traitors kill Her Majesty's personal guards and try to kidnap her?"

"Not exactly," said Vlad.

"Wait a minute," said Savn. "Were *you* involved in that? Is that why you had to—"

"No," said Vlad. "I was involved, I suppose, but only in trying to stay out of the way."

"Well, what did happen?"

Vlad shook his head. "For the most part, I don't know. There was almost a war, and there was conscription, and there was blood, and then it was over."

"What's conscription?"

"When they put you in the army or the navy and send you off to fight."

"Oh. I should like that, I think."

Vlad gave him another quick glance, then almost smiled, and said, "I wouldn't know, myself. I've never been in the army."

"Well, but you've killed people. It's the same thing, isn't it?"

Vlad laughed briefly. "Good question. There are soldiers who would disagree with you. I tend to think you're
right, though. Who's to say?"

"I used to dream about being a soldier," said Savn.

"Did you? That seems odd. On the one hand a soldier,
on the other a physicker."

"Well, but . . . I see what you mean. But when I wanted
to be a soldier it was, I don't know, different."

"I know," said Vlad. "When one dreams of being a soldier, one imagines killing the enemy but not seeing the enemy bleed. Or seeing friends bleed, for that matter."

Savn nodded slowly. "I was young and—" He shrugged
and smiled a little. "I thought the uniforms looked so
nice."

"And the idea," said Vlad, "of getting away from here?"

"Maybe, though I never thought about it that way. Have
you ever known a soldier?"

"I've known warriors," said Vlad.

"What's the difference?"

"Another good question. I'm not sure, but that's how
they described themselves."

"What were they like?"

"Arrogant, but not unpleasantly so."

"Did they frighten you?"

Vlad laughed. "At one time or another, nearly everyone
I've ever known has frightened me."

"Even your friends?"

"Especially my friends. But then, I've had some unusual
friends."

"Yes, and one of them is a vampire."

"Indeed."

"That would frighten me," said Savn thoughtfully.
"There's something about the idea of someone who should
be dead that— You still say His Lordship is undead?"

"Yes."

"Do you really mean it?"

"Yes."

Savn shook his head. "I still don't believe it."

"I know."

"How do you talk to someone who's undead? I mean, isn't it creepy?"

Vlad shrugged. "You get used to—" He stopped, his eyes straying toward the door. "Ah. You must be prescient. The minstrel, I suppose."

Savn turned, and, indeed, a lady was just coming in the door to the smiles of Tem and the few patrons of his house. She wore a travel-worn white blouse and pants, with a green vest and a light green cloak. She carried a pack slung at her hip, and hanging at her back were a long-necked kordu and a shiny black horn- or pipe-like instrument that Savn didn't recognize. Savn thought she was very pretty.

"An Issola," remarked Vlad.

"Green and white," agreed Savn. He was always excited when a minstrel arrived, but especially so when it was a noble, because they always had a wider variety of instruments and songs, and could tell stories of what happened in the courts of the highborn.

By whatever magic caused news to spread, people were beginning to drift into Tem's house already, before the minstrel had finished speaking with Tem, presumably making arrangements for a room and meals in exchange for songs and stories, news and gossip.

Vlad said, "I'm going to have to speak with her, but that can wait."

"Oh? Why?"

"Minstrels know things."

"But will she speak to you?"

"Why not? Oh. Because I'm an Easterner? I suspect that won't be a problem."

Savn started to ask why, but changed his mind. He was, he decided, beginning to be able to anticipate when he was reaching a subject the Easterner wouldn't want to discuss. The minstrel finished her discussion with Tem, and, with a surprisingly shy-looking smile directed at everyone present, she went back toward the chambers that Tem let out to travelers.

Tem cleared his throat and said, "She'll be back and

play for us in a few minutes, after she's refreshed herself."
This seemed to be a pleasing prospect to everyone. More
and more people drifted into the house.

As they did, Savn couldn't help but notice that many,
perhaps most of them, looked at him sitting with the Easterner, then quickly looked away. He caught a glimpse of
what might have been disgust in Firi's expression, and
dark-haired Lova, who was sitting next to Firi, seemed
faintly puzzled. Lan and Tuk were sitting together with
some of their friends, and, though Tuk only looked at the
table in front of him, Lan seemed, for a moment, to be
looking at Savn unpleasantly.

For the first time, he began to seriously question
whether he ought to be seen with Vlad so much. Vlad
looked at him with a slightly amused expression, and Savn
wondered if his thoughts were being read. But Vlad said
nothing, and presently the minstrel returned.

She had changed to a loose, clean, white blouse with
green embroidery, and her leggings were a light, fresh
green. Her hair was brown, with a subdued but unmistak-
able noble's point, and her eyes, very dark, stood out
sharply in contrast to her complexion and clothing. She
carried both of her instruments, and set them at a table in
the corner that was hastily cleared for her. Her teeth were
white when she smiled.

"Greetings, my friends," she said in a melodic, carrying
voice. "My name is Sara. I play the reed-pipe and the
kordu, and I sing, and I even know a few stories. If there
were a drink in front of me, I might play something."

The drink was provided quickly. She smiled her thanks
and sipped from whatever she'd been given, nodded ap-
proval, and poured some of the liquid over the mouthpiece
of the long black flute.

"What's she doing?" whispered Savn.

Vlad shrugged. "It must be good for it. She wouldn't
wreck her own reed."

"I've never seen one of those before."

"Neither have I."

"I wonder what it sounds like."

This question was answered almost at once, when a low, rich dark sound emerged and at once spread as if to fill every corner of the room. She went up and down the scale once or twice and the instrument went both higher and lower than Savn would have guessed. Then she began to play an eerie, arhythmic tune that Savn had never heard; he settled back to enjoy the music. Vlad's face was expressionless as he studied the minstrel.

She sat on a table, one foot resting on a chair, tapping slowly and steadily, though Savn could not find a rhythm that she might be tapping to. When the tune ended, she played another, this one more normal, and, while Savn couldn't remember its name, it was very familiar and seemed to please Tem's guests.

After playing the pipe for a while, she picked up the other instrument, quickly tuned it, and with an expression of sweet innocence, began singing a scandalously bawdy song called "I'll Never Trust a Shepherd, I'll Never Trust a Thief," that, without ever saying anything directly, implied things about her character and pleasures that Savn found unlikely. Everyone pounded on the tables, laughed, and bought Sara more drinks.

After that, she could do no wrong, and when she began singing an old, sweet ballad about Chalara and Auiri, everyone sighed and settled back to become lost in music and sentimentality. In all, she performed for about two hours. Savn liked her singing voice; she chose good songs; and there were stories he had never heard before, as well as some that were as familiar to him as his sister's face.

Eventually Sara stood and bowed to the room at large, making it seem as if she were bowing to every man or woman present. Savn found himself whistling and slapping the table with everyone else. She said, "You are all charming and very kind. With your permission, I will have something to eat, and then, if you wish, I will play again in the evening and tell you what news I have."

Everyone in the house did, indeed, so wish. Sara bowed again to acknowledge the compliment, and carefully set her instruments down.

For the first time since the minstrel had begun, Savn remembered the Easterner sitting next to him, and said, "Did you enjoy the music?"

"Hmmm? Oh, yes, it was fine," said Vlad. He was looking quite fixedly at the minstrel, and his thoughts seemed to be elsewhere. Savn decided against asking what he was thinking about; he sipped his watered wine and looked around the room. Once more he noticed people at other tables surreptitiously glancing at him, at Vlad, or at both of them.

Savn drank slowly and let his mind drift, until, after perhaps a quarter of an hour, Vlad suddenly stood up.

"Are you leaving?" asked Savn.

"No, I wish to speak with this minstrel."

"Oh."

Vlad walked over to her. Savn stood up and followed.

"Good evening, my lady," began Vlad.

The minstrel frowned at him briefly, but said, "And a good evening to you as well."

"My name is Vlad. May I join you for a moment?" As he spoke, he seemed to show her something in his hand. Savn looked at her face in time to see her eyes widen very briefly.

Then she recovered and said, "By all means. Please sit down. It is a pleasure indeed to meet you, Vlad. Who is your friend?"

"My—" Vlad turned, and Savn realized that the Easterner hadn't known he'd been followed. For an instant he seemed annoyed, but he only shrugged and said, "His name is Savn."

"How do you do, Savn?"

Savn found his voice and made a courtesy. "Very well, m'lady."

"Would you both do me the honor of sitting with me?"

They sat. Vlad said, "Please accept my compliments on your performance."

"Thank you," she said. And, to Savn, "You seemed to be enjoying the music a great deal."

"Oh, I was," said Savn, while he wondered if the

Issola's remarks contained a hint that she had noticed how little attention Vlad had actually been paying to the music. If so, Vlad gave no sign of it.

"First things first," said Vlad. He handed her a small piece of paper, folded so that Savn couldn't read it.

The Issola opened it up, glanced at it, put it into her pouch, and smiled. "Very well, my lord," she said. "Now, what can I do for you?"

'My lord'? thought Savn, startled. *How can an Easterner be 'my lord'?*

"I have a few questions for you. Perhaps you can answer them, perhaps not."

"I will certainly try," said the minstrel.

"Do you know Baron Smallcliff?"

"Indeed, yes. I gave him a performance yesterday."

"Excellent." He paused, thinking, then glanced at Savn. "I wonder," he said, "if you would be so good as to return to the table, Savn. I'd really rather make this private, if you don't mind."

"I don't mind," lied Savn. He stood and gave the minstrel another courtesy. "It has been an honor to meet you, my lady," he said.

"And a pleasure to meet you, Savn," said the minstrel.

As Savn walked back to the table he felt that everyone was either staring at him or pointedly not staring at him. He glanced at his friends, and this time there was no mistake; Coral, who was speaking to the others, was at the same time directing a look of unconcealed hatred at Savn.

The feeling of being the center of hostile attention suddenly became so strong that before Savn could reach his seat, he found that he had turned and begun walking toward the door.

And by the time he reached it, he was running.

How long he ran or where he went he did not know, but at last he found that he was lying on the soft grass of a hill, staring up at the dead night sky, breathing in the smell of autumn leaves.

He tried to account for his friends' behavior, but he

couldn't. He tried to understand his own reaction, his panicked flight, but his mind shied away from the subject.

He thought about going back to Tem's house and asking his friends to tell him what the problem was. But what if they did? What if, as they were almost certain to do, they berated him for associating with the Easterner? What would he say?

And, for that matter, why *was* he spending so much time with the Easterner?

He stood up and looked around. He was west of town, not far from Master Wag's, and quite near the road. The way home would take him past Tem's house. He thought of taking a long way round, but chided himself for cowardice.

He climbed up to the road and turned toward town. It was late; Mae and Pae would be starting to worry about him soon. He broke into a jog. He passed Tem's house. It was quiet, and he thought about going in, but quickly rejected the idea; he had no intention of confronting his friends tonight—not until he knew what to say to them.

His lengthening shadow, cast by the lamp from Tem's, preceded him down the road out of the cluster of buildings he thought of as "town." As it disappeared, he nearly ran into an indistinct shape that appeared in front of him. He stopped, and the shape resolved itself into several, he thought three or four, individual areas of darkness darker than the night around them. It took the length of two breaths for Savn to realize that they were people.

The panic that had gripped him before was suddenly back, but he resolved not to give in to it. If it was only his imagination at work, he'd look ridiculous if he ran away. And if it wasn't, running probably wouldn't help.

"Hi," he said. "I can't see who you are."

There was the sound of soft laughter, and he knew, with stomach-dropping certainty, that his fear was not misplaced.

"Who are you?" he said, trying to think of something to say that might get him out of this.

"We're your friends," said a voice he recognized as

Coral's. "We're your friends, and we want to know why
you don't introduce us to your new buddy?"

Savn found that he had some difficulty swallowing.
"You want to meet him? Sure. I mean, he's just a guy.
You'd like him. Why don't we—"

"Shut up," said Coral, and, at the same time, someone
pushed Savn.

He said, "Coral? Look—"

"Shut up," repeated Coral.

He was pushed again, this time so hard that he fell over.
His fall was cause for more laughter. He wondered who
else was there. He thought uncomfortably about how big
Lan was.

He thought about trying to run, then, but one of the
three was bound to catch him, and it would probably make
it worse if he tried to run. He stood up slowly, trying to
think of something to do, and not succeeding.

Coral called him a name and waited. Savn didn't do
anything. He was sent sprawling once more, and once
more he got up. He thought about charging them, but he
couldn't make himself do it; some part of him kept hoping
that they'd be satisfied just to push him around a bit, although he knew the hope was vain.

Then the boy next to Coral called him another name,
and Savn recognized Lan's voice. He guessed the third to
be Lan's brother Tuk, and this was confirmed in a moment.

Savn stood and waited, feeling as if none of this could
really be happening. Someone pushed him yet again; then
someone else pushed him, and this continued for a dizzy-
ing time until he fell to the ground again. He wondered
what would happen if he just lay there, and decided they'd
probably kick him. He stood up slowly, wondering in a
distant way if they could see him well enough to hit him.

Then someone punched him in the stomach, knocking
the wind out of him and doubling him over. *Answers that
question,* he thought, beginning to feel as if he were somewhere else.

"Here, let me," said Lan, and Savn waited.

DORR TOWNSHIP LIBRARY
1807-142nd AVE.
PO BOX 128
DORR, MI 49323

* * *

Her mate was trying to tell her there was a problem, and she didn't understand what he meant. Well, she understood the part about there being a problem, but not what it was. She tried to tell her mate this, and he, in turn, got confused.

They wheeled about in the sky.

After a time, he managed to convey what he wanted, if not why he, or, rather, the Provider, wanted it done. She didn't have any real objection, but she didn't understand how they were to tell one of them from the others.

Her mate seemed to think that this didn't matter, that things would work out anyway. This was somewhat puzzling, but she trusted him.

He led her through the sky, below the overcast.

On the ground, a grey wildcat prowled the night, leaving her nest briefly unattended. She called her mate's attention to this, but he insisted that this other matter, whatever it was, should be attended to first.

They came to a place, and through the darkness, she became aware of a group of animals, much like the Provider himself, huddled together as if in a herd.

They circled, and, after a time, it began to look as if one was being singled out by the others, either to be driven off, or to be mated with, or for some other reason. Was that the one? she wondered. No, all of the others.

Very well, then. Now?

Now.

They flew down together. She felt her wings cup the air, and she was suddenly very close to one of them, his face white and ugly in front of her—

And, her mate insisted in her mind, they were not to bite. How could she not bite? How?

Very well, she would do her best for him.

She hissed and veered away, looking for another, but the others were already running away. Would her mate allow pursuit? Yes, he would allow pursuit. A little, at any rate. She set off after them.

When her mate thought they had frightened them

enough, she pulled up, swirled around her lover, held her breath, and they climbed above the overcast once more, taken again by the sudden beauty of the countless stars. They danced there for a while, laughing together, then turned to where the Provider waited for them with, her mate told her, his thanks.

Just his thanks? Wasn't there something tasty to go along with his thanks?

Of course. Wasn't there always?

Chapter Eight

I will not marry a guzzling drinker,
I will not marry a guzzling drinker,
He'd be no lover and no thinker.
Hi-dee hi-dee ho-la!
    Step on out . . .

SAVN STEPPED INTO the house, shutting the chill out behind
him. The fire on the hearth had died down to coals, but the
stove was still giving off heat. It seemed very safe; but he
didn't feel any sense of relief. This was strange, and it occurred to him that he hadn't felt frightened—that he hadn't
felt much of anything.

"Where have you been?" said Mae, in a dim, distracted
sort of way, as if she expected a reasonable answer, and
would be satisfied with almost anything.

Even while Savn was wondering what to say, he heard
his own voice explaining, "A minstrel showed up at Tem's
house, so I stopped and listened to her."

"Oh, that's nice," Mae said. "Perhaps tomorrow, after
the harvest is done, we'll all go together. Was she good?"

"Yes, Mae," said Savn, wondering how he was manag-
ing to answer.

"Well, go to bed now. Your sister's already asleep, and
we have a big day tomorrow."

"I will, Mae."

Pae listened to this mild interrogation with abstracted
interest, and made no comment.

There is much that I do not understand, thought Savn, looking at Mae and Pae. *Everything has changed somehow, and nothing makes sense anymore. Why don't I care? What is happening to them? What is happening to me?*

Savn found his place next to Polyi, who was already asleep. He got into his nightclothes and crawled in among the furs, warmed by the low fire in the stove. It was starting to get chilly at night. Funny he hadn't noticed it earlier this evening. Or maybe not; he'd been occupied with— with other things.

He lay back and stared at the ceiling, his thoughts running in circles like mating tsalmoth.

Tomorrow morning would see the end of the harvest.

Then would come the Festival.

Then would come ... what?

He didn't want to stay in Smallcliff anymore, but the idea of leaving was dim, impossible, unreal—as unreal as the experience outside the house, as unreal as those things he'd learned from the Easterner, as unreal as what had happened that night. He was caught between leaving and staying, but the choice was somewhere off in the distance.

The idea of the morning was also dim, impossible, and unreal. And the day that was ending could not have happened. Maybe it was a dream. He'd have to tell Coral about it. . . .

Coral ... the jhereg ... the same ones? Vlad ...

What do you do when nothing makes sense? Stare at the ceiling and watch it dissolve into wavy lines, and wonder if your future is engraved therein.

Savn slept, and if he dreamed, he had no memory of it. The next thing he knew it had become morning, and with the morning came the familiar sounds of everyone stirring around and the smell of the tea that Pae, always the first one up, brewed fresh for the family every morning. Savn's arms were stiff and sore; he had fallen asleep with them locked behind his head. He made fists and shook his arms, then stared at his hands as if they were not part of him. He remembered that Vlad had looked in the same way at his maimed hand.

Everything had an odd, ethereal feel, as if time had become disconnected. Savn stood outside the house and realized that he didn't remember breaking his fast, yet he felt the warmth of the bread in his stomach. Later he stood behind Polyi, holding a sack, and didn't remember getting there, nor how the sack had become so full.

Pae was in the bins, already beginning to seed and strip the plants, preparing to send them off to town, while Mae was counting and weighing the sacks in order to make the account, so Savn and Polyi were alone in the field. Occasionally Polyi would say something, and Savn would realize a little later that he had answered, but he had no memory of the conversation.

They finished the harvest, and he hardly noticed. Polyi cut the last plant, Savn put it in the half-full sack, tied it, and hauled it in to Pae. There had been no need for such caution; it hadn't rained. But then, if they'd neglected to store everything in the bin, it probably would have. Was that really true? Was anything really true?

Savn set the sack next to the full ones. He felt Polyi standing behind him. Pae looked at the sack, and gave Savn a smile which he felt himself responding to.

"That's it," said Polyi.

"Well," said Pae, standing, his knees cracking. He wiped his hands on his leggings, and said, "Fetch the bottle, then. You know where it is."

He's an old man, thought Savn suddenly. But that thought, too, was distant.

"Mae's getting it already," said Polyi. "Are we going to drink it here?" She looked around the bin, full of sacks. The smell of linseed oil seemed to hang in the air.

"Why not?" said Pae. "Well, perhaps we can step out into the air."

It's odd, thought Savn, *that none of them think I'm acting strange. Even Polyi didn't notice while we were working. Maybe I'm not acting strange at all. Maybe I just feel funny, and no one can tell.*

Mae came in with the bottle and four of the special mugs, set on the silver tray. She unwrapped the top, pulled the wax from the bottle's mouth, and handed it to Pae to pour. Savn was keenly aware of the faded black lettering against the green label, and found himself wondering who had written that label— Was it done where the wine was made? Who made the bottle? Did he live in a big city somewhere? Did he ever wonder who would buy the bottle, and what would go in it, and who would drink from it?

For that matter, Savn thought, *where does all of this flax go? That last plant we cut down, what will happen to it? Will the fiber be thrown away, or turned into linen? What will the linen be used for? Sheets? Perhaps a gown for a lady? Who will wear it? The seeds will be turned into oil blocks, and then it will be put in the coolhouse, and then packed into barrels and sent somewhere. Who will use that bit of oil? And for what? Probably it will be made into linseed meal to feed the livestock. Or maybe given to His Lordship to sell.*

His Lordship . . .

Could he really be undead?

Savn shuddered, and became aware that he was now back in the house, standing in a huddle with Mae, Pae, and Polyi, and that the ritual wine-drinking had ended, and he felt a dim sadness that he hadn't been aware of it—he only knew he had participated from the sting on his tongue, the cool ceramic in his hand, and the faint ring of half-remembered words in his ear. He recalled the end of harvest from all the other years, and the memories blended together as tears threatened to come to his eyes, but even this sadness was far removed from where he drifted, in the center of his emotions but not part of them.

"I can't believe it's over," he said.

"Hunh," said Mae, who was drinking while sitting on the cushions below the loft. "It's over for you, perhaps, but we still have to—"

"None of that, Mae," said Savn's father. "The hard part is over, and the children can enjoy themselves today."

Savn wondered if they'd still be "the children" when they had survived a millennium and had children of their own. Probably. He made a note to himself, for the hundredth time, not to refer to his own children that way after they reached their sixtieth year. Well, seventieth, maybe. On reflection, he *had* been pretty young at seventy.

After eating, for which they allowed a good, long time, and after the dishes had been cleaned, Savn and Polyi took a slow walk around what had been the garden, jumping from stone to stone and playing sticks and bricks. Polyi chatted about how sore she was, and how she hadn't even noticed at the time, and about how it was such a shame that by the time harvest was over it was too late to swim, and did he remember the sweater she'd been working on all summer, and did he think the color was right for her. Savn said that this was the first harvest he remembered where he *wasn't* sore afterwards, and attributed it to the way he'd spent most of the summer rearranging Master Wag's house, and that he, too, would enjoy swimming, and did Polyi know a girl named Lova and what did she think of her.

It was, in all, one of the most pleasant mornings Savn had had since summer, and he felt sad that he wasn't really there to enjoy it.

He heard Polyi suggesting that they go to Tem's house early; she had heard that a minstrel had arrived last night. Savn heard himself agreeing. *Tem's house? Yes, there will be a minstrel. And Vlad will be there, and perhaps Coral and Tuk and Lan. Why aren't I afraid?*

Mae and Pae didn't mind their leaving early.

What had Pae said? Something about having done well this year. Savn put the big kettle over the fire to prepare bath water for himself and Polyi, then stood in the door, looking out over the stubble of the harvested fields, and a little later he realized that he was now wearing clean clothes, and his hair smelled of soap. Polyi was saying that she was ready to go, and asking if Savn was.

He shook his head, as if he could clear it of whatever strange mood had fallen upon him, then nodded to Polyi. She looked slightly puzzled, then seemed to forget about it as they set off for town.

The morning was still bright around them, the air cool

with the promise of autumn. The red, yellow, and gold of
the leaves, already starting to fall, exploded all about them
as they walked. Polyi sang "Dung-Foot Peasant," and
didn't seem to notice that Savn wasn't joining in.

They passed the place where, as near as he could guess,
he had been attacked the night before by his best friends.
Why aren't I afraid?

As they came into town, Savn noticed Bless on the
other side of the street, along with his apprentice, Ori. Ori
was looking at them, but then he looked away and said
something to Bless, who glanced at them quickly, took Ori
by the shoulder, and turned him in the other direction
while saying something in his ear. *Why don't I care?*

Polyi had not noticed them, which seemed odd, too;
Polyi, like all the other girls in town, always noticed Ori.
*Maybe it's a disease, and I've given it to Mae and Pae and
Polyi. I could ask Master Wag. Only I won't. Perhaps I
should ask Bless, but I don't think he wants to talk to me.*

Tem's house was empty except for Tem and Vlad, the one
behind his counter, the other at the far end of the room. The
minstrel was not in sight. Savn looked at the Easterner, and
found that he had begun to tremble.

"What is it, Savn?" said Polyi.

So, she's noticing something, he thought. "Nothing. I
don't feel well."

"Here, sit down."

"Yes."

Vlad was not looking at him.

He realized, and wondered why it had taken him so
long, that the Easterner had, somehow, been responsible
for the two jhereg who had chased Coral, Lan, and Tuk
away last night. Yes. It had really happened. They were
going to beat him—had actually hit him—and then there
was the flapping, and the small, horrible shapes, wings
dark in the darkness. It had been real. It had all been real.
And, somehow, the Easterner had done it. Polyi went to
fetch ale for him and watered wine for herself while Savn
sat and trembled.

To have such power . . .

He glanced at Vlad, but the Easterner was sitting back in his chair, staring at the ceiling as if deep in thought. Savn's intention had been to ignore Vlad; and if Vlad had even looked at him, he would have been able to do it. But it was as if Vlad, by ignoring him, was saying, "I understand that you don't want to be seen with me, and it's all right." And that was something Savn would hate.

Polyi came back and set a glass down in front of him. He stood up and said, "I'll be back in a minute," and walked over to Vlad's table. The Easterner glanced up at him, then looked away as if he didn't recognize him.

Savn hesitated, then sat down.

Vlad looked at him again. "Good morning," he said. "I didn't expect you so soon."

"Harvest is done," said Savn. "We finished early."

"Congratulations. I suppose there will be a festival before too long."

"Yes."

"You'll enjoy that, I think."

"Yes."

Vlad looked at him closely, his eyes narrow. "What is it?" he said.

"Nothing."

"Crap. What's wrong?"

"I don't know. I feel funny."

"Funny, how?"

"Disconnected."

"Mmm. How long have you had this feeling?"

Savn suddenly wanted to laugh, because Vlad was sounding like Master Wag. He did not laugh, however. He said, "I guess since this morning. No, last night, I suppose."

Vlad nodded, slowly, still watching Savn's face. "It'll pass," he said. "I know the feeling. Believe me, I know the feeling."

Savn whispered, "Why did you do it?"

"I beg your pardon?"

He cleared his throat. "Why did they do it?"

"Do what?" said Vlad.

Savn tried to find some indication in the Easterner's face that he knew what Savn was talking about, but Vlad seemed to be frankly inquiring.

"My friends tried to beat me last night."

"Oh," said Vlad. "I'm sorry."

"But why?"

"I don't know," said Vlad. "Fear, perhaps."

"Of me?"

"Of me."

"Oh." Savn could feel Vlad's eyes on him. He looked back, then said, "What did you do?"

"I?" said Vlad. "Nothing."

"But I would have been beaten if—"

"If something happened that prevented a beating, consider yourself lucky and don't ask any questions."

Savn watched him for a while. "You've been beaten before, haven't you? I mean, when you were younger."

"Oh, yes."

"Because you were an Easterner?"

"Mostly."

Savn felt himself smiling a little. "Well, you survived; I suppose I will too."

"Very likely," said Vlad. "Only . . ."

"Yes?"

"Nothing."

"Did you have a friend who helped you?"

The familiar enigmatic smile came and went. "Yes, I did."

"Did he ever explain why he helped you?"

"No," said Vlad slowly, as if the thought had never occurred to him. "No, she never did."

"Did you ever wonder?"

"I still do."

"Maybe I always will, too, then."

"No," said Vlad. "I suspect one day you'll know."

Savn nodded, and decided that this was all the information he was likely to get. "How was your talk with the minstrel?"

"Satisfactory. I got some of what I was after; I'm hoping to get more."

"Then I don't doubt that you will," said Savin. "I'll see you later," he added, standing.

"Are you certain?"

"Oh, yes." Savn felt a small smile come to his lips and wondered if he was starting to copy Vlad's mannerisms. He said, "I still want to impress girls." He walked back to the table where he'd left his sister, and discovered that she was watching him.

"What were you talking to him about?"

"Just passing the time," said Savn, picking up his ale. As he sipped, he realized that whatever mood or spell had been on him had broken; he was himself again.

He finished his drink in silence, then announced, "It's time for me to go."

"Already?"

"Yes."

"All right. I'll wait here for the minstrel."

"Your friends will probably be joining you."

"Maybe," said Polyi, as if she couldn't have cared less.

Savn looked at her for a moment, then leaned over and kissed the top of her head.

"What was that for?" she said.

"Because," he said. "Not everyone has a sister." He stood up and headed for the door. Just before he walked out, he turned and looked at Vlad, who was watching him. Savn inclined his head toward Vlad, and set off to spend the day with Master Wag.

He stopped about twenty paces outside the door, just to take in the day—doing what Master Wag called "Enjoying the now of it all," though Savn thought that was a silly way of putting it.

The row of thin maples that marked the Manor Road wagged in the odd dance of mildly windswept trees, looking as if there were an entirely different breeze for each one. The sky had greyed, covering the overcast and hinting at the rain that Savn had been expecting each day of the harvest. Polite of it, he decided, to wait until they were done.

There was almost no one in sight, perhaps because of the threatening weather. Savn rather enjoyed being rained on, unless it was also cold and windy, but most people seemed not to like—

His meditations were interrupted by the odd sight of six or seven strangers walking around from behind Plaster's hut, just across the way from Tem's. They were all armed with long, heavy swords, and dressed in black, and Savn fancied he could see that above each breast was the Athyra crest of His Lordship.

What would seven of His Lordship's men-at-arms be doing here, now?

He didn't consciously answer his question, nor did he consciously decide to do anything about it, but he turned at once and went back to Tem's to find Vlad.

When he entered once more, Polyi, who was still seated near the door, said, "What is it, Savn?" which was the last clear thing he remembered; all the rest of it he reconstructed afterwards from what Polyi told him and the fragments of memory that remained.

He shook his head and walked over to Vlad's table, according to Polyi. Savn remembered how the Easterner was staring off with a distracted look on his face. Before Savn could say anything, however (Savn was never certain what he was going to say, in any case), Vlad rose abruptly to his feet; the table at which he had been sitting tipped over, landing on its side with a loud *thunk*. Vlad moved so quickly, Savn could hardly see him, which Savn later remembered as being the point at which he realized that Something Was Wrong.

There was a heavy step behind him, and he turned and saw one of the soldiers he'd noticed earlier, now holding his sword and charging through the door, directly at Savn.

No, he realized suddenly, at Vlad.

Savn never remembered deciding to get out of the way, but somehow he was against the counter, watching more soldiers enter the door. They stepped over the body of the

first one—Savn had not seen what happened to him—and
Savn realized the scream in his ears had come from his
sister.

He looked back at Vlad, who was now standing on a table, holding a sword in his right hand, and swinging what
looked like a gold chain in his left. The sight of the Easterner's shiny black boots on top of Tem's table imprinted
itself on Savn's memory and brought back older memories, of a dancer who had come through town a long, long
time ago.

There came a splash of red on the boots, and Savn's
eyes traveled up Vlad's body until he was aware of an
ugly slash along the Easterner's side. He didn't know how
he'd gotten it. He also saw one of the soldiers writhing on
the floor, and there was the glint of steel reflecting the
lamps on Tem's walls.

Somewhere, far from Savn's conscious thoughts, he was
aware of Tem and his guests all scampering out of the way
through doors and windows, but this seemed unimportant;
Savn, unable or unwilling to move, stared at the scene before him.

For just an instant, he was able to watch the swordplay,
three soldiers against the Easterner, all four blades slicing,
thrusting, and whirling as if they went through the move-
ments of a beautiful, terrible dance, and when one slipped
through and struck Vlad deeply in the upper thigh, that,
too, was planned and necessary.

The illusion shattered when Vlad suddenly teetered and
fell, amid tables and chairs. At the same time, one of the
soldiers fell back and turned around. At first, Savn thought
the man's hand had been injured, and then Savn realized
that the man was clutching his throat, which had been horribly cut open. He watched the man fall, and felt ill.

And two familiar, winged shapes flew into the room and
struck at the backs of the two soldiers who still stood, and
two more soldiers came in from the back of the room.

Savn remembered thinking very clearly, *Well, if I had
any doubts about the jhereg, this should settle them.*

There was an instant that was filled with swords flailing

against the air, and then it all stopped, and the two jhereg flew back out the door.

One of the soldiers said, "Where did he go?"

Another said, "Get the healer!"

Another said, "It's too late for Tevitt."

Savn stared at the place where Vlad had been, and where now there were only reddish stains; then, without a thought for the injured soldiers or his terrified sister, he turned and fled out the door. He ran around to the back of Tem's house and hid behind the stables, trembling.

Chapter Nine

I will not marry a starving painter,
I will not marry a starving painter,
I'd get skinny and just grow fainter.
Hi-dee hi-dee ho-la!
      Step on out . . .

SAVN HEARD THE heavy tramp of feet leaving Tem's house.
He waited a little longer to be sure, then made his way
back inside. Polyi sat where she had been, looking awestruck and slightly ill. There were no injured or dead in
sight, but Tem was already cleaning the floor where blood
had been spilled.

He sat down next to Polyi and noticed that his hand was
shaking. He put it on his lap under the table. She said,
"Aren't you late for going to Master Wag's?" as if nothing
out of the ordinary had happened.

"I guess so," he said.

After a moment, she said, "Why did you run out?"

"I was too frightened to stay," he said.

"Oh. Me, too."

"Then why didn't you run out?"

"I was too frightened to move."

"Are you all right now?"

"I think so. I'm shaking."

"Me, too."

He noticed that several people had come in, attracted to
the scene of the excitement by some magic he didn't un-

derstand. They were talking in low tones, and pointing to
the overturned tables and chairs that Tem was in the process of straightening.

"You should go home," said Savn.

"I will," said Polyi. "Are you going to Master Wag's?"

"Yes, I—I'm not certain. I just want to sit here for a
moment."

Polyi's eyes widened suddenly. "I can't wait to tell Slee
about this." Before Savn could say anything, even if he'd
thought of something to say, she was up and out of the
door, running.

Savn considered what he wanted to do. Master Wag was
expecting him, but Vlad was out there somewhere, hurt.
But there was no way to find Vlad, even if he wanted to.

After a moment of thinking, he went up to Tem, who
had finished cleaning the floor. He asked Tem for some
food, which he put into a large sack that Tem supplied.
Tem didn't seem curious about what Savn wanted these
for, or maybe the Housemaster, too, was so stunned by
what had happened that he wasn't thinking clearly. Savn
got a large jug of water, sealed with a wax plug, and put
it into the sack with the food, working it down to the bottom so it wouldn't crush everything else.

He slipped into the back and found an empty bedchamber,
from which he removed a towel, a sheet, and a blanket. Vlad
would be able to pay Tem back for these, if . . .

He went out the back way, and wondered where to begin looking. Vlad had certainly teleported, and done so
faster than Savn had thought possible. How long had it
taken? In fact, he didn't know; everything had happened
so fast. But it was certainly much quicker than it had before.

What was it he had said? Something about if you were
in a hurry . . . Yes, it was about setting up a place to teleport to, which could be anywhere; there was no way to
know—

He suddenly remembered his first sight of the Easterner,
standing next to the Curving Stone, making lines on the
ground with a dagger.

But he had said that was witchcraft.

But he was certainly capable of lying.

Savn began running down the Manor Road, convinced he knew where Vlad was. As he ran, he realized that he had no idea why he was going to all of this trouble, and he wondered, too, about the heavy sack in his hand, which was making running so tiring as it bumped against his hip. He shifted it to his other hand and slung it over his shoulder as he reached the top of the hill and started down the long, bending road that lead to the Curving Stone.

Why am I doing this? he wondered, and the answer came as quickly as he'd formed the question.

If he ignored Vlad, he'd never learn anything more, and what he'd learned felt like a door that had opened just enough to let him see that on the other side was a place he desperately wanted to visit, maybe even to live. And he knew he would always berate himself for cowardice if he let himself be driven away from the Easterner.

He could try to sneak around, and still spend time with Vlad without being seen, but that didn't feel right either, and he suspected that he wasn't much good at sneaking around. And to be found out would be worse than being openly seen with him.

But if he continued associating with the Easterner, how would he continue to live here? There wouldn't always be friendly jhereg to—

He shook his head, shying away from wondering how it had happened that, just when he faced being beaten by his friends, out of nowhere there came . . . No. He didn't want to think about it, not yet.

And so, naturally, it was just then that he noticed a rustling in the trees overhead, and, yes, of course there were two jhereg, arrogantly sitting in the branches, almost as if they were watching him. He stopped abruptly and stared back at them.

They were the same size and color as the two he had seen—when was it? He'd been walking with Polyi, and then he'd gone to Master Wag's, which was the day Dame Sullen's arm had been broken, so that would be . . .

The same day Vlad had shown up.

They were the same two, of course; it was silly to try to deny it. The same two who had rescued him, and who had rescued Vlad, and who he'd been seeing, again and again, since Vlad had appeared. Maybe it had even been one of them that had been sitting on the roof of Tem's house, listening in on everything that was said.

He tore his gaze away and covered the remaining twenty or thirty feet to the Curving Stone, breathing hard, and looked for traces of blood on the ground. He found them right where he expected; large red splotches.

Where had the Easterner gone? He tried to find a trail of blood, but there didn't seem to be one.

He turned back to the jhereg, who were still watching him. If he spoke to them, could they understand him? Of course not. He frowned.

"Well?" he said aloud. "What do you want? Why are you following me?" He swallowed, hearing the echo of strain in his own voice. In the back of his head he heard Master Wag talking about hysteria. The jhereg stared back at him impassively. He shut his eyes, took a deep breath, and opened his eyes again. He spoke again, this time slowly and carefully. "I've brought food for him. Where is he?"

The smaller of the two jhereg spread its wings, then refolded them, looking hesitant. When folded and seen from the side, each wing formed an almost perfect triangle, as if nature had intended to give the beast a shield against the arrows of men. Yet seen from the front, it looked like there was a snake's head bobbing up and down between the walls of two houses that had been built too close together.

It spread its wings again, and this time left its perch. It dropped just a little until it caught the air, and then rose quickly and flew over Savn's head. Its mate followed it, and Savn turned to watch them fly.

They made a high circle, climbing until he thought they were going to vanish into the overcast; then they flew back down so quickly he thought they were about to attack him, but they landed some distance away. He could barely see them through the trees—about forty feet from the road.

Savn plunged into the thicket after them. Just below the tree in which they rested he almost tripped over the Easterner's sword; no doubt Vlad had dropped it as he'd stumbled along. He picked it up by the hilt, noticing that the blade was still stained with blood. He wondered what it was like to hit someone with it. His musings were interrupted by a hiss from one of the jhereg. He jumped, startled. They were, apparently, impatient for him to find Vlad.

Very well, then. He looked further ahead, and at once saw a dark object, not far away at all, that looked like it didn't belong. A few steps closer and he realized that it was the bottom of Vlad's boot, toe pointed toward the sky.

Savn knew, even before he reached Vlad, that the Easterner was alive, because his breathing was obvious—quick and shallow. Breathing like that meant something, he knew, but he couldn't remember what. Or maybe there were several things it could mean. Was it blood loss? It wasn't a concussion, he was sure of that. It occurred to Savn that one of Vlad's lungs might have been punctured, in which case he'd be unable to do anything except watch the Easterner die.

Savn came up next to him, knelt down, and studied his face, seeing at once that his skin had an odd grey tint and that his lips were blue, and, in fact, so were his eyelids and ear lobes. The colors meant something; he was sure of it. Savn shook his head and thought, *He's dying.*

And so he seemed to be. Not only did his lung appear punctured, but it looked like his neck had been broken—the veins and the windpipe stuck out horribly from the throat, and at a funny angle, down toward the Easterner's left side.

He was muttering as well, but only incoherent sounds, grunts and squeaks, as if his ability to make words were gone. His arms and torso were moving weakly, and without any apparent purpose. A terrible sorrow filled Savn—he was convinced that Master Wag would be able

to heal him, punctured lung and broken neck or not, but
Savn himself just didn't know enough. If Master Wag
were here, he'd . . .

Savn frowned. If Vlad's neck was broken, could he
move about like that? Savn tried to think of what the Master had said about such injuries, but he couldn't remember
hearing about them. The Master had spoken about the
neck as the stream that fed the mind, and that if the spine
were severed, the brain would starve from want of
thoughts. Maybe this was what he meant; this was what a
body did when there were no thoughts to guide its actions.
It was horrible.

And then, as if to underline the ghastly sight, Vlad's delirious babbling ceased long enough for Savn to hear an
awful sucking, bubbling sound that came from somewhere
on his body.

As Vlad began mumbling again, Savn wondered what
could cause the sucking noise. If the lungs had been
pierced, that might account for a wheezing, but would the
escaping air sound like that? Probably, he decided. But
still . . .

There was a dagger at Vlad's belt. He removed it and
one of the jhereg hissed at him.

"Shut up," said Savn abstractedly. He cut open Vlad's
jerkin down the middle and pulled it aside, exposing a
chest full of dark, curly hairs. Was that normal for Easterners? He didn't stop to give it further thought, because he
saw the wound at once—about halfway down on Vlad's
right side. There wasn't all that much blood—Savn almost
wished there were more, so that he wouldn't have to look
at the pink tissue that was lying open—but what there was
of the escaping blood bubbled and frothed.

Vlad's breath was still coming rapidly, and was very
shallow. Oddly, though, only one side of his chest—the
left side, away from the wound—was rising and falling.
And what bothered Savn most about the queer chest movement was that he'd seen or heard of such a thing before.

Where? When?

He looked at Vlad's face once more; it was grey, but

seemed no more so than it had a moment before. He looked again at Vlad's chest, watching the left side rising and falling rapidly, while the right side hardly moved. It was familiar, and it wasn't. He closed his eyes, and tried to recall Master Wag's words.

"I found it because I was looking for it. It isn't the sort of thing you can see easily. . . ."

That couldn't be it, because it *was* easy to see.

"I was looking for it because I found the broken rib. And I found the broken rib because it was hit in the side."

Wait, though. "It"?

". . . the sort of thing you can see easily in a pig." Yes! Cowler's stud-hog, butted by their goat. Cowler had spent ten minutes on his knees begging Master Wag to look at it, because Birther was off somewhere, and Master Wag had finally agreed only because he thought Savn might be able to learn something useful. "We're a lot like pigs, inside, Savn," he'd said, and refused to make any jest on the subject. Yes.

Vlad was still mumbling. Savn tried to ignore him and remember what the Master had said. It hadn't been *that* long ago. ". . . knocked a hole in the Cave of the Heart, so the lung collapsed . . . no, not the heart, the *Cave* of the Heart, where the heart and the lungs live. Same thing can happen to a man, you know. You'll learn about that some day. Now, go fetch a bottle with a plug, and you'll learn what I can do with a couple of reeds. Good thing this was a hog; they have the same sort of lungs we have, which I told you half an hour ago, though you probably weren't listening, as usual. You'll learn about that, too, someday. Run along now, before this smelly beast up and dies and makes a fool of me."

The procedure came back to him, and with the memory came the fading of hope. He had the water, which he'd brought for Vlad to drink and to repel the Imps of Fever from the wound, and there was even a wax plug in it, but he had no reed, nor anything that could be used as one; none of the plants that grew around here were both hollow and wide enough to work, and it would take hours to reach the river and return. Vlad didn't look like he would live for hours.

He glanced at the sword which he'd dropped next to Vlad. If it was hollow, it would be perfect; long and flexible . . .

He stared at the empty sheath at Vlad's hip. How well-made was it? Savn had drunk from leather flagons; leather could certainly be made watertight.

He had to hurry, but there was still time for thought. He'd waste less time if he figured out what he had to do, every step, before he did anything else. Finding the sheath was enough to give him hope; he began to think that everything he needed was here if he could just find it; what he had to do was get it right the first time. How could he make the puncture? No, he didn't have to; the sword that had cut Vlad had made a fine puncture; all he had to do was to seal it up while he was working on it, and then again afterwards. How?

Well, for the first step, his hand would do well enough, but how about later? The sheet he'd taken from Tem's house certainly wasn't airtight; could it be made so? Was something that was watertight also airtight? It had to be; how could air get through if water couldn't? Well then, if he could find a candle, he could melt wax onto the cloth from the sheet.

He took Vlad's belt off, found his belt pouch, dumped it out, and looked at the contents. There was a piece of flint (why would a sorcerer need flint?), a few odd-looking sewing-needles (but no thread), a few scraps of paper, a purse with several gold coins in it as well as some silver, a bit of wire, a few small clay vials of the kind that Master Wag kept potions in, but no candles. Well, that made sense, why would a sorcerer need a candle? Then he frowned . . . the wax plug on the water bottle? He'd have to melt it, but it might work. So he'd need a fire. Okay, there was plenty of wood around, and he could set the cloth near the fire, and then cut shavings from the plug and set them on top of the cloth where they could melt and make an airtight seal to put over the wound; it wouldn't have to be very big; the wound itself was less than an inch wide.

He should cut the strips first, before doing anything else, so he could have them ready. And he'd have to cut the bottom of the sheath. . . . What about the second tube? Oh, yes, there was the sheath for Vlad's dagger. That was also leather. Would they both fit in the jug?

He felt an instant's panic at the thought that he'd dropped the food sack somewhere, but it was sitting next to him, where he'd set it down while he looked at Vlad. He took out the water jug he'd gotten from Tem. Yes, the mouth was good and wide. It would be hard to jam the leather sheaths through the wax plug though, and he'd have to be careful not to push the plug out, or rather in. Well, he had the dagger, he could cut holes in it.

How much water should be in it? He wished someone would make a jug one could see through. Well, about half-full would be easiest, because then he could be certain that the long sheath was in the water and the short sheath was out of it—or was it supposed to be the other way around? No, that was right: "wound to water, air to air," Master Wag had said. "Why?" Savn had asked. "Because it works," the Master had replied.

Savn went through the entire procedure in his mind, and when he was sure he had it right, he cleared a three-foot circle of ground, gathered a few twigs and leaves and struck a small fire with his own flint an arm's length from Vlad. He got it going, added a couple of branches, and found a few rocks to set next to it. While they were getting warm, he cut several strips from the bedsheet he'd taken from Tem's house and set them on the stones.

The jhereg hovered around, looking interested; Savn tried not to think about them. Vlad seemed greyer. His arms and legs were still moving about without purpose, and he'd shifted his position slightly. The odd angle of his throat seemed to be worse, too. His speech was still unrecognizable. Savn remembered that Master Wag had said something about the heart being crushed if the Cave of the Heart became too small. Savn started working faster.

The dagger was sharp enough to cut through the leather of the sheaths with little difficulty. Savn made the cuts at an angle, so there was almost a point on them.

He took another look at Vlad. The process—whatever it was—was accelerating; he could almost see Vlad's skin getting greyer. "Don't die," he said aloud. "Don't you *dare* die. You hear me?"

He took the water jug and made two holes in the plug with the dagger, then widened them as much as he dared. "You just hold on there and breathe, and I'll fix you up, but if you die I'll kick you in the head." He measured the two sheaths against the bottle, and made marks on them with the dagger at the appropriate levels. "Breathe now, you Eastern son of a kethna. Just keep breathing."

The smaller of the jhereg watched him raptly. "Okay," he told it, "here's the first hard part." The sword sheath slid into the hole with surprising ease, and the sheath for the dagger just as easily. He held a piece of hot wood near it to melt the wax, then blew on the plug; there was now a water jug with two leather sheaths sticking out of it, looking like the remains of a flower arrangement that hadn't been very pretty in the first place.

"Hmmm," he told the jhereg. "That wasn't bad. Now for the first test." He blew into the open end of the sword sheath, and was rewarded by a bubbling sound from the bottle, and the feel of air against his left hand held over the other sheath.

"Airtight," he announced to the jhereg. "This might really work. I'm glad he has such well-made stuff."

He sat next to the Easterner and put a hand on his chest. Vlad didn't react to the touch, so maybe he was too far gone to notice what was about to happen. This part was scary, and Savn was afraid that if he hesitated at all, his courage would fail. "Here we go," he said to the jhereg, and opened up the wound with his fingers.

The puncture was small but ugly, between the fifth and the sixth ribs, still not bleeding much, but still bubbling and frothing, and making a burbling sound that ought never to come from a body. The end of the sheath would fit over the puncture easily, but he'd have to get past the outer edge of the wound, which might be too big.

Savn started to bend the sword sheath, but the bottle almost tipped over. He cursed, let go of the wound, and bent the sword sheath with both hands, putting a kink into it. That would never do.

He felt himself trembling, and almost gave up the whole idea, but instead he gritted his teeth and played with the position and angle of the bottle until he could draw the long sheath smoothly all the way to the wound with no sharp bends in it.

Once again he opened the wound with the fingers of his left hand and tried to put the point of the sheath into it. It was a tight fit, and the skin actually tore slightly, but he was able to cover the puncture while wrapping the outer edge of the wound over the sheath. He held it in place as tightly as he could, wishing he had thought of a way to secure it without using his hand. Well, with any luck, Vlad's skin would provide the seal, and it wouldn't have to be there long.

It took a long couple of seconds to bend over to the bottle without changing the position of the sword sheath, but he managed, and, while he had the chance, exhaled.

Then he put his mouth over the dagger sheath, made sure of the grip of his left hand, and inhaled through the sheath.

The results were astonishing.

There was a bubbling sound in the bottle and Vlad gave a twitch; Savn was only barely able to keep the sword sheath in place over the wound. But he held tight, and when he dared to look at the Easterner, he could hardly believe the change. Both sides of his body were now expanding evenly, and his throat was no longer angled so oddly—Savn had thought that even if it worked, it wouldn't happen so quickly. Since it had, he was suddenly fearful that he'd overdone it somehow, though he didn't know if that was possible, or what the results would be.

He wished he'd paid more attention to Vlad's normal color, but his skin was certainly losing its ashen appear-

ance, and his lips no longer looked blue. He had stopped
waving his arms about, and his breathing was deeper and
slower.

"That was quick," remarked Savn to the jhereg. The
smaller one hissed, spread its wings, and was still, which
Savn hoped meant that it was pleased.

The next step, however, was the hard one: sealing the
wound without letting Vlad's lung collapse again.

His left hand still held the sheath against the wound in
Vlad's side; he increased the pressure as much as he could,
and took the dagger into his right hand. One of the jhereg
hissed. "Shut up," he said distractedly. "I'm trying to help
him."

Manipulating the knife to shave off bits of the wax plug
while keeping a firm grip on the wound was perhaps the
hardest thing Savn had ever done—he would have been
unable to do it at all if he'd had to hurry. As it was, he
was concentrating so totally that he hardly noticed when
Vlad began speaking again, this time in words, but with no
apparent thought behind them. Savn heard him speak but
paid no attention.

When he had a shaving of wax on the flat of the knife,
he set it on one of the cloth strips that was resting on the
rock near the fire, then went back for another shaving before he could take the time to consider how difficult this
really was. He dropped the next one, left it on the ground,
and went back for another, which he managed to bring
over to the cloth. Then a third.

That should do it.

The wax had melted, and what had been a cloth now
ought to be an airtight patch. He picked it up by an end
and waved it around enough to cool it off.

"Here it goes," he told the jhereg. The jhereg watched
him mutely.

Savn held the patch next to the wound, and at as close
to the same time as he could, withdrew the makeshift tube
and slapped the cloth over it.

Vlad moaned once, but fortunately didn't begin thrashing. Savn watched his chest motions, but they never wavered. He held the patch in place and took some of the longer strips to wind them about Vlad's body.

One problem that he hadn't anticipated was how hard it would be to get the cloth under the Easterner's back while making sure the patch didn't slip from the wound, which would open up the Cavern of the Heart and he'd have to do everything all over again. In the end, he had to let go of the patch for an instant, but fortunately the wax seemed to hold it against Vlad's skin long enough for Savn to slip the cloth strip under him. He positioned it carefully, then tied it tight around the Easterner's stomach, making sure it held the patch in place. Then, just to be sure, he wrapped two more strips around Vlad, again making them as tight as he could.

He let out his breath as if he'd been holding it the entire time, and said, "I don't believe I did it." He stood up and staggered over to a nearby tree to rest his back. He noticed that his hands were shaking. That was stupid. Why should they shake now, when everything was all right? Well, it was a good thing they hadn't been shaking before.

The smaller jhereg hissed at him angrily. It seemed to be staring intently at Vlad's left leg, where blood had soaked through his leggings.

"Oh," said Savn wearily. "Yes. Well, he can't be bleeding much, or he'd be dead already." The jhereg resumed hissing at Savn. He sighed and went back to Vlad, made a slit down his legging and pulled it back to expose the wound, which was still bleeding, though not profusely. He splashed water over it so he could see it better, and because water was always good for keeping the Fever Imps from a wound.

The small jhereg was staring at Savn, as if waiting to hear the report of his examination. "The seam itself is but shallow," he said, imitating Master Wag's tones, "yet the scar will go from his knee to his ankle, and it will take a great deal of cloth to cover it. I hope I have enough," he added to himself. Then he noticed how bloody the water was, and resolved to find a stream and get clean water as soon as he could.

Vlad was still talking to himself. Savn made certain his breathing was all right and that his throat looked straight, then set about cutting the rest of the sheet into strips, wondering why his throat had been fixed at that funny angle, and what had caused it to return to normal. He would have to ask the Master about that.

Master Wag would, no doubt, consider that today had been well-spent in learning his future trade, but Savn had no intention of telling him about it.

He gave Vlad a last inspection. As far as he could tell, the Easterner would be fine; he'd even stopped mumbling. For a moment Savn just stared at the Easterner, amazed that someone who had been so close to dying a few short minutes before now appeared to be sleeping peacefully, as if nothing at all was wrong with him. He felt unreasonably annoyed, as if Vlad's apparent health were mocking all the work he'd done. Then he shook his head. "I'll never understand how people are put together," he muttered.

She perched in one of the thick lower branches of a friendly maple and watched her mate, waiting for the signal to kill, but it didn't come.

She was not unhappy with the battle she'd been in earlier, but when the Provider had been hurt, her mate had screamed as if he'd been the one who was injured. She wished she'd understood what the fight had been about, since no one had seemed interested in eating anyone, but she was used to this. She also wished her mate would decide once and for all whether this soft one below her was a friend or an enemy.

Her mate continued watching it, and she felt his moods—now suspicion, now amusement, now something not unlike affection—but never a firm decision. She whipped her tail with impatience, but he didn't notice, and just then she suddenly realized that the Provider was going to live. This surprised her, although she hadn't been aware of how she knew he was dying, either.

And at about this same time, her mate suddenly turned, took to the air, and landed beside her.

Very well, then, they'd let the soft one live. She hoped either it or the Provider would supply some food soon; she was hungry, and she hated hunting.

Chapter Ten

I will not marry a wealthy trader,
I will not marry a wealthy trader,
He'd keep me now and sell me later.
Hi-dee hi-dee ho-la!
    Step on out ...

SAVN BECAME AWARE that the shadows had lengthened, and wondered if he'd fallen asleep, sitting with his back to the tree. Perhaps he had. Everything was very still. He checked Vlad's breathing, which was all right, then checked the bandage on his leg, which had soaked through. He removed it and inspected the wound. It was no longer bleeding, at any rate—or, rather, it hadn't been bleeding until he removed the bandage. He knew there was a way to take bandages off without starting the wound to bleeding again, but he couldn't remember what it was. It annoyed him that he could have managed something as tricky as getting Veld's lungs working again but couldn't remember how to treat a wound.

But he cleaned it once more, using the water sparingly, then wrapped it in what remained of Tem's fine cloth bedsheet. He noticed again how bloody the water looked, and wondered if it really mattered; it was, after all, Vlad's own blood; perhaps it was good for him.

He leaned against the tree again. He wondered if he ought to go to Master Wag's where he was expected, but he didn't want to leave Vlad alone; he preferred not to take any chances on someone or something, by accident or design, undoing all of his work.

As this thought formed, he realized that he felt rather fine; he had managed a very difficult procedure under far from ideal conditions, in spite of having only the vaguest idea of what the problem was, much less the solution. He looked at Vlad and smiled, then looked at the two jhereg, who were now seated next to each other on the ground, their wings folded.

"I feel like I can do anything," he told them.

The smaller one looked at him for a moment, then curled around and rested its head on its neck, looking at Vlad. What was the relationship between Vlad and the jhereg? It had something to do with witchcraft, he knew, but what was it exactly? Would he ever know? Would he ever be enough of a witch to do such things himself?

Why not?

If he could save a man's life with a jug of water and two pieces of leather, he ought to be able to perform spells, especially after everything he'd been shown. He remembered that odd state of mind, which felt like a dream, but where his thoughts were sharper than being awake—distant, but present. Why shouldn't he be able to get there himself? He remembered how Vlad had done it; he should be able to do it on his own.

He leaned back against the tree, pretending he was sinking into it. Slowly, methodically, he took himself through the procedure that Vlad had shown him, relaxing his head, neck, shoulder, arms, and every other part of his body. By the time he reached the soles of his feet, he felt curiously lethargic—he knew he could move if he wanted to, but he didn't want to; he was held motionless by his own will. It was an odd feeling, but not quite what he wanted.

Sink, he told himself. *Back into the tree, down into the ground. Feel heavy. I am a beam of light, and empty, and I will travel in and down. I am heavy, so I will fall. There are steps that lead into the tree, past its roots. I will take each, one at a time, and with each step, I will go deeper.* And, almost to his surprise, it worked—he felt light as air, heavy as stone; his vision was as intense as a dream, yet he could control it.

He was very aware of his own breathing, of the sounds of the small, scurrying animals around him, of the light through his eyelids. He wished to remove himself from all of these things that were part of his world, so: *Again, deeper. Deeper. Draw in and down.*

Savn imagined his body sinking further through the dirt and the clay and the stone, and with each layer, he became more distant from himself, from Vlad, from the world he knew. He was aware of controlling his descent, and so he gave up the control, and drifted.

Falling through the ground to the spaces beneath, alone, spinning in place, seeing without eyes, walking without legs, coming to an emptiness where emotion is pale and translucent, and sensations are the fog through which thoughts are observed. He regarded himself, reflected in narrow seclusion, and realized that, in fact, he was not alone, had never been alone. His sister, his mother, his father, Master Wag—they slowly spun around him, looking away; his own gaze retreated and advanced, went past them all, past his friends, past the Easterner.

He created a vast forest to walk through—a forest the like of which he'd never seen, where the trees rubbed shoulders and their tall, thick branches created a roof. At his feet was a large silver goblet. He picked it up and carried it with him for a while, enjoying the coolness he imagined against his fingers. Or did he imagine it?

There was a break in the forest, a clearing, and tall grasses grew there. He was barefoot now, and he loved the way the grass felt between his toes. In the center of the clearing was a pond of clear water. He dipped his goblet into it, and drank. It was very cold, yet he knew that he could dive in and it would be as warm as a spring afternoon. He thought of doing so, but now was not the time.

He walked on, and before him was a high stone wall. In the way of dreams, it had appeared before him with no warning, stretching out to the sides forever, and towering high above him. For a moment he quailed, as if it were a threat rather than an obstacle, but he thought, *This is my dream, I can do as I will.*

And so he took to the sky, like a jhereg, circling once, then up, past the wall and out over the chasm of the future, into which he could climb or jump, the choice arbitrary but full of significance.

Like a jhereg?

There was a jhereg there—no, two of them—flying about over and under him, saying, *Isn't it grand to fly to fly to fly? But now you must choose must choose must choose.*

It annoyed him, to be told what he had to do by jhereg, so he refused to choose, but instead continued once he was over the wall, continued aloft, light as the air, warmed by the winds of chance, until the burden of his own power threatened to pull him down.

"I need wings," he said to the emptiness below him.

"No," said a voice which he did not recognize. "You *are* wings. You do not fly, you are flight."

The surprise of hearing a voice where nothing could exist outside of his will was buffered by the words themselves—What did it mean to be flight? He was now wrapped in the dream fabric he had created, and in his confusion chasm and world disappeared, leaving him bodiless and nowhere, yet he scarcely noticed, for the sensation of flight never left, which, he realized suddenly, was the answer.

"I can go anywhere, then; do anything."

"Yes." The voice was quiet, and echoed oddly in what were not his ears, its age and sex impossible to determine, and irrelevant.

"But this is only my dream. When I am awake, I can't fly and there is only one path."

"This place will always be here."

"But it isn't real."

"Real? No. It is not. The trick is to find this place along the one path you think you have. Then, perhaps, you will find others."

"I don't understand."

"I know."

"This is where Vlad lives, isn't it?"

"Sometimes."

"Are you G'mon, the Lord of Dreams?"

The answer was accompanied by a laugh that reminded him of Polyi's. "No."

"Then who are you?"

"It does not matter."

Below him, around him, there were points of light. He knew without trying that he could focus on any of them, and learn of it, and it would be as important as he chose to make it. How, then, to choose among them?

"What does matter?" he said.

"You matter, and he matters."

"He? Vlad?"

"Yes."

"I need his help."

"Yes, you do. But he needs you more than you need him, you know."

"I saved his life."

"Yes. And he will need you again."

"For what?"

"Be kind," said the voice, trailing away in an impossible direction. He tried to follow, and rose up, up, up. The world he had built was gone, so he thought to build another as he rose. He was climbing now, and weaving in and out of thick strands that were the roots of the tree of the world. There was a strange sound, and it was a coolness on his face. The darkness had become light, yet he was unaware of the transition. Sensations grew, and seemed real: a stiffness in a shoulder, the fluttering of a bird, the smell of the trees and the brush.

He opened his eyes.

"You were far away," said Vlad.

Savn stared. The Easterner still lay on his back, but his eyes were open. In his hand was the wax plug from the bottle, and the two leather sheaths that were still thrust through it.

"You're awake," said Savn.

"Yes."

"How do you feel?"

"Pleased to be alive, as well as surprised."

"I—"

"No," said Vlad, "don't tell me." He looked at the odd device in his hand, inspecting the blood at the cut end of the sword sheath. "I think I'd rather not know how you did it."

"All right."

"But I owe you my life, and I won't forget that. Where did you go?"

"I was, uh, I guess I was exploring."

"How was your journey?"

"It was . . . I don't know. I'm not sure where I went."

"Tell me about it."

"Well, I was alone, only then everyone was there, and I made a forest and walked through it, and then there was a wall, and I flew over it, and there was a voice. . . ." He scowled. "I don't think I can describe it."

"That was sufficient," said Vlad. "You went to visit your dreams."

"Yes. I knew it was a dream, and I knew I was making it up."

"Did you like your dream?"

"Yes," said Savn, sitting up suddenly. "I did."

"That's a good sign, then. You should always like your own dreams."

Savn didn't know what to say. On the one hand, he wanted to talk about it, but on the other, it seemed too private. He waited for Vlad to ask him a question, but the Easterner just closed his eyes.

"I have some food," said Savn.

"Not now," said Vlad.

"Do you think you can move?"

"No."

"Oh. I'd like to get you somewhere safer."

"Then you know I'm in danger?"

"I saw the fight."

"Oh, yes. Sorry. It's a little hazy. How did I do?"

"How did you—"

"Never mind. Perhaps it will come back to me."

The two jhereg rose, took a couple of steps forward, and flew off. Savn tried to follow them with his eyes, but they soon became lost in the trees. A moment later, Vlad said, "There is no one around."

"Still," said Savn. "I'd like—"

"In a while. I'm feeling very weak, right now; I need to rest. You don't have to stay, however. I'll be fine."

Savn grunted. Vlad started to say something else, but instead he closed his eyes again. Savn ate bread and cheese, then took a chance and carried the water jug to the nearest stream and filled it, which took over an hour. When he returned, Vlad was still sleeping, but presently his eyes snapped open and he said, "Is someone pounding nails into my side?"

"No, you—"

"Just wondering."

"It hurts?"

Vlad didn't see fit to answer this question; he just closed his eyes tightly, then opened them again, then closed them once more and fell asleep. Savn felt his forehead, which he remembered to be the first place the Imps of Fever liked to attack, once a wound had allowed them into the body—he remembered how Master Wag had sat up with Lorr from Bigcliff for three days, bathing his head and chanting. But Vlad's forehead seemed, if anything, slightly cool. Perhaps Easterners had cooler blood than humans.

It occurred to Savn that wet applications and chanting couldn't hurt, in any case. He took some bloody scraps of the first bandage he'd made, dampened them, and put them on Vlad's forehead, while pronouncing as much as he could remember of the ward against Fever Imps. He also tried to make Vlad drink water, and had some success, though much more water dribbled down his face than went into his mouth. Savn continued the chanting and the applications for about half an hour, until he noticed that Vlad was awake and watching him.

"How do you feel?" said Savn, who, for some reason, felt self-conscious.

"Weak," said Vlad. "My side hurts like . . . It hurts."

"Can you eat?"

"No."

"You should eat."

"Soon."

"All right. Want some water?"

"Yes."

Savn gave him some water.

"I've been having some odd dreams," said Vlad. "I can't tell how many of them are real. Did I just have a fight with about six very large people with swords, wearing livery of the Athyra?"

"Seven, I think."

"And one of them got me?"

"Two or three."

"And I got a few of them?"

"Yes."

"So that much was real. I was afraid it might be. Did someone harness me to a horse and use me as a plow?"

"No."

"I suspected that was a dream. Were there three little tiny people standing around me arguing about who got what pieces of my body, and what to do with the rest?"

"No."

"Good. I wasn't sure about that one." He winced suddenly, his jaw muscles tightening and his eyes squinting. Whatever it was passed and he let out his breath. "My side really hurts," he said conversationally.

"I wish there was something I could do," said Savn. "I don't know much about stopping pain—"

"I do," said Vlad, "but witchcraft would kill me, and sorcery would make my brain explode. Never mind. It will pass. I hope. Did I talk during my dreams?"

"You were mumbling when I got to you, but I couldn't hear any of the words. Then, later . . ."

"Yes?" said Vlad, when Savn didn't continue.

"You said things."

"What sorts of things?"

Savn hesitated. "You said some names."

"What names?"

"Cawti, was one."

"Ah. What were the others?"

"I don't remember. I think you called 'Kiera.' "

"Interesting. What else did I say?"

"The only other thing that I could make out was 'wind it the other way.' "

"Hmmm. I imagine that was terribly important."

"Do you think you can move?"

"Why?"

"I don't know. It makes me nervous to leave you out here. We aren't far from the Manor Road, you know, and—"

"And they may be looking for me. Yes. Unfortunately, I really don't think I can move."

"Then I should get you some more blankets, and water, and food."

Vlad seemed to study Savn's face, as if looking there for the solution to some mystery. Then he closed his eyes.

"There's fresh water in the jug," said Savn. "And some food."

"I'll be fine," said Vlad.

"All right," said Savn, and turned back toward the Manor Road, which would take him back into town.

Savn heard the mob before he saw them, which gave him the opportunity to slip off the road before they reached him. He was just coming up over the last hill before Tem's house, and there came an unintelligible assemblage of voices, followed by the tramp of many feet. Savn hid in the flatbushes that grew along the road and watched as the townspeople came over the hill and passed in front of them. There must have been twenty-five or thirty of them, and he recognized several faces. Most of them were carrying hoes and rakes, and he saw knives in a few hands. They seemed grim but excited.

Savn waited for a few minutes after they'd passed, then

rushed down to Tem's house. It was, as he'd expected, empty except for Tem, who was wiping tables, and the minstrel Sara, who was sitting alone with her instruments and a cup. Tem looked up as Savn entered. "You missed them," he said.

"Missed who?" said Savn.

"Everyone. They've gone off to look for the Easterner."

Savn felt as if his heart dropped three inches in his chest. "Why?"

"Why? He killed some of His Lordship's men, that's why. His Lordship sent a messenger telling us that since it happened here, it was our responsibility to look for him."

"Oh. Then they don't know where he is?"

"No, they don't," said Tem. He looked hard at Savn. "Why? Do you?"

"Me?" said Savn. "How would I know? Did everyone in town go?"

"Everyone who was here except me and old Dymon. I stayed to spread the word to anyone who shows up late."

"Dymon didn't go with them?"

"No. He said it was none of our business, and tried to talk everyone out of it. I think he may have had a point, too. But no one else did. He called them a bunch of chowderheads and stormed off."

"Where are they looking?"

"Everywhere. And they're spreading the word, so your Mae and Pae will probably hear about it. You should get on home."

"I guess so," said Savn. He moved toward the door, then stopped and looked back. Tem was ignoring him; Tem didn't want to be part of the mob, either. Nor did old Dymon, whom Savn didn't know well. But what about the rest? What about Lova, and Coral, and Lem, and Tuk? Why was nearly everyone in town so certain that finding and maybe killing Vlad was the right thing to do? Or, put the other way, why was he, Savn, not sure? Had he been enchanted? He didn't *feel* enchanted.

He noticed that the minstrel Sara was looking at him.

On impulse he went up to her table, and without preamble, said, "What about you?"

"I beg your pardon?"

"Why aren't you trying to find Vlad?"

The Issola looked at him. "I'm certain that I would be of no use to them," she said. "And I don't live here, so I don't believe it would be proper for me to interfere."

"Oh. But what about *him*?"

"I'm sorry, I haven't understood you."

"I mean, aren't you worried about what they'll do to him?"

"Well," she said. "One can't go around killing men-at-arms, can one?"

Savn shook his head, and, in so doing, noticed Tem going back toward the pantry, which reminded him why he had come in the first place.

"Excuse me," he told Sara. "I'd best be going."

"Perhaps I'll see you again," said the minstrel.

Savn bowed as well as he could, and continued past her and through the curtain to the guest rooms. He found the room Vlad had stayed in, identifiable by the leather pack on the floor, and picked up this pack, along with a neatly folded blanket that lay at the foot of the bed. He rolled them into a bundle, which he tied with his belt, looked out the window, and then slipped through it.

The afternoon was giving up the battle with evening as he made his way out to the Manor Road, only to be hailed by a call of "Savn!" before he had left the last buildings of town behind him.

He almost bolted, stopped, almost bolted again, then turned and peered into the darkness, realizing that he knew the voice. "Master?"

"You didn't come today. I was expecting you."

"No, Master. I—"

"You were off searching the green for this monster with whiskers, along with everyone else?"

"Uh, no, Master."

"No? Why not?"

"Why aren't you?" asked Savn.

Master Wag snorted, and came closer. "Is that how you talk to your Master?" He didn't wait for Savn to answer, however. He said, "I don't know this Easterner, and he didn't do anything to me, so why should I hunt him down? Now, what about you?"

Savn, not quite knowing why he did so, said, "I want to help him."

"Hmmph. I suspected as much. Why?"

"Well, because . . . I don't know. I saved his life, and if they find him—"

"You saved his life?"

"Yes, Master. He'd been injured."

"Tell me about it."

Savn, as coherently and quickly as he could, gave a brief summary of the fight, explained the odd wound, and described what he'd done about it.

"Hmmph. Not bad. Did you perform the rituals against infection?"

"Not very well, Master. I don't really know them, and I haven't any herbs."

"Hmmph. Then you can bet the demons have infested him by now."

"I think he's past the worst of the wound—"

"Not if he's burning up inside."

"But I can't move him, and he'll need blankets, so—"

"So, nothing. We can find the herbs we need as we go, if we go now, while there's still light."

"*We*, Master?"

"We'll also need torches."

"Torches?"

"It's dark in the caves, and I can't think of anywhere else he'll be safe. There are torches at Speaker's house, but I'd better get them myself, in case Speaker hasn't gone with the others—I don't think you could survive his questions. Wait here while I get them; then we'll go see what we can do for your friend."

Chapter Eleven

I will not marry a filthy hermit,
I will not marry a filthy hermit,
Such a life I could not permit.
Hi-dee hi-dee ho-la!
     Step on out . . .

MASTER WAG, TO Savn's surprise, led them through the woods by paths that he, Savn, had never known. He had always assumed, without really thinking about it, that no one over the age of ninety or so, except perhaps for trappers and hunters, knew anything about the woods. The idea that Master Wag knew, or at any rate remembered, the forest near town startled him.

They made good time, even with a few stops to gather knotweeds and blowflowers, and they found Vlad as daylight was failing. The two jhereg were still there, and hissed suspiciously at Master Wag, who jumped back and began waving his arms around, as if to shoo them away. They didn't move, but kept staring at him as if wondering what his peculiar gestures were intended to accomplish.

"It's all right," Savn said; then he repeated the words, this time speaking to the jhereg. He felt Master Wag looking at him, but the jhereg calmed down, moving closer to Vlad and watching carefully.

"When there is time," said the Master, "you must explain this to me." Then he knelt next to the Easterner. He moved his hand slowly, watching the jhereg. When they remained motionless, the Master touched Vlad's forehead and cheek, and frowned. "He seems feverish," he said, "but I don't know about Easterners—perhaps they have warmer blood than we do."

Savn touched Vlad's forehead and said, "He was cooler than this when I left."

"Well, then."

"What do we do?"

"We get him to a cave, and then we bring his fever down. First, wrap him in the blanket."

"All the blankets? Do we need to keep him warm?"

"No, no. It's just easier to carry him that way. We have to keep him cool, not warm."

"That's what I thought."

"Roll up the blanket first, just a little on each side so we can grip— No, the other way. Good. Now lift his head and I'll slide this— Good. Now lift up his waist. That's right. Now his feet. Good. You're younger than me; you take that end."

"Just a minute," said Savn, and picked up the sack containing the food and the water jug. He looked around for a moment, trying to figure out how to carry it, until Master Wag set it carefully on the Easterner's legs. Savn opened his mouth to object, but could find no reason to. He felt his face turn red and was glad there was so little light.

Savn picked up the blanket at Vlad's head, Master Wag picked it up at Vlad's feet. They had no trouble lifting him. "Master," said Savn, "it's getting dark—"

"I know the way. Let me get turned around . . . There. Now, be careful; we'll have to go slowly."

He led them deeper into the woods, but he must have struck some sort of path, because they didn't have to stop or even slow down. They began to go down a gentle slope, and there were not even twigs brushing against Savn's face, although Vlad seemed to get heavier with each step. Savn recalled the dreamwalking he had done, and wished this journey were as easy.

They came to the loose stone of the slopes above the caves and went down sideways, never quite losing their balance, but feeling the strain of maintaining it. Savn began to feel the effects of carrying the Easterner, light though he was. At about this time Vlad began to moan softly. Savn asked, "Vlad, are you awake?" but the Easterner said nothing that sounded like a response. A little later Savn said, "Master, maybe we should try this one?"

"I don't remember how to get back to the water. Do you?"

Savn blinked back his surprise. "Yes, I think so."

"All right. This way, then. Stop; this is far enough. I have to light a torch, or have you learned how to see in the dark?"

"How can we hold a torch and still carry Vlad?"

"I'll drill a hole in your head for it."

Savn considered himself answered. After carefully setting the Easterner on the floor of the cave, Master Wag brought one of the torches to light. He put it into his fist so it stuck out to the side, then indicated that Savn should pick Vlad up again.

They made their way back into the cave, Savn leading, until they could hear water dripping. "This is as far as we can go," said Savn. "To get to the stream we have to go over this ledge and down a very narrow—"

"I understand. Set him down and let's see how his fever is doing." Vlad moaned again, and muttered something that sounded like "Do it yourself."

Master Wag felt his forehead and said, "Start bathing his face with cool water, and find something to fan him with. I'm going to find the infection and see if we can exorcise it. Here, wipe this on his face, too. I have to find somewhere to put the torch—look!"

Savn looked in the direction Master Wag was pointing, but saw nothing except the two jhereg, who were sitting on the floor of the cave, wings folded, watching the proceedings. "What is it?" he said.

"They followed us!"

"Oh. Well, they've been doing that."

"Mmmmm," said the Master. "All right."

He found a place to wedge the torch in between a pair

of rocks, lit another, and set that on the other side of the cave. His two shadows performed an odd dance as he returned to the motionless Easterner. Savn continued bathing Vlad's face and fanning him with the leather pouch taken from his room.

Master Wag peeled back Vlad's shirt, and carefully removed the bandage. "Not bad," he said.

"Master?"

"You could have done worse with this. But there are no signs of infection, which puzzles me. The fever—"

"Perhaps his leg," said Savn.

Master Wag looked at the bandages wrapped around the Easterner's thigh (which was hairy, like an animal's, though Savn had not noticed this before), and began removing them. "Keep fanning," he said.

Savn did so, and presently Master Wag said, "Yes, indeed."

The wound had changed in the few hours since Savn had bound it. It was red, swollen, and puffy, and there was a thick white fluid coming from it. Savn stared, more fascinated than disturbed.

"Bathe his face again and keep fanning him."

"What are you going to do?"

The Master didn't answer, but began to remove things from his pouch—a sprig of laith, a vial labeled "essence of dreamgrass," another vial with a light brown powder, mortar and pestle—and set them out around himself along with the knotweed and blowflower he'd collected on the way. Once more, watching the fluid efficiency of his hands while he worked, Savn was reminded of Vlad.

"Bathe his face," repeated the Master, and Savn started guiltily, and complied. As he was doing so, his hand touched Vlad's forehead; it had become even warmer in the time it had taken to get to the cave.

Savn began to fan him, but the Master said, "Wait, hold his head up so I can make him drink this."

"What is it?"

"Crushed root of prairiesong, knotweed, and water. Tip

his head—there. Down now, and begin fanning him again. Above all, he must be kept cool."

Master Wag began touching and pressing the wound, and probing it with a thin, silvery tool that Savn could not recall having seen before, and, as he worked, the Master began to chant softly under his breath. Savn wanted to ask about the incantation, the tool, and the procedure, but he didn't dare interrupt the spell. The Master broke off long enough to nod toward a pile of herbs and say, "Mash them well and add a little water."

Vlad began speaking again, muttering phrases of which only a word or two was understandable. Master Wag looked up. "We do not pay attention to the ravings of those under our care," he said, then returned to his soft chanting.

Savn did not answer. He handed the mortar to the Master, who took it without breaking off and poured the contents over the wound. Then he handed the empty vessel back to Savn and said, "Clean it, crush a small handful of those, put in three drops of this, and add more water to it. When it is done, make him drink it."

Savn did so, holding Vlad's head up. Vlad was still speaking, which made it easier to get the liquid down his throat. The Easterner coughed and half-choked, but did manage to swallow it.

The Master stopped his chanting and probing. "Notice," he said, "how the edges of the wound are red. Are your hands clean? Then touch, here."

Savn did so, tentatively. The wound seemed even warmer than Vlad's forehead. "Sometimes," said Master Wag, "it is possible to find the cause, the vehicle on which the Imps rode into the body. This time we were able to."

"What?" said Savn.

"See, on the end of the probe?"

"What is it?"

"I believe it is a piece of his clothing, which was driven into the wound."

"Clothing?"

"We wear clothing, why cannot the Imps? When a piece

of cloth enters the body, it is almost certain that the spirits are riding it to a new home. It is our task to expel them. Thus I poured onto the wound the purest water I could find, mixed with laith, which demons hate, and blowflower leaves which purify. And through his mouth we give him dreamgrass to help him sleep, and prairiesong which cools the soul."

"I see."

"Now I push—here—and we expel the Imps. You see how thick and grey is the solution? That is the grey of death. Necromancers are known to use it for evil purposes, so we catch it on a cloth, which we will then burn thoroughly. Here. Set it aside for now, until we have the chance to build a fire. Hand me a clean cloth."

Savn did these things. Master Wag's mention of necromancers made him think of His Lordship, but he put the thought out of his head, telling himself sternly to concentrate on the task at hand. As he was reaching for the clean cloth, both jhereg suddenly rose as one, stared down the cave, and hissed.

Savn looked but didn't see anything. "Who's there?" he said.

The answer seemed to come from a long distance away, and it was full of echoes. "Savn? Where are you?"

The Master looked at him, his eyebrows raised.

Savn got one of the torches and began walking down back through the cave, the jhereg, still hissing, at his heels. "No," he told them, "it's all right." He wasn't certain if they believed him; at any rate, they continued hissing.

He found Polyi about fifty feet away, apparently caught between several diverging paths. "What are you doing here?"

"Following you," she said.

"Why?"

"To see what— Eek!"

"It's all right," said Savn. "They won't hurt you." He hoped he was right.

"Are those the same—"

"Never mind that. Come with me. We're trying to heal the Easterner."

"I know. I saw you."

The jhereg watched Polyi suspiciously, but didn't seem inclined to attack her. Savn led the way back to where Master Wag was tending Vlad.

"It's my sister," he said.

The Master grunted, then said, "Get back to work."

Polyi didn't speak.

Savn knelt down and touched Vlad's forehead, which was still warm, as well as wet with perspiration.

"Bathe his head," said Master Wag. "And I will teach you the spells. We will recite them together, and we will wait."

"Savn—" said Polyi.

"Not now," said Savn.

Less than an hour later, Master Wag touched Vlad's forehead and said, "His fever has broken. We must let him sleep now."

"My throat is sore," said Savn.

"You must practice chanting," said Master Wag. "Sometimes you will spend hour after hour doing nothing but sitting and reciting the spells. Your Easterner friend is lucky."

Savn nodded. "How long will he sleep?"

"There's no way to know. Probably a long time. But when he wakes, he will require water and—"

"*Murmumph,*" said Vlad. His eyes were open, and his expression was intelligent and aware. The two jhereg, forgotten by the side of the cave, began to hop around near his head. Polyi, who had not spoken for the entire time, just watched, her eyes wide and gleaming in the torchlight.

"I can't understand you," said Savn to Vlad.

The Easterner opened his mouth, closed it again, and said, "Who?"

"This is Master Wag. He treated your fever."

"Fever?" His voice was just above a whisper.

"Yes."

Vlad glanced quickly at the jhereg and at Polyi, then nodded to Savn.

Master Wag said, "Would you like water? Food?"

"Yes," said Vlad. "And yes."

The Master nodded to Savn, who helped Vlad drink from the wineskin. "Do you have food?"

"Yes. I have some bread, and cheese, and spring onions, and beets, and a few seasonings."

"Help me sit up," said Vlad. Savn looked at Polyi. She hesitated, then helped Savn assist Vlad. It seemed to be quite an effort for the Easterner, but at last he was in a sitting position, his back very straight. He took slow, deep breaths. Something about the flickering of the torches made his face seem even more gaunt than usual. "More water," he said.

Savn helped him drink.

"Back down," said Vlad.

Savn and Polyi helped Vlad lower himself, and when he was flat once more, his breathing was labored. He shut his eyes, and in a few minutes his chest rose and fell normally. Savn became aware for the first time of the smell of Vlad's sweat—very much like the smell of a human who had been working hard or was ill.

About the time Savn had decided that Vlad had fallen asleep, the Easterner opened his eyes again and said, "Food?"

Polyi said, "Where—?"

"I'll get it," said Savn.

He found the sack and rummaged around in it until he found the food. As he tore off a piece of bread, he noticed that his hand was trembling. "What should I give him?" he asked the Master.

"The bread is fine, and perhaps some cheese."

"Put a spring onion on it," said Vlad, "and whatever herbs you have."

Savn did so, and then frowned. "Is it all right?" he asked Master Wag.

"Yes," said the Master. "You may season the cheese. You must not put another scallion on it."

Savn held Vlad's head. Vlad managed a couple of laborious bites before he shook his head and asked for water. Savn supplied it, and Vlad leaned back once more, and this time he did fall asleep. While he slept, Savn tried a bite. Not bad, he decided. He offered some to his sister, who declined with a quick shake of her head.

"He'll sleep for a while now," said Master Wag. "Let's start a fire."

"Is it safe to leave him here?"

"Probably. But if your sister wants to help you find wood, I can watch him."

"Would you like to help, Polyi?"

"All right," she said in a small voice.

They took one of the torches and made their way out to the woods. "Savn," said Polyi when they were alone. "What is—?"

"Why did you follow us?"

"I thought you'd know where he was."

"Well, you were right. Now what? Are you going to tell Speaker where we are?"

"I don't know."

They gathered sticks and fagots from the thinly wooded area above the caves. "Why are you helping him?" she said.

"Because he's my friend, and because everyone else is after him, and he didn't do anything."

"Didn't do anything? You saw Reins."

"What makes you think he killed Reins?"

"What makes you think he didn't? And what about all those men of His Lordship's?"

"They attacked him."

"Well, but what's he doing here, anyway? Who is he?"

Savn remembered some of the things Vlad had uttered while feverish, and didn't answer.

They brought the wood back into the cave. "Where shall we put the fire?" asked Savn.

"Over here," said the Master. "Even though his fever is broken, we don't want him getting too warm. Burn the cloth, keep the fire going, and I'll return tomorrow. You should sleep, too."

Savn nodded. The three of them built the fire together, after making certain there was enough of a draft to carry the smoke out of the cave.

"Tomorrow," said the Master.

"I'll still be here," said Savn.

"You will?" asked Polyi.

"Yes."

Master Wag left without another word, taking one of the torches to guide him out. Savn made a pillow out of Vlad's pack, another out of one of the blankets, and stretched out on the hard cave floor. "I'm tired," he said. "We'll talk more after I've slept." Actually, he doubted that he'd be able to fall asleep, but he didn't know what to tell his sister.

As it turned out, he was wrong; he fell asleep almost at once.

Savn woke up to a not-unpleasant, wet warmth in his ear, accompanied by a nibbling that was almost affectionate and tickled. He rolled away from it, but the hard floor of the cave woke him more fully, and as he realized what was licking his ear, he sat up abruptly with a half-stifled scream. The smaller of the jhereg scurried away, then turned to look at him, its wings folded in tightly and its snakelike head bobbing up and down. Savn had the feeling that he was being laughed at.

"What happened?" said Polyi.

"Nothing," said Savn, feeling himself blush and hoping Polyi couldn't see his face in the dim light. The fire had gone out and so had one of the torches. The other torch was burning strongly.

Savn glanced at Vlad, who was awake and staring at the ceiling, apparently oblivious to the comedy being performed around him.

"How do you feel?" asked Savn.

"Water." His voice seemed no stronger than it had before. Savn wondered how much time had passed, and was surprised to learn that it had been almost four hours.

"A moment," said Savn. He lit a new torch and replaced the one that had gone out, then stepped into a side cave and relieved himself. When he returned, he found the skin and made sure there was still water in it, then helped Vlad to drink. Vlad seemed to have some difficulty swallowing. When he had done so, he said, "Weak."

"Food?"

"Later."

"If you need to ease yourself, there is a place not far from here, but you'll have to get up and—"

"I'm all right for now," said Vlad.

"Over there?" said Polyi. "I'll be right back."

The jhereg who had nuzzled Savn did the same to Vlad, who attempted a smile. Savn, watching, had mixed feelings. A little later, Vlad announced that he was ready to eat, and Savn and Polyi helped him do so. The bread was going stale but was still edible. Vlad had another drink of water. Then, with Savn's help, he pulled himself over to the nearest wall so he could sit up and lean against it.

With no warning or explanation, both jhereg suddenly turned and began flying out of the cave. Vlad did not appear surprised. Savn wondered if they could see in the dark, like bats and dzur.

"What are we going to do?" asked Polyi.

"I don't know," said Savn. "It depends on Vlad."

"Do?" said the Easterner weakly. "About what?"

"Well, they must still be after you."

"Yes."

"Can you teleport out of here?"

"Not now."

"Why?"

Vlad searched Savn's face. "Too weak," he said at last.

"Oh."

"Must recover first," said Vlad.

"And then?"

Vlad looked slightly puzzled, as if Savn had asked him whether harvest came before or after planting. "Then I must kill Lord Smallcliff, of course," he said, and, as if producing such a long sentence had exhausted him, he fell back asleep.

She felt his unhappiness as if it were a cord that connected them, though she didn't express it to herself that way. But there was a feeling of painful unease that made its way into her consciousness, and it was connected to the Provider, to his injuries.

They spiraled up from the caves, stopping below the overcast, and they began their search out over the bare fields between the town and the woods.

She hated hunting.

She enjoyed flying, and she enjoyed searching the ground for food, but she didn't like chases, and she certainly didn't like fights. In one case, she was certain to get tired; in the other, she might get hurt. And—

There was a movement, small and furtive, almost directly below her. She told her lover, but made no sudden moves. They rose and described a slow, leisurely turn. Her straining eyes picked out a patch of brown that didn't quite blend with the surrounding grass and weeds. They continued past it once more, dividing up and selecting the best angles from which to attack. If one had to hunt, it was better together.

And sometimes, one had no choice.

Chapter Twelve

I will not marry a fat old cook,
I will not marry a fat old cook,
For the larding pan I'd be forsook.
Hi-dee hi-dee ho-la!
    Step on out . . .

AFTER THE SILENCE that followed Vlad's declaration, Polyi echoed Savn's own thoughts: "He can't mean it."

Savn stared at the sleeping Easterner, but the things he'd said while delirious wouldn't go away. "I don't think so either," said Savn at last. "But . . ."

"But what?" said Polyi when he didn't continue.

"But I don't know. Let's get the fire going."

"All right."

They managed to get the fire started, and after some discussion, decided there was enough wood to keep it going for a while without having to leave the cave again, which neither of them felt inclined to do.

"Mae and Pae must be pretty worried about us," said Polyi.

"Yeah," said Savn.

"Well, I think we should tell them where we are," said Polyi.

Savn shook his head. "They'll tell Speaker, sure as drought in summer."

Polyi stared at the sleeping Easterner, and Savn could

practically feel her thinking, *So what*? And the worst of it
was that he didn't know how to answer that thought.

A few minutes later there was the sound of flapping
wings. Polyi jumped and stifled a shriek, and the two
jhereg landed on the floor of the cave.

"It's all right," said Savn. "They're tame."

"Tame?" said Polyi, sounding on the verge of hysteria.

"Well, I mean, they're friends of his."

She stared at the Easterner wide-eyed, while the larger
of the jhereg deposited what looked like a dead norska.
They walked triumphantly over to Vlad and sat down near
his head.

Polyi looked a question at Savn, who said, "I guess he
wanted meat."

"But how—?"

"Let's find something we can use as a spit."

Polyi looked at him, questions dancing on her face, but
she didn't ask any of them. They looked through the wood
they'd collected and found something suitable, while the
two jhereg seemed to be arguing with each other about
whether the norska should be eaten right away. Savn settled the issue by taking it away from them and proceeding
to skin it as best he could, which earned him an angry hiss
from the larger jhereg.

"Sometimes," said Savn, "people say really funny
things when they're feverish. Once Needles had the Dry
Fever for almost two days, and she—"

"It doesn't matter," said Polyi. "He can't mean it."

"Yes. No one can kill His Lordship anyway, because of
the box."

"That's right."

Savn set the bloody skin aside for the moment, wondering what to do with it so it wouldn't attract pests. They
worked the makeshift spit through the norska.

"What should we set it on?" asked Polyi.

"I don't know. Two of the logs?"

"What if they catch fire?"

"Well, we don't have any big stones or anything."

"We could just sit on each side of the fire and hold it."

"I guess. How long will it take to cook?"

"I don't know."

"Can you tell when it's done?"

"Can you?"

"Maybe," said Savn, and motioned Polyi over to the other side of the fire. "Best to keep it as high as we can, so we don't burn it."

Blood and fat dripped on the fire, sending the flames higher and making the cave alarmingly bright, but after only two minutes Polyi announced, "My arm's getting tired."

"Mine too," Savn admitted. "I don't think this is going to work."

"Well, what should we do?"

They moved away from the fire and set the slightly warmed norska down on the floor of the cave. Savn glanced at Vlad, and observed that the Easterner was awake, and watching him intently.

"Why don't you see if you can find something," said Savn.

"Me?" said Polyi.

"You," said Savn.

She started to argue, then scowled and got up. "Take a torch with you," he said. She didn't answer.

Savn turned to Vlad and said, "They brought you some dinner; we're trying to figure out how to cook it."

He nodded. "Pour wine over it," he said. "My flask—"

"All right," said Savn, and continued, "You said some funny things while you were feverish."

Vlad's eyes narrowed. The torchlight illuminated the side of his face nearest Savn, and the shadow of his forehead made his eyes seem very dark. "Tell me," he said. His voice was forceful, in spite of its weakness.

"You used the word 'Morganti' several times."

"Did I? I'm not surprised." He paused to collect his strength. "You know what it means?"

"Yes. It's a weapon that kills, not only the body, but—"

"Yes. Well, that's probably what they'll use on me if they catch me."

"Who?"

Vlad didn't answer for a moment, and Savn thought he had fallen asleep again, because his eyes were closed. Then he opened them and said, "The people who are after me."

"That isn't what His Lordship's men used."

"No," said Vlad, frowning, "it isn't." He screwed his eyes tightly shut, then opened them again. He stared straight ahead, looking puzzled, then shook his head as if dismissing a line of thought. "What else did I say?"

"Lots of stuff. Most of it I couldn't understand. And there were names and things."

"And?"

"And you said, 'I won't kill for you anymore.'"

"Oh." Vlad seemed to consider this. "Anything else?"

"Just before you fell asleep, you said you were going to kill His Lordship."

"Did I? I must have been very tired."

"To think it?" said Savn. "Or to say it?"

Savn waited, but Vlad made no answer to this. Savn said, "Why do you hate him so much, anyway?"

Vlad's widened nostrils flared. When he spoke, his voice was almost normal. "He's a necromancer. He works with souls. When he needs one, he takes it, and does what he will. Do you understand what I'm saying? Does that mean anything to you? Would you like it if your life was snuffed out one day, with no warning, and for no crime, just because someone needed your soul, the way you might need a yard of cloth? What sort of person does that, Savn?"

Then he fell back, and he seemed to fall asleep at once.

A few minutes later Polyi returned. "I've found a couple of stones that might work," she said. "But you're going to have to help me roll them in."

"All right," said Savn.

"Did he wake up?"

"Yes."

"Did he tell you anything?"

"Yes. He really is going to kill His Lordship."

The smell of cooking norska filled the cave, and Vlad still slept as Savn and Polyi continued their discussion. "I still say we should tell someone," said Polyi.

Savn shook his head. "Even if no one will believe us?"

"Even so."

The jhereg watched them, seemingly fascinated. Savn doubted they could understand the conversation, and hoped he was right.

"And even if His Lordship isn't in any danger?"

"How can you know that?"

"No one can kill him, because he hides his soul in a magic box."

"Well, we should still—"

"And even if they kill Vlad, if they find him?"

"He might be lying about that, you know," said Polyi.

"I don't think he is," said Savn.

Polyi started to speak, looked at the sleeping Easterner, and shut her mouth. Savn turned the spit once more. Fat dripped; the fire blazed up, then died down again. Savn's mouth was beginning to water and his stomach was growling.

"How long?" asked Polyi, who was evidently feeling the same way.

"I don't know. How do you tell when it's done?"

"Well, it's brown on the outside. Pae always cuts it open, though."

"Yeah, but what does he look for?"

"I guess if it looks like it's ready."

Savn scowled and found Vlad's dagger, and cut open the norska. Some of the flesh was white, but some of it seemed translucent. "Well?" he said.

"I don't know what norska should look like," said Polyi. "I've never eaten any."

"Well, I don't think it's done. Let's let it cook some more."

"I'm hungry," said Polyi.

"Me, too."

She stared at the fire and the roasting norska, and said, "Why does he hate His Lordship so much?"

"I don't know, exactly. But he thinks His Lordship killed Reins, and—"

"He couldn't have!" said Polyi.

"Why not?" said Savn.

"Well, because, he just *couldn't* have."

"I don't know. But Vlad thinks so, and I guess he liked Reins or something."

"Liked him? Were they, you know, lovers?"

"I don't know."

"They must have been," said Polyi. "I mean, you don't go killing somebody just because he killed someone you like, do you? If people did that, we'd have killed every soldier in the army by now."

"Well, I don't know if it's the same thing."

"Why not?"

"Because . . . I don't know. Maybe you're right."

"I'll bet they were lovers."

"So now you think maybe His Lordship really did kill him?"

"Well, no, I'm not saying that."

"Then what?"

"Well, just that maybe Vlad thinks so."

"He seemed pretty sure."

"So? He's an Easterner; maybe they're always like that."

"Maybe," said Savn, and fell silent.

This was, he realized, what anyone would call an adventure, and it felt like it. Yes, in a way it was terrifying, but it also had an odd, storylike quality to it—it wasn't quite real.

Savn had never seen people killed before his eyes, and yet here was this Easterner talking very seriously of killing His Lordship. None of it had a sense of being his own memories; it was as if these were things he heard of in a

song. The cave was real, and the feeling that he had em-
barked on something that he'd be able to tell stories about
for the rest of his life; but the death and danger were off
in the distance, not actually present, like when he had been
standing outside of his house.

He kept coming back to that experience, he decided, because it puzzled and intrigued him, and because it seemed
to mark a starting point. It had seemed, at the time, to be
the beginning of something, but he hadn't expected it to be
the beginning of a time when he would be going through
one thing after another that seemed unreal. In retrospect,
though, it made a certain kind of sense.

He looked at Polyi. Was it real for her? She was wearing a frown of great concentration. He hoped that whatever her thoughts, they were not carrying her into a place
she'd have trouble coming back from, because that would
be truly, truly sad. For that matter, how was it going to af-
fect *him* when it was over? Would he have nightmares for
the rest of his life? Would he and Polyi wake up screaming
for no reason that they could explain? He shuddered.

He caught Polyi glancing at him speculatively, and it
occurred to him that she had seen him with the Easterner,
and heard him agreeing that something that she
might—no, *would* see as a great crime—was reasonable.
He thought about trying to explain things to her, but realized that he really had no explanation; he was going to
have to wait until she brought it up herself, if she ever did.

After a time, she said hesitantly, "Savn . . ."

"What is it, Polyi?"

"Will you tell me something?"

"Sure."

"Do you *like* Lova?"

"Vlad, wake up," said Savn. "I think the food's ready."

"I'm awake," said the Easterner in a voice so low Savn
could hardly hear it. "Let's see the norska."

Savn suddenly wondered how much of the conversation
Vlad had overheard, and decided it had been stupid to talk

about it right in front of him in any case. He took the spit off the stones and showed it to Vlad.

"It's done," announced the Easterner. "Help me sit up."

Savn and Polyi put the spit back on the stones, then helped him sit up.

"Now I want to stand."

Savn said, "Are you sure you should—"

"And help me to the latrine."

"Oh. All right."

They took his arms and helped him up, and guided him to the other cave, and held him up until he was done. Then they brought him back and helped him sit up against the wall of the cave. The jhereg scampered along with him all the way. He sat there for several moments, breathing deeply, then nodded. "Let's eat," he said.

While they'd been helping him, part of the norska had burned slightly, but the rest was fine.

They ate in silence at first. Savn thought it was one of the best things he'd ever eaten. He wasn't certain what Polyi thought, but she was eating with great enthusiasm.

"Do you know," said Savn suddenly, "it just occurred to me that if there are people looking for us, and if they are at all nearby, the smell will bring them right to us." He took another bite of roasted norska.

Vlad grunted and said, "Should my friends take that as a compliment on their choice of food?"

Savn took his time chewing and swallowing, then said, "Yes."

"Good. I think the cave is deep enough that no smells will escape."

"All right," said Savn.

Polyi was still eating and not talking. Savn tried to decide if she was looking sullen, but he couldn't tell.

"It's the wine that does it," said Vlad. His voice seemed slightly stronger; at any rate, he seemed to have no trouble talking. "Cooking over an open flame is its own art, and doesn't have much to do with oven cooking or stove cooking. I'm not really good at it. But I know that wine always helps."

Savn wondered if it was the wine that made the norska taste so good, or if it was really the circumstances—if it wasn't still the feeling that he was on some sort of adventure. He knew there was something wrong with thinking about it this way, but how could he help it? He was sitting in a cave with a man who spoke of killing His Lordship, and he was eating norska taken with magic—

"Vlad," he said suddenly.

"Mroi?" said Vlad. Then he swallowed and said, "Excuse me. What?"

"I had always heard that it was bad luck to hunt with magic, except for finding the game."

"I've heard that, too."

"Well, then," said Savn. "What about—"

"Oh, this? Well, it wasn't exactly magic. At least, not directly."

"I don't understand."

"Never mind. It isn't important."

Savn decided that he was probably never going to understand what Vlad thought important. The most trivial things seemed to provoke the biggest reactions, like when Savn had mentioned that His Lordship's men hadn't been using Morganti weapons. Savn shook his head, wondering.

All of a sudden Polyi said, "You can't kill His Lordship."

Vlad looked at her without speaking.

Savn said, "Polyi—"

"Well," she said to Vlad. "You can't."

"Of course not," said Vlad.

"But you mean to. I know it."

"Polyi—"

"Just out of curiosity," said Vlad, "why couldn't I kill him?"

"He's a wizard."

"So?"

Polyi frowned. "They say that he can never die, because his magic protects him. They say that there are rooms in his keep where he just walks in and comes out younger, and that he is only as old as he wants to be. They say—"

"And how much of this do you believe?"

"I don't know," said Polyi.

Savn said, "If it's true, though—"

"It's true that he's a sorcerer."

"Well, then?"

"No matter how subtle the wizard, a knife between the shoulder blades will seriously cramp his style."

Savn couldn't find an answer to that, so he didn't make one. He looked at Polyi, but she was just staring angrily at Vlad. There was a sense of unreality about the entire conversation—it was absurd that they could be talking about killing His Lordship as if discussing the price of linen. There had been a time, some five years before, when he, Coral, and Lan had drunk wine until they had become sick. The thing he remembered most clearly about the incident, other than walking around for the next week hoping Mae and Pae didn't find out about it, was sitting with his head bent over, focusing on nothing except the tabletop, slowly memorizing every mark on it. The memory came back to him with such a rush that it almost brought along the giddy, sickly, floating feeling he had had then.

At last he said, "But what if he is undead, like you say?"

"He is," said Vlad. "That makes it a little trickier, that's all."

"Then you admit you're going to do it," said Polyi, in the same tone of voice she used upon discovering the piece for her game under Savn's blankets.

"What if I am?" said Vlad. "Do you think I should just let him kill me?"

"Why don't you teleport away?" said Savn.

"Heh," said Polyi. "Teleport? If he could do that, he could have fixed his finger."

"Polyi—" said Savn.

"First of all," said Vlad, looking at Polyi. "I'm not a physicker. A physicker who knew sorcery could have healed my hand if I'd gotten to him quickly. Now it would be very difficult, and I haven't been in touch with anyone that good in some time.

"Second," he continued, looking now at Savn, "never attempt complicated sorcery—and teleportation is complicated—when you're weak in the body. It upsets the mind, and that can be fatal. I've done it, when I've had to, and I will again, if I have to. But I've been lucky, and I don't like to depend on luck.

"Third," he said, addressing them both, "I do, indeed, intend to kill Loraan—Baron Smallcliff. But I'm in no shape to do so now. He knows I want to kill him; he killed Reins in order to draw me in, so that when I tried to kill him he could kill me. I don't know everything that's going on yet, so I don't know how I'm going to kill him. If I did, I certainly wouldn't tell you. I wouldn't have told you this much if I hadn't betrayed myself already, and if I didn't owe it to you.

"But there it is," he said. "I've told you my plans, or as much of them as I have. If you want to betray me, I can't stop you."

He looked at them and waited. At last Savn said, "I don't know what to do."

"I think we should go home," said Polyi.

"Then what?" said Savn.

"I don't know."

Savn looked at the Easterner, who was watching them carefully, his expression blank. "She's right," said Savn. "We really should go home."

"Yes," said Vlad. "I'll be all right here."

"Are you sure?"

"Yes. And, whatever happens, no one is going to be able to take me by surprise."

Savn glanced at the jhereg and nodded.

Vlad settled back against the wall of the cave and closed his eyes. "I believe I will sleep now. Will you help me to lie down?"

When they were done eating, they gave the bones to the

jhereg, who seemed well pleased with them. Savn wanted to say goodbye to Vlad, but the Easterner was sound asleep. He and Polyi left the cave together, blinking in the bright afternoon sun.

They started for home.

Chapter Thirteen

I will not marry a handsome soldier,
I will not marry a handsome soldier,
He would not want me when I'm older.
Hi-dee hi-dee ho-la!
     Step on out . . .

BY UNSPOKEN AGREEMENT they took the long way, not passing through town; as a result they didn't see anyone. Savn wondered if there were still parties out looking for Vlad, and if Mae and Pae had joined them. Thinking of Mae and Pae filled him with a vague unease over and above his fear of whatever punishment they'd inflict on him for staying out all night. He thought about it, trying to figure out why, and eventually remembered how oddly they'd acted the night Vlad had come to their home, at which point Savn realized that he wasn't afraid of what Mae and Pae would say; he was afraid of what they wouldn't say.

It was as bad as Savn had feared, or worse. Mae looked up, nodded at them, and went back to stripping seeds. Pae, who was counting sacks, just gave them a brief smile and said, "Savn, isn't it time for you to be at Master Wag's?"

"Yes, Pae," said Savn, trying to keep his voice from trembling.

"Well, be on your way, then."

Savn watched Polyi, who was obviously trying to conceal how upset she was. She said, "Don't you want to know where we've been?"

"Well," said Mae, straightening up and stretching her back, "you're here, aren't you? You've been fine, haven't you?"

"Yes, but—"

Savn caught her eye and she fell silent.

"We'll be going, then," said Savn.

Mae and Pae nodded abstractedly and returned to their work. Savn and Polyi didn't speak until they reached the house, where Savn gallantly offered to let Polyi bathe first.

She ignored his offer and said, "What's wrong with them?"

"With who?"

"Cut it out," said Polyi. "You know what I mean."

Savn started to protest, then gave up and said, "I don't know. I think— No, I don't know."

"What do you think?"

"Never mind."

"Is it something Vlad did to them?"

Savn looked away and repeated, "I don't know."

"Maybe he—"

"I don't know."

"All right," she said, pouting. "Don't yell at me."

"Do you want to bathe first, or should I?"

"I don't care. Go ahead. No, I will."

"Let me, I have to get to Master Wag's."

"Then why did you ask?"

"I don't know. I'll hurry."

Savn bathed quickly, and leaving the house, cut across the fields away from the counting bin so he wouldn't have to face Mae and Pae again. He also skirted the town, although he was frightfully curious about whether they were still searching for Vlad.

When he arrived at Master Wag's, he was greeted with the words, "I didn't expect you to be here today. How's our patient?"

"He was well when I left him, about five hours ago."

"Had he eaten?"

"Yes."

"No fever?"

"None."

"Still weak?"

"Very."

"Did he empty his bowels?"

"No. Liquid only."

"Hmmm. Not good, but not yet bad, either."

"Are they still looking for him?"

The Master nodded. "Not with any great intensity, perhaps, but Speaker insisted that they keep searching the
area until they were certain he had left."

"That sounds like they think he did."

"Speaker probably does, but that doesn't much matter.
They'll keep looking, I'm afraid, and eventually they'll
find the caves."

"It may take a long time."

"Oh, yes. It would take days to just search the caves—
they're immense, convoluted, and lead all the way back
into the cliff. But still—"

"Yes. I hope they don't get to them soon."

"In any case, Savn, the Easterner shouldn't be alone for
very long. He could relapse at any time."

"All right," said Savn. "I'll return at once."

"No, as long as you're here, you may as well relax for
a while. We can discuss that procedure you performed. I
want to show you just what you did, and why it worked,
so you can be more certain next time."

Which is what they did for the next hour; the Master explained the problem and the cure, while Savn listened
more intently than he ever had before. It was different, he
realized, when you knew exactly why you were doing
something, when you'd actually seen someone with the injury and were learning how to save him.

After that, the conversation drifted onto other matters of
the healing arts, and even here Savn noticed a difference
in the Master's attitude: he was less brusque and somehow
more respectful of Savn—as if by saving the Easterner,
Savn had proven himself to Master Wag.

At one point, the Master stopped in the middle of explaining the sort of thoughts that must be kept out of the

head of a person in danger of fever, and said, "What is bothering you, Savn? You seem disturbed about something."

"I'm not certain, Master."

The Master looked at him closely. "Is it," he said, "that you aren't certain you should have saved the Easterner? Because, if that is the trouble, it shouldn't bother you. Saving lives is our trade—all lives. Even, sometimes, that of livestock. Yes, if it is a choice between saving the life of a human being and saving the life of an Easterner, that is one thing. But in this case, you found someone who was injured and you cured him. It is no betrayal of His Lordship for you to perform your calling."

"It isn't that, Master. I think it's Mae and Pae."

"What about them?"

"Well, they've been acting funny, that's all."

"Funny? What do you mean?"

"Well, they seem distracted, like they're far away."

"Explain what you mean, Savn. Be precise."

"It's hard to, Master. It's a feeling I have. But when Polyi and I were out all night, they didn't say a word to us about it."

"You're growing up, Savn. They recognize this, and feel you can be trusted more. That's all it is."

Savn shook his head. "I'm afraid Vlad put a spell on them."

The Master cocked his head. "A spell? What sort of spell, and why would he do something like that?"

"A witchcraft spell."

"Witchcraft!" said the Master. "Nonsense. If you believe all of the rubbish that— Hullo, is someone there?"

There did, indeed, seem to be someone clapping at the door. Savn got up and opened it, and was startled to find himself looking up at Fird, the fruit-seller from Bigcliff.

Savn stared, open-mouthed, his thoughts racing. For one thing, he had forgotten how tall Fird was. For another, Vlad had been asking about him just the other day, and . . . Savn realized he was being rude. He closed his mouth, opened it again, and said, "May I be of some service to you?"

"I be here looking," said Fird, in his low, careful voice, and with the odd grammatical formulations of Bigcliff, "for Master Wag."

"Who is it?" called the Master from inside.

"Please come in," said Savn, stepping out of Fird's way.

"My thanks to you for that," said Fird, ducking his head as he passed under the Master's doorway. Over his shoulder was a large sack, which Savn assumed contained the fruit he'd been selling.

The Master rose as he entered, and said, "What seems to be the matter, goodman?"

"A note is sent me to you, by for this Eastern devil. You know him?"

"Eastern devil?" said Master Wag and Savn with one voice. The Master gave Savn a look, then continued. "Do you mean the Easterner, Vlad?"

"The same as him, yes," said Fird.

"I know him. He sent you a note?"

"That were, or the mountains grew him."

Savn had to stop and figure this one out, but Master Wag said, "May I see it?"

"To you be done, then," said Fird, and handed a small piece of pale, almost white parchment to the Master. The Master, in turn, frowned, read it several times, and, with a look that asked permission of Fird, handed it to Savn.

At first, Savn mentally *tsked* at the Easterner's penmanship; then he wondered how Vlad had written it. It had probably been done in wood-ash using a dagger's point. It read: "Sorry I missed you I've been hurt ask Master Wag to bring you to me I'll pay gold."

Savn handed it back to Fird, while the Master asked, "How do you know him?"

"How? As one will know another. Gold he is offered to me, and then he is not where his promise is. I be curious, I be finding fruit in sack, I be finding note, I be reading, I be coming here. But you he is knowing, and this I be in wonder at."

"He's hurt, as he said," said the Master. "I helped him."

"So?" said Fird, shrugging. "He is hurt. I have mangoes and apples, which will cure like a physicker."

"Maybe," said the Master, sounding doubtful.

"Apples. Apple's the thing. Where with to—"

"Savn here will lead you to him."

"Master—"

"You think it's a trick?"

"Well—"

"If His Lordship, or Speaker, or anyone else knows enough to attempt this sort of trick, it doesn't much matter if we fall for it."

"Not to us, but—"

"Think about it, Savn. Think about how much they would have to know."

"Trick?" said Fird. "Is what this—"

"The Easterner," said Master Wag, "is hurt because some people tried to kill him. Savn is concerned that—"

"Ah. Well, is to careful, then, but I—"

"Yes, I know," said the Master. "Savn?"

"All right. Should we go now?" Both Fird and Master Wag nodded.

"I may join you later, to check on our patient, or else I'll see you tomorrow."

"Very well, Master," said Savn, and led the way out the door and down the road toward the Curving Stone.

He was saved from the necessity of deciphering Fird's speech by the fact that Fird didn't seem inclined to make conversation, and Savn, for his part, didn't know what to say. Just past the Curving Stone he led the way into the woods, through them, and out over Bigcliff. Fird looked down with interest at the beach where, though he probably didn't know it, Savn had first pointed him out to Vlad.

Savn still wondered what the Easterner wanted with the fruit-seller. As they approached the cave, Fird stopped, sniffed the air, and said his first words since they set out: "Norska is been roasted."

Savn smelled it too, and repressed a chuckle. So much

for the smell not getting out. "This way," he said, and led
Fird into the cave. "Can you make a light?"

Fird grunted, and a soft red glow filled the cavern. They
went through the first, large chamber, and Savn led the
way unerringly into the correct passage, and another large
chamber. Here, even though Savn half expected it, he was
startled by the flapping of wings as the jhereg appeared
before him. Fird jumped, and his sorcerous light wavered
for a moment as Savn said, "It's all right, they won't hurt
us." Fird didn't appear convinced, but watched the jhereg
closely and kept a short knife in his hand.

The jhereg flew around the opening for a moment, then
disappeared.

"Is Easterner magic to tame carrion-eaters?" asked Fird.

"I guess," said Savn.

Fird's mouth twitched. "Then is onward."

They continued, Fird ducking to traverse corridors that
Savn was able to walk through upright, until they saw the
flickering glow of the torches.

Savn called out, "Vlad? It's Savn. Fird, the fruit-seller,
is with me."

There was a rustling sound ahead, and in the dim light
Savn was able to make out Vlad turning his head. "Good,"
he said in a hoarse whisper.

"How are you feeling?"

"Weak. But a little better, I think."

"Great."

"Sorry I missed our appointment, Fird. Glad you got the
note."

Fird was watching Vlad carefully. He said, "Note is arrived, but the wondering is from its means of travel."

"Does it matter?"

"Magic is that of the Easterner, is to wonder what else
you is to have done or will do?"

"For one thing," said Vlad. "Give you a certain amount
of gold, in exchange for answering some questions. Have
you been to—" He paused and looked at Savn.

"Would you like me to leave?"

"Please," said Vlad. "I'm sorry, but I'd rather this not
be overheard."

Savn shrugged his shoulders as if he didn't care, and,
taking one of the burning torches, wandered back out of
the cave. To his surprise, the larger of the jhereg accompanied him. He was even more surprised to realize that this
no longer bothered him. Finding a comfortable-looking
spot beneath a tree just outside the cave, he put out the
torch and settled down with his back against the trunk.
The jhereg perched on a low branch of the same tree.

Savn looked up at it, and it looked back, as if waiting
for Savn to start the conversation. "I would like to know,"
said Savn obligingly, "what they're talking about in there."

The jhereg stared at him with unblinking, reptilian eyes.

"And while we're on the subject," he continued, "I'd
like to know how close the searchers are getting to this
cave. If I knew how long we had, I—well, I don't know
what I'd do. But I'd like to know.

"And, since I'm asking questions, just what *did* Vlad do
to Mae and Pae? I know, I know. He put a spell on them."

He frowned and studied the ground between his feet.
He'd known since last night that Vlad had enchanted
them, but it seemed to take a long time for the fact to
make its way into his bones. There was something so *evil*
about doing such a thing—about magically clouding someone's eyes, muffling his thoughts—that he couldn't really
think of it as something done by the Easterner lying helpless a hundred yards into the hill.

And the thought that, even now, Mae and Pae were
under the influence of whatever spell Vlad had cast was
utterly foreign to his emotions; he didn't know how to
look at it. The anger that ought to be his natural response
simply wouldn't appear.

He tried to imagine himself confronting the half-dead
Vlad and telling him off for it, but his imagination failed.
He thought about doing nothing until Vlad felt better, but
that didn't seem right either.

"What would you do?" he asked the jhereg.

It ducked its head under its wing and cleaned itself, then

seemed to settle more fully onto the branch and looked around with, Savn imagined, an expression of mild curiosity.

"So, what am I waiting for? I'm not going to ask him about Mae and Pae. Why am I here? In case he has a relapse? But am I going to heal him after what he did? Of course I am; I can't let him *die*."

He stared at the jhereg, who seemed completely uninterested in his problems. He scowled at it. "What I *should* do is abandon Vlad and see what I can do for Mae and Pae. Sure. Good idea. But what can I do for them? They've been enchanted; I don't know anything about enchantments."

He stopped, feeling his eyes grow wide. "But Bless does. Bless knows all about curses of the gods, and whatever this Easterner did, it can't be *that* bad. That's it. Vlad can take care of himself; I have to find Bless."

And, with no more reflection or questions, he stood and dashed off toward town.

Twilight made the outlines of the livery stable indistinct as Savn came up over the top of the hill. He stopped and surveyed the city. There were a few people on the outskirts, talking, as there always were; Savn could make out Tif from her posture and Boarder from his hair, and there were others he didn't yet recognize. At the far end a few people moved about, but they were too far away to identify. However, he was certain he saw a two-horse wagon not far from Speaker's, and Bless was one of the few (as was Savn's family) who drove two horses.

He started down the hill, and couldn't help but notice how the gossips outside of Feeder's stopped talking and watched him pass. It was creepy. But they didn't say anything to him, and he didn't see any of his friends.

Bless and Ori came out of Speaker's house and climbed into the wagon. Savn ran up to them, waving. Bless saw him, checked the horses, and waited. Ori looked at him with mild curiosity. Bless's face was round, his eyes were very widely set, and the look on his face seemed suspicious, as if he wasn't certain Savn was doing what he was supposed to do.

"The evening's rain to you, sir."

"And to you, young man. Where have you been this last day?"

"Where have I been, sir?"

"Yes, the whole town has gathered to look for this East-erner, and your absence was noticed."

"I didn't know. Why were you looking for him, sir?"

"That is none of your concern, young man. You should be glad that it is I and not Speaker who wants to know, or you can be sure the questions would be rougher in the ask-ing and quicker in the answering."

"Yes, sir." Savn didn't look at Ori, but he was aware of him there, watching, and it made Savn angry and uncom-fortable.

"So where *were* you?" asked Bless.

Savn heard himself answer, "I was looking for him, too."

"*You* were?"

"Yes, sir. I saw what happened, and he was hurt, and I thought he might need physicking, and—"

"*Physicking!*" thundered Bless. "Of all the nerve! This Easterner killed—actually *killed*—three of His Lordship's men-at-arms, and you want to physick him?"

"I'm sorry, sir."

"I should hope so! He has already done more evil here than you can imagine."

"I know, sir. That's what I wanted to ask you about."

That seemed to catch Bless up short. "Eh? Is there something I don't know about?"

"Yes, sir. It's Mae and Pae."

"Well? What about them?"

"I wonder if you could . . . that is, I think they've been enchanted."

Bless made a peculiar sound with his mouth and nose. "Enchanted?" he said. "And by whom?"

"By Vlad, the Easterner."

"Oh, he's a wizard, is he?"

"No, sir, a witch."

"Rubbish," said Bless. "A witch can't do anything to you unless you believe he can. Have you spoken to Master Wag about this? What does he say about witches?"

"The same as you, sir, only—"

"Well, there you have it."

"But—"

Bless sighed. "Very well. What makes you think this witch has done something to them?"

"They've been acting funny. I mean, *really* funny."

Bless sniffed. "Maybe they're concerned about you."

"That's just it. They're *not*."

"What do you mean?"

"Well, they don't seem to care what I do."

"Eh? That's the first time I've heard that complaint from a young man. What did you do that they didn't care about?"

Savn realized that he was in dangerous waters. He wanted to say enough to convince Bless to do something, but not so much that Bless would know what he'd been up to.

"Well, I stayed out playing, and they didn't do anything about it. They didn't seem to even notice."

"I see. And because of this you think they're enchanted?"

"Well, yes. If you'd seen the way they've been acting—"

"I saw them two days past, and they seemed quite fine to me."

"It hadn't happened yet."

"Young man, I believe that you are suffering from a disease called bad conscience. Instead of seeing mysterious enchantments everywhere, I'd recommend you start doing what you should be doing, and I suspect everything will be fine."

"But—"

"But at the moment, I've got bigger problems. While this Easterner may not be casting spells on everyone's mother, he *is* out there somewhere, and I must see to it that he is found before he does any more damage. Now be on your way."

Without waiting for Savn's answer, Bless motioned for Ori to drive off. Savn clenched his fists with frustration. Why did everyone only see what he wanted to?

Savn looked around to make sure he hadn't attracted any attention, and saw, to his dismay, Lan and Tuk walking by on the opposite side of the street, staring at him. They looked away when he stared back, which was almost worse than if they'd tried to beat him up again.

He turned and headed for home. Maybe Polyi would say something that would cheer him up.

The walk home was long, and it was nearly dark by the time he got there. Mae and Pae were still busy, and when they bid him a good day, it seemed that they were even further away than they had been.

Savn wondered if perhaps he was exaggerating their condition to himself. He couldn't be sure, but he didn't think so.

Polyi was in the house, and her first words were, "Are they sick, Savn?"

He thought about giving her an honest answer, but couldn't make himself do it. He said, "I don't know what's wrong, Polyi. I just don't know."

"Should we ask someone?"

"Who?"

"Well, Master Wag, maybe?"

"I don't think they're sick."

"Well *something's* wrong with them."

Savn sighed. "Yes, I know. Let me think about it."

"What good will thinking about it do? We have to—"

"I know, we have to do something. But I don't know— What in the world was that?" There had come some sort of rapping, scraping sound from the roof.

Polyi rushed out the door, Savn right at her heels. They turned and looked up at the roof. Polyi screamed. Savn, though he had become used to such things, felt very much like doing the same.

* * *

For an hour or so after the large soft one left, the Provider seemed fine, and even after that, she couldn't really tell that something was wrong, but her lover began to grow agitated, then worried, and finally almost frantic. He began to fly around, nearly hurting himself against the cave walls.

She came to understand that the Provider was not well, and she wondered if the large soft one had done something to him, and if she should track him down and kill him. No, she was told, it had nothing to do with that one, it had to do with how he had gotten hurt before.

This puzzled her, because it seemed that one would either be injured or healthy; the Provider had been injured and was now getting healthy again, so how could the same injury account for two illnesses? But her lover was in no mood to explain such things, so she didn't ask.

As he grew more frantic, however, she began to catch his mood. Desperate to do something that would alleviate his misery, she at last suggested that, if he had been cured before by something one of the Provider's species had done, couldn't it happen again?

Her lover calmed down at this suggestion, only to become angry again, this time at himself, because he seemed to feel he ought to have thought of that before. But he seemed disinclined to waste too much time with such thoughts; almost at once he turned and flew out of the cave.

She had nothing better to do, so she followed.

Chapter Fourteen

I will not marry a sly intendant,
I will not marry a sly intendant,
I'd make money and he would spend it.
Hi-dee hi-dee ho-la!
      Step on out ...

POLYI CLUTCHED SAVN'S arm and stared. The day's light was nearly gone but there was enough to see, without possibility of error, what was sitting on the roof. Even to Savn, there was something horribly invasive in the jhereg's perching on his own house; whatever they were, and however friendly they were, they didn't belong here.

It was only much later that it struck Savn as odd that neither he nor Polyi thought of calling Mae and Pae, which would have been their automatic reaction only three days before.

At last Polyi said in a whisper, "What are they doing?"

"Watching us."

"I can see that, chag-brain. I mean *why* are they watching us."

"I don't know."

Savn stared back at them, refusing to be intimidated. That there might actually be intelligence behind those quick, tiny eyes made it worse. *Well*, he wanted to say. *What do you want with me?*

Could Vlad have sent them?

Maybe. But, if so, why not give them a note, like he gave to Fird?

Perhaps because he couldn't.

But, if he couldn't, how could he have sent the jhereg?

Savn scowled. He just didn't know enough about Vlad's relationship with these things. It was a matter of witch-craft, and—

Witchcraft.

Just like the spell he'd put on Mae and Pae.

He broke free of Polyi, turned, and walked away from the house. Behind him, Polyi was asking something, but he didn't really hear her.

Vlad was in trouble, maybe dying; that was the only possible explanation.

Vlad had, for whatever reason, laid enchantments on Mae and Pae.

Vlad needed help.

Vlad didn't deserve help.

Savn slammed back into the house and got a small cooking pot, two wooden bowls, a little barley (Vlad could pay for that at least, and he'd better!), and some three-season herb, which was another thing Master Wag had rec-ommended against fever.

Polyi came back in. "Where are you going?"

"Vlad's gotten sick again," he growled.

"How do you know?"

"I just do."

He rolled up his sleeping furs and tied them into a bun-dle.

"Aren't you coming back?" said Polyi.

"Yes, I'm coming back, I just don't know when."

Prairiesong grew next to the road; he could pick some on the way. What else did he need?

"What do you mean, you don't know when?"

"I'm going to stay with Vlad until he's well, or until he dies, or until they find us. And, when he's well, I'm going to make him—I'm going to talk to him about some things."

He carefully wrapped Pae's best kitchen knife in a towel and stowed it among his furs.

"But," said Polyi, "that could take—"

"I know."

"Mae and Pae—"

"Won't even notice."

Polyi shut up. Savn continued to pack as quickly as possible, ending up with one large roll that fit over his shoulder and a light sack that he could carry.

"I'm going with you," announced Polyi.

Savn looked at her in the light of the stove. Her hair, which always gave her trouble, looked completely disorganized; her thin brows were drawn together in a line, and her mouth was set in an expression that he'd often seen before and thought of as stubborn; now it looked determined. He wasn't certain what the difference was, but he knew it was there.

"Of course you are," he said. "Hurry up and get ready. We have to take the long way around, and I don't want to waste any time."

The two jhereg shadowed them as they walked. It was too dark to see them, but Savn and Polyi heard the occasional *thwp thwp* of their wings, which made Savn nervous, though he didn't mention it. Polyi didn't mention it, either. In fact, Polyi didn't say anything at all, though a couple of times Savn tried, halfheartedly, to engage in her conversation. The only thing she said was, "How are we going to see in the cave? It's bad enough out here."

"I left a torch just outside; maybe we can find it."

Their progress through the woods was very slow. There was no light at all save for the diffuse glow from the sky and the faraway beacons from His Lordship's manor house, which, faint as it was, got fainter as they went further from Manor Road and into the woods above Bigcliff. Savn was afraid they would miss the path altogether and step off the cliff itself. He made Polyi take hold of his arm, and he went very slowly, feeling for low branches with his free hand and exposed roots with his feet.

"I'm glad you came along," he said. "This would be even scarier alone."

Polyi didn't answer.

Soon the light from the manor house was gone entirely, and Savn was afraid he'd lose his sense of direction and wander the woods all night, but shortly thereafter they emerged, and he realized that the soft glow from the sky was enough to allow him to pick his way with care down the path to the caves.

Finding the torch proved difficult indeed, and he might not have managed it if he hadn't bumped into the tree he'd been leaning against earlier. He scraped his cheek slightly, but was otherwise unhurt, and by feeling around at the tree's base, discovered the torch he'd brought out of the cave.

It was only then, with the unlit torch in his hand, that he realized that it was chilly. "Are you cold?" he asked Polyi.

"Yes," she said, "but I'm all right. Hurry up and light the torch so we can go."

While Polyi waited by the cave mouth, Savn pushed together a pile of leaves that weren't too damp and succeeded in making a fire. The glow hurt his eyes so much, he had to look away while igniting the torch, and once he'd managed to do so, he had to look away from both while he stamped out the fire. When he'd done this, he hesitated, wanting to wait until his eyes adjusted to the light, but not wanting to remain outside the cave where the light could be observed.

As he stood, undecided, Polyi said, "Come *on*, Savn," so he squinted as best he could and headed into the cave. The jhereg, visible now in the torchlight, stayed with them, as if to be certain they completed their journey.

At last they reached the chamber where Vlad lay. Savn put the torch in the wall, lit another from the stack on the floor, brought it over to the Easterner, and gasped.

"Savn, what's wro—"

"Hand me the sack, Polyi. Thanks. Now, find the mortar and pestle. Quick."

"Where? Oh, here it is."

Savn dumped the contents of the sack on the floor, and found the prairiesong. "Crush this up with some water," he said.

"Where's the water?"

"I don't know, look around. Wait, in the wineskin, against the wall, below the torch. No, the brown wineskin; that one still has wine. Yes."

"How much water?"

"After you've crushed the prairiesong, fill the bowl. Wait, give me the water first."

Savn inspected Vlad, looking at each wound carefully, then got a cloth wet and put it around Vlad's head. Then he began fanning him.

"What happened?" said Polyi.

"The Imps of Fever have entered his body, but I don't know how. His wound isn't infected."

"What do we do?"

"Have you mixed the prairiesong yet?"

"Yes."

"Then we will help him drink it."

"Then what?"

"Then we'll get the fire started again. Is there any wood left?"

"Not much."

"After he's had the prairiesong, take a torch with you and get some wood. Don't stay out there any longer then you have to. Be careful not to be seen."

"All right. What will we do when we've got the fire going?"

"We will sit here with him, keeping him cool, chanting the charms against fever, and feeding him water with prairiesong until his fever breaks."

"What if it doesn't break?"

"It will," said Savn.

"But what if it doesn't?"

"It will. Here. I'll hold his head, you open his lips and pour. Slowly, we don't want to spill any."

They helped the Easterner drink. He was only semiconscious, but he was able to swallow normally. His skin was

still very hot. Savn wiped Vlad's forehead again, while
Polyi got the firewood. He reviewed the chants against fever, while he ground up more prairiesong and set it aside,
then began fanning Vlad. *I'll have to send Polyi out for
more water*, he thought, *but that can wait until the fire's
going.*

He began the chant clumsily. It was difficult to perform
the invocation with the proper rhythm while fanning Vlad,
until he managed to adjust his fanning to the rhythm of the
incantation. After that it was easier.

Polyi returned with the firewood, and built up the fire,
got more water, then sat down next to Savn. "How is he?"

"He burns," said Savn, his voice already hoarse.
"Come, listen to the chant so you can help me with it. I'll
fan him, you make sure the cloth on his forehead stays
damp, and we'll perform the healing together."

"All right," said Polyi.

Vlad moaned softly then, and mumbled something.
Polyi made a soft exclamation. Savn glanced at her and
said, "We do not pay attention to the ravings of those
under our care." Then he resumed chanting. Presently his
sister joined him.

Several hours later, when both of their voices were raw
and sore, when Savn felt more exhausted than he ever had
in his life, when he was afraid that his arm lacked the
strength to lift up Vlad's head one more time, he felt his
forehead and found it was cool to the touch.

"You can stop, Polyi," he said.

She kept chanting, stumbling a little, slowing down,
then at last ran down like a spinning doll at the end of its
string. She looked at him blankly, as if unable to compre-
hend the silence. Perhaps they said something to each
other—Savn later had a memory that they exchanged a
hug, but he was never certain. All he knew was that within
a minute after the sudden silence boomed through the
cave, he was sound asleep.

When Savn awoke, the first thing he did was stifle a cry
and look at Vlad. Then he realized that he'd only dreamed

that he'd fallen asleep while Vlad's life was still at stake, and he relaxed. The Easterner slept, but his color looked good and his forehead felt cool, though perhaps slightly clammy.

The next thing he did was make sure Polyi was all right. She was still asleep (or, for all he knew, asleep again). He badly wished for tea. Then he noticed a dead norska lying by the fire. He looked at the two jhereg who stood over it, either guarding it or showing off, and said, "Now, I suppose, you're going to want me to skin it and cook it, aren't you? Haven't we been through this already? Fortunately for you, I have a stewpot, because I wouldn't want to risk the smell of roasting it again."

The smaller of the jhereg hopped over to him, jumped coolly onto his arm, and licked his ear. Savn wondered why this didn't bother him, and, moreover, how the jhereg knew it wouldn't bother him.

He built up the fire, skinned the norska, and put it in the pot with water and more three-season herb than probably ought to go in. That was all right; it might make the stew a little sweet, but it should still be edible. The smell woke up Polyi, and, at almost the same time, Vlad.

Savn realized the Easterner was awake when the two jhereg suddenly stopped nibbling at the norska skin and flew over to land next to his face. Savn followed them, knelt down, and said, "How are you?"

Vlad blinked, cleared his throat, and said, "What did I say this time?"

"I have no idea," said Savn. "You sound stronger than you did yesterday."

"Do I? I think I feel a little better, too. How odd."

"Did Fird do something to you?"

"No, I don't think so. I don't think he could have done anything I wouldn't have noticed, and he doesn't seem to be the type that would try anything, anyway. No, I think it just happened."

"You *do* sound better."

"Thanks. I really didn't say anything?"

"I wasn't paying attention. What was Fird doing here, anyway?"

"Giving me some information I'd paid him to find out."

"Oh. I hope it was worth it."

Vlad laughed, weakly. "Oh, yes. It was worth it."

Savn grunted and stirred the stew, spilling some, which made the fire hiss, and thick smoke curled up into his eyes. He waved it away and stepped back. He added a little wine, figuring it couldn't hurt anything and remembering Vlad's comments last time.

He glanced back at Vlad, who had struggled to a sitting position on his own, and was leaning against the wall, breathing heavily, his eyes closed.

"You're going to make it," said Savn quietly.

"Eh?" said Vlad.

"Nothing. Rest now and I'll wake you when the food's ready."

"Thanks, but I want to be awake. I need to think."

"Are you afraid they'll find you?" He didn't think the stew smelled as strongly as the roasted norska had, and hoped that the smell wouldn't manage to sneak its way out of the cave.

"Are they still looking?" asked Vlad.

"Yes."

"Hmmm. Well, that's part of it. If they found me now I wouldn't be able to give them much sport. But even if they don't find me, I have to figure out what to do."

"About what?"

"About Loraan, of course. Excuse me, I mean Baron Smallcliff."

"Oh."

Eventually the food was ready. Polyi splashed water on her face, visited the cave they'd designated as a privy, and rejoined them, still looking groggy. They ate in silence, not even commenting on the quality of the stew, which Savn thought was fine (although, as he had feared, a bit sweet), even if it was not as exciting as the roasted norska had been the first time.

They had to share bowls, since Savn had only thought

to bring two, but they finished every morsel. When they had given the bones and scraps to the jhereg, Vlad rested for a while. Savn thought he was looking better and better, but resolved not to leave him unattended until he was certain there would not be another relapse.

Polyi, who, as usual, had been the last to finish eating, watched Vlad as he rested. Savn wondered what she was thinking about, a question which was answered when she suddenly said, "What did you mean about not wanting to work again?"

Vlad opened his eyes. "Excuse me?"

"When you were feverish, you said you never wanted to work again, and you wouldn't, and swore by Verra. Or maybe at Verra, I couldn't tell."

Vlad looked reproachfully at Savn, who said, "When did he say that, Polyi?"

"While we were chanting."

Savn looked at Vlad. "I didn't notice," he said.

"I meant," said Vlad, "that, basically, I'm a pretty lazy fellow. What else did I say?" The Easterner was staring at Polyi, and Savn felt the intensity of that stare.

"Stop it," he said.

Vlad turned to him. "Excuse me?"

"I said, stop it."

"Stop what?"

"Whatever you were about to do to her."

The Easterner seemed genuinely confused. "I wasn't about to do anything to her; what are you talking about?"

"You were about to cast a spell on her."

"No, I wasn't. What makes you think I was?"

"I saw how you were looking at her, and I know what you did to Mae and Pae."

"Oh," said Vlad softly. His features were still and silent; only his eyes seemed troubled as he looked at Savn.

"*What?*" cried Polyi, rising to her feet.

Damn my big mouth, thought Savn. He stepped between her and Vlad and said, "Wait—"

"*What did he do to them?*"

"How did you know?" said Vlad quietly.

Savn ignored him, gripped his sister's shoulders and said, "Polyi, please—"

"How long have you known?" said Polyi.

"I guessed yesterday, when we went home, but I wasn't certain."

She tried to twist free, but Savn was stronger. He said, "Wait, Polyi. Let us at least listen to what he has to say—"

Vlad, abruptly, started laughing. Polyi stopped struggling and stared at him. Savn did the same. "What's so funny?" he asked.

"I'm almost tempted," said Vlad, still laughing, "to tell you to let her go. After everything I've done, the idea of falling at last to the wrath of a Teckla girl appeals to my sense of irony. And right now, she could do it. At least," he added, sobering suddenly, "it wouldn't be Morganti."

Savn felt his stomach turn at the word. At the same time, he noticed that the two jhereg were watching Polyi with, it seemed, great intensity, and he remembered that they were poisonous—it was certainly best that Polyi be kept from attacking Vlad, even if Vlad was, as he claimed, "almost tempted."

The Easterner continued. "In any case, I wasn't about to put a spell on your sister. I wasn't doing anything except, maybe, trying to intimidate her a little."

"Why should I believe you?" said Savn.

"Why indeed?" said Vlad. "At any rate, I haven't denied what I did to your Mae and Pae."

"No, but you've lied about everything else."

Vlad shook his head. "Very little, in fact," he said. "I've mostly refused to answer because I really don't like lying to you. Although I'm willing to do so, if it will preserve my life and my soul."

His voice hardened as he said this, but Savn refused to be put off by it. "How did putting a spell on Mae and Pae help preserve your life?"

Vlad sighed and looked away. "I'm not sure it did," he said eventually. "I was being careful. How could you tell there was a spell on them? And, for that matter, how did you know it was me?"

Savn snorted. "Who else could it have been? And it wasn't very difficult to see they'd been enchanted. They've been acting like they're living in a dream-world. They haven't seemed to care what Polyi and I do. They—"

"I see," said Vlad. "I overdid it, apparently."

"What were you trying to do?"

"It's a long story."

"I'm not going anywhere."

He looked at Polyi, who hesitated, then sat down and looked at the Easterner expectantly.

Vlad took a deep breath and nodded. "I thought I might need your help," he said. "And, in fact, I did, though not the way I had anticipated." He smiled a little, looking down at himself as if to inspect Savn's work.

"How had you anticipated you'd need my help?"

Vlad shrugged. "Once I knew what had happened to Reins, I thought I might need the eyes, ears, and memory of a local. And I did, but it didn't turn out to be you, because I found Sara and Fird."

Polyi said, "What does that have to do with putting a spell on Mae and Pae?"

Vlad sat up, resting his back against the stone wall. He spread his hands. "If I wanted you to look around for me, I couldn't have you disturbed by parents wanting to know where you were and what you were doing. It wasn't supposed to be that strong, however."

Savn nodded. "You did it when you brought me home that night, didn't you?"

"That was when I triggered it, you might say, but I'd already set it up."

"How? You weren't anywhere near them before that."

"Yes." Vlad sighed. "Remember that green stone I gave you?"

"What green stone?"

"Remember when we met?"

"Sure. On Manor Road, by the Curving Stone."

"Yes. I gave you something."

"I don't remember ... Wait. Yes. You said it was the

custom of your land—" He broke off suddenly. "Why had I forgotten that? What did you do to me?"

Vlad winced, then looked away. After a moment he shook his head, as if to himself. "Not very much, actually," he said. "You can blame my friends here"—he gestured at the jhereg on the ground, who were still watching Polyi and Savn—"for not keeping good watch. You saw me doing something I didn't want known, so I gave you that stone, and through it, I suggested that you not talk about me, and that you not remember the stone. And I used the stone to work the other spells, the ones you noticed. When I took you home that night, I'd already prepared—"

Savn stared. "You've been putting spells everywhere, haven't you?"

"It may seem like that—"

"What did you do to Polyi?" he said fiercely, ready to strangle the Easterner, jhereg or no.

"Nothing," said Vlad. "But, as I said, I did use the stone to cast a spell on your parents, through you, that would allow you to be more useful to me. So if you're looking for a grievance, you have one."

Savn spat, then glared at the Easterner. Vlad met his eyes calmly.

"Well, I've been useful, haven't I?" said Savn bitterly. "I've saved your life—"

"I know."

More implications began to sink in. He said, "I assume you made me physick you? That was why I found you so easily?"

"No," said Vlad.

"What do you mean, No?"

Vlad adjusted his position against the wall. "I was unconscious, and even if I wasn't, it wouldn't have occurred to me that you'd be able to heal me." He paused. "How *did* you find me?"

"I remembered what you said about spells to make teleports easier, and I remembered what you'd been doing in

the road, and I thought about how quickly you'd teleported, and I just put it together."

Vlad gave one of his characteristic laughs—a small
chuckle that never left his chest. "Virtue, I've been told, is
its own reward."

"What does *that* mean?"

"I almost blocked out your memory of what I'd been
doing, but I didn't want to do more to your memories than
I had to."

"That's bleeding noble of you," said Savn.

"So to speak," said Vlad.

"How can you do things like that?" said Polyi, in a tone
more curious than reproachful.

"I'll do what I have to, to save my life," said Vlad, giving her the briefest of glares. "Who wouldn't?"

"I wouldn't," said Polyi firmly. "Not if to save my life
I had to go into people's heads and change them. That's
evil. It's better to just kill them."

"Maybe it is," said Vlad. "But if they're alive, they can
change again, and perhaps recover. If they're dead, it's all
over."

"But—"

"But yes, I know, altering someone's mind is an ugly
thing to do. Don't think I don't know it. But don't think
that you can pretend these questions are easy, because they
aren't, and anyone who says they are is lying."

"You'd know a lot about lying, wouldn't you?" said
Savn.

"Yes," said Vlad. "I've done a great deal of it. Also killing. Also, tricking people into doing what I wanted them
to do. I'm neither proud nor ashamed of any of this—I do
what I must."

"It sounds," said Polyi, "like you'll do anything to anyone, as long as it's useful to you."

Vlad took a deep breath, as if he was about to shout at
her, then let it out slowly. "You may be right," he said.

"Is that why you taught me witchcraft?" said Savn.
"Because you thought it would be useful to you?"

Once again, the chuckle. "No." Vlad shook his head and closed his eyes. Savn waited. After a moment, the Easterner sighed. "I guess, what with one thing and another, I owe you the truth."

Savn nodded, but didn't say anything. He felt Polyi looking at him, but she, too, waited.

Vlad said, "The first time, here in this spot, I didn't teach you anything. I just put you to sleep for a while so I could explore."

"I don't understand. Why did you bother putting me to sleep?"

Vlad turned his palms up. "I didn't want your company while I explored."

"Then why have me along at all?"

"You knew where this place was," he said, gesturing at the cave around them.

"This place? I don't understand."

"I knew there had to be an underground waterway, and Dark Water can be useful against the undead, and I was looking for a way into Loraan's manor house. I thought you might know how to find it, so I—"

"So you asked me leading questions until I found it for you."

"Yes," said Vlad. "That's right." He closed his eyes briefly. When he opened them again, his face was, once more, without expression.

"And the second time you pretended to teach me witchcraft? What was that about? That time, you even had me convinced you'd taught me something."

"I did. That time there was no trickery, Savn. I taught you because you wanted to know, and because I'd started to like you. I hate to sound trite, but you remind me of myself. Take that for what it's worth."

"I will," said Savn, hearing the bitterness in his own voice. Then he said, "Do you remember when we were talking about Athyra?"

"Yes."

"Do you remember how you said those who explore the

world see people as objects, and mystics act like people don't really exist at all?"

"Yes," said Vlad. And, "Oh."

He looked down, and chewed on his lower lip. No one said anything, because there seemed to be nothing more to say.

Chapter Fifteen

I will not marry an acrobat,
I will not marry an acrobat,
He'd always think that I'm too fat.
Hi-dee hi-dee ho-la!
    Step on out . . .

AT LAST VLAD broke the silence. "Maybe you're right," he said. "Maybe I'm no better than your Baron. But all I know is that he's killed someone who once helped me. And years ago he nearly destroyed a close friend of mine. And now he is cooperating with a Jhereg assassin who plans to kill me—"

It took a moment before Savn realized that when Vlad said Jhereg he meant the House, not the animals. Then Savn gasped. "What?"

"That's what Fird told me, though I'd already guessed it. There's an assassin staying with Baron Smallcliff at the manor house, and I don't think he's here because he likes linseed-flavored wine. The Baron is cooperating with the Jhereg to assassinate me."

"I don't believe you," said Savn.

Vlad shrugged.

"Why would he do that?" said Savn.

"They both hate me; it makes sense that they'd work together."

"The Jhereg hates you?"

"Oh, yes."

"Why?"

"I picked an unfortunate method of terminating my relationship with them."

"What do you ... you mean, you're a Jhereg?"

"I used to be."

"What did you do?"

Vlad took a deep breath and met Savn's eyes. "I killed people. For money."

Savn stared at him, but couldn't think of anything to say.

"I reached a point where I couldn't do it anymore, and I left. In the process, I killed someone important, and I threatened the House representative to the Empire—sort of like your Speaker. So now they want to kill me. I can't really blame them, but I'm hardly going to cooperate, am I?"

"I don't believe you," said Savn.

"Then I doubt I can convince you. But don't you wonder why the Baron attacked me?"

"Because you killed Reins—or because he thought you did."

"Is that the way justice usually works around here? If someone is suspected of a crime, your Baron Smallcliff sends his soldiers to kill them? You'll notice they made no effort to arrest me."

"I don't know," said Savn. "I never said I understood everything. But I know His Lordship wouldn't hire an assassin."

"Not hire," said Vlad. "Merely help."

"He wouldn't do that."

"Why is it that, just at the time I happen to be coming by, Loraan decides to leave his home and take up residence in his manor house, which just happens to be near the place I'm passing by? You think this has nothing to do with me?"

"I don't know."

"And then Reins dies, which is enough to keep me here—"

"I don't believe you."

Vlad sighed and shook his head. "Why does everyone only see what he wants to?"

Savn twitched, started to speak, then realized he had no answer. He sat on the floor of the cave, looking down.

At length, Vlad broke the silence. "What are you going to do?" he said.

"About what?" said Savn.

"I'd like to know if you plan to tell your Baron where I am, or perhaps the townspeople."

"Oh. Well, you never told me your plans; why should I tell you mine?"

Vlad chuckled. "Well taken. Whatever you decide, you should probably get home soon."

"What difference does it make?"

"I would think," said Vlad, "that your Maener and Paener would be getting worried by now."

Savn looked at him closely. "Is it that easy?"

"To undo? Yes. The spell, at any rate, is easy to undo. And there shouldn't be any direct aftereffects."

"What do you mean, 'direct'?"

"I mean that they'll probably figure out that they've been under a spell. I don't know what that will do to them. Maybe nothing."

Savn glanced at Polyi, who was staring at the ground and frowning.

"Do you want to go home?" Savn asked her.

She looked up. "Do you?"

"Not right now. I want to stay for a bit and—"

"See how it comes out?" said Vlad ironically.

Savn shrugged and asked Vlad, "What do *you* intend to do?"

"I'm not sure. It depends how much time I have. If I had to teleport right now, I might be able to. Then again, I might not. I'd rather not have to. If I can get a couple of days to recover, I'll have the choice of getting out of here to someplace safer. If, on the other hand, I'm found, I'll have to try to escape as best I can."

"So your intention is to get out?"

"Oh, no. That's only if I have no choice. You know very well what I want to do."

"You're crazy," said Polyi. "You can't kill His Lordship! No one can."

Vlad shook his head. "I'm going to kill him. The only questions are when and how. If I can't do it now, I'll have to wait for a better time. But now would be best. I'd like to have it over and done with."

"Heh," said Polyi. "You won't feel that way when it *is* over and done with."

Savn knelt down next to Vlad and felt his forehead. He was relieved to find that it was still cool, though his face seemed a trifle flushed. Vlad watched him intently.

"How do you feel?" said Savn.

"Tired. Weak. Not bad other than that."

"You should rest."

"I doubt I can," said Vlad. "There's too much on my mind."

Savn was suddenly and comically reminded of how he would explain to Maener that he was too excited about Pudding Morn to go to sleep, and how she would smile and tell him that he should just rest his eyes then, and how he would fall asleep. He said, "That's all right, just close your eyes and—"

Vlad laughed. "Very good, Paener. I get the idea. Wake me if they come to kill me."

He slid over to his blankets, threw one arm over his eyes, and, as far as Savn could tell, went instantly to sleep.

They watched him sleep for an hour or two; then Savn decided they should talk. He whispered to Polyi, and she agreed, so he took a torch and guided her back through the cave until he was certain they were far enough away that Vlad couldn't hear them.

"What should we do?" he said.

"I think we should go home," said Polyi. "If Mae and Pae really are worried—"

"What will we tell them?"

"The truth," said Polyi.

"Oh?"

She frowned. "Well, it isn't our problem, is it? Savn, you heard him. Now we *know* he wants to kill His Lordship. I mean, we know he can't, but what if he does?"

"Well," said Savn. "What if he does?"

"We have to stop him, that's all."

"Do we?"

"You heard what he is. He's an assassin. He kills people for money. He—"

"He *used* to be an assassin. And what about His Lordship?"

"You don't believe all that stuff he said, do you?"

"I don't know. Why would he admit to being an assassin, then lie about everything else? It doesn't make sense."

"He's an Easterner; maybe it makes sense to him."

"That's no answer."

"Why not? Do you know how they think?"

Savn didn't answer; in his mind, he kept hearing Vlad's voice, echoing his own: *Why do people only see what they want to?* An unanswerable question, certainly. If Master Wag would even admit that it was true, he'd just say that it didn't matter. And maybe it didn't; maybe it was always going to be frustrating for someone who knew things that most people didn't want to know. Maybe it was the way of the world.

But if what Vlad said was true, then, within a day, he'd been on both sides of the problem. He didn't much like either one. How were you supposed to know what to believe, anyway?

"Come on, Polyi," he said, and started back to the cavern where Vlad slept.

"You want to stay here?"

"I don't know, but right now I want to talk to Vlad."

"You know," said Polyi, "I'm getting tired of this cave."

Savn was tempted to tell her that she was along by her own choice, but decided it wouldn't be nice. He wedged the torch once more into the rocks and sat down next to Vlad. The jhereg, at first watching him carefully, seemed to relax and go back to resting. Funny how they knew he didn't intend to hurt Vlad. Maybe they had some means of knowing the truth. Maybe they were the only beings in the world who knew what was really going on, and they were secretly laughing at everyone else.

He laughed at the thought, and Vlad's eyes opened.

"What's funny?" said Polyi.

"I've just had a revelation," said Savn. "Truth is in the eyes of the jhereg."

Vlad blinked and shook his head. "Water?" he croaked.

Savn got him some, and said, "How do you feel?"

"Better," he said. He drank more water, then looked at Savn patiently.

"Vlad, how do you know what the truth is?"

The Easterner didn't laugh. He considered for a moment, then said, "Help me sit up."

Savn did so, then helped him to the wall, which he rested against for a few minutes, recovering his breath. To Savn's eye, he seemed to have made some improvement.

"Very often," said Vlad, "I learn what is true by trying something and having it fail."

"Oh," said Savn. "I know about that. Master Wag talks about learning from errors."

"Yes. I don't recommend it."

"You don't?"

"No. It's far better not to make mistakes, at least when your life is on the line."

"Well, yes."

Vlad chewed his lower lip. "It's not that I've never thought about it," he said. "I have. That happens when you associate with philosophers. The trouble is, you get different answers depending on whether you really want to know, or if you just want to argue about it."

"I don't want to argue about it," said Savn.

"I suspected that. That makes it harder."

Polyi said, "Savn, what are you doing?"

Vlad answered for him. "He's trying to make a very difficult decision."

Polyi snorted. "Savn, you're going to ask *him* how to

decide whether you should turn him in? Well, that really makes sense, doesn't it?"

"I think it does," said Savn. He turned back to Vlad. "What were you saying?"

Vlad was frowning at the floor. He didn't look up. "I wasn't saying anything. I was thinking."

"Well?"

Then he did look up, squinting at Savn. "Let's start with this," he said. "Suppose everyone you know says there's no cave here. Is that the truth?"

"No."

"Good. Not everyone would agree with you, but I do."

"I don't understand."

"It doesn't matter." Vlad thought for a moment longer, then suddenly shook his head. "There's no easy answer. You learn things bit by bit, and you check everything by trying it out, and then sometimes you get a big piece of it all at once, and then you check *that* out. I know what your problem is. Everyone thinks that your Baron can't be killed, and, furthermore, he's a great guy, and here I am with a different story, and you don't know who to believe. I understand the problem. Sorry, I can't give you any answers.

"But," he resumed suddenly, as if a thought had just occurred to him, "I can point out a few things. First of all, the only reason you think he's so wonderful is because you know people from Bigcliff, who have a real scum of a Dzurlord. So what makes your Baron so great is that you have someone horrible to compare him with. As I recall, you weren't very impressed when you learned that I could have done worse things to you than I did, and you were right. As far as I'm concerned, saying someone could be much worse is not much of a recommendation."

Savn shook his head. "But he's never done anything to us."

Vlad's eyebrows twitched. "Doesn't he come by and pick the best portion of your crop, and take it for himself?"

"Well of course, but that's just—"

"I don't want to argue it," said Vlad. "There's no point
in talking about all of the things you take as the natural order of life that I don't think are. But that's part of the answer to your question, which is just to ask questions of
everyone, and of yourself. Try to identify the assumptions
you make, and see if they stand up. Master Wag, you said,
scoffs at witchcraft, doesn't he?"

"Yes."

"Well, why do you chant to drive fevers away? The in-
cantations you use resemble witchcraft more than a little."

"Maybe they do," said Savn. "But I know witchcraft
works, so why shouldn't the chanting?"

"Sure," said Vlad. "But how does Master Wag explain
it?"

"Well, it's because the Fever Imps—"

"How do you know there are Fever Imps at all?"

"Because the chanting works."

"Fair enough. Why, then, do you also use herbs, and
why go to such effort to keep me cool?"

"You need all those things."

"Are you sure? Maybe the herbs would work by themselves. Maybe the chanting would work by itself. Maybe
all I'd need is to be kept cool. How do you know?"

"Well, I assume, since it's been done that way for
years—"

"Don't assume, find out."

"You mean, I can't know anything until I've proven it
for myself?"

"Hmmm. No, not really. If someone learns something,
and passes it on, you don't have to go through everything
he learned again."

"But, then—"

"But you don't have to accept it on faith, either."

"Then what do you do?"

"You make certain you understand it; you understand it
all the way to the bottom. And you test it. When you both
understand why it is the way it is, and you've tried it out,
then you can say you know it. Until then—"

"But can you ever *really* understand something?"

"Yes, I think so."

Savn fell silent. Eventually, Vlad cleared his throat and said, "I'm afraid I haven't helped you much."

Savn looked up at his odd face, with the thick black hair down in front of his ears and above his thin lip, more dark hair falling in waves inelegantly to his shoulders, with wrinkles of age on his forehead where none should yet be. Savn wondered how many people he had killed, and how rich he had become doing it, and why he had stopped.

"No," he said. "You've helped me a great deal."

Vlad gave a terse nod.

Savn said, "Would you like to tell me what you're going to do now?"

"What, before I know whether you plan to help me or betray me?"

"Haven't you been asking me to trust you, in spite of all the reasons you've given me not to?"

"I suppose I have," said Vlad.

"Well, then, why shouldn't I ask you to trust me, in spite of those very same reasons?"

Vlad looked at him for what seemed to be a long time. Never before had Savn wished so much to know what someone's thoughts were; he was very much aware of the two jhereg, sitting patiently at Vlad's side, with their poison fangs barely concealed by their reptilian jaws. Then, abruptly, Vlad laughed. "Well taken. I can't argue, so I concede. But what about you?" he added, looking at Polyi.

She stared back at him, then turned to Savn. "Whatever you do, I'll go along with it."

"Are you sure?" said Savn.

"Yes."

Savn turned back to Vlad. "Well?"

The Easterner nodded. "If you follow the waterway, you'll find it seems to run into a wall. If you go under the wall, it splits into several streams, none of which has much water, and all of which end in identical walls that look natural. Some of these—four, as far as I can tell—actually lead into the basement of the manor house. They are probably sorcerously controlled."

"Can you get past them?"

"Yes, given enough time."

"How?"

"You mostly wear your way through with diligence, patience, and a chisel."

"Can't you knock it down with sorcery?"

"Not without alerting him; he's very good."

"Then why can't he find you?"

"Because I'm very well protected against being found."

"So is that what you're going to do? Break through the wall and . . . and murder him?"

"Not a chance. He may be expecting me to do that, he may not, but he'll certainly be guarding against it. I might, however, make him think that's what I'm doing. It's the obvious way in."

"Then what will you do?"

"I haven't decided yet. I've got a few things going for me, but I haven't figured out how to make them work."

"What things?"

"The assassin. He's not getting along with Loraan at all."

"How do you know that?"

"Because he's been there for more than a week, and Loraan made that attack on me."

"I don't understand."

"The Jhereg," said Vlad, looking straight at Savn, "want me to be killed with a Morganti weapon. Loraan's attacks were not bluffs—he tried to kill me and almost succeeded. He—"

"Wait a minute. Attacks?"

"Yes. There have been two so far."

"I only know of the one at Tem's house."

"The other happened the day before. I got careless and allowed myself to be seen too close to his manor house, and he made a sorcerous attack on me."

"And it failed?"

"I have," said Vlad, "a few tricks up my sleeve. I was really sloppy in staying at Tem's house long enough for them to find me. My only excuse is that it's been some years now since I've had to worry about that sort of thing. In any case, neither attack would have been Morganti; neither would have satisfied the Jhereg. So my conclusion is that Loraan is just barely cooperating with them, and they are just barely cooperating with him. They need each other, because this is Loraan's area and because the Jhereg have the expert assassins. But neither of them like it. That's what I hope to use. I'm not certain how to go about it, though."

"I see," said Savn.

"Have I answered your questions?"

"Yes."

"Then, do you care to tell me what you're going to do?"

"I won't turn you in," said Savn.

That seemed to satisfy Vlad, who closed his eyes and breathed deeply, leaning against the wall.

"You tire easily, don't you?"

"I think," he said, "that I'll be able to begin healing myself in a day or two. After that, it shouldn't be long."

"So the idea is to keep you safe for two days."

"More or less. Less, I hope."

"Do you think this place is secure?"

Vlad frowned, then looked at the jhereg, who rose and flew out of the cave. "Maybe," said Vlad. "But, in any case, we will now be warned of anyone approaching, so, as long as they don't put a teleport block up over the entire area, I'll have a chance to get out."

"A *what* over the area?"

"Never mind. Loraan would either have to know exactly where I was, or be willing to use a great deal of power to cover the entire area."

"I don't understand."

"Skip it. I'm saying that whatever happens, at least we'll be warned."

Savn stared at the place where the jhereg had disappeared into the narrow corridor that accompanied the subterranean stream. "Yes," he said. "At least we'll be warned."

* * *

Savn and Polyi cleaned up the cooking pot, which Savn put back into the bag. He carefully wrapped the good kitchen knife. They assisted Vlad once more to get to his blankets; he needed less help than he had before.

It didn't seem to matter that outside the cave, which was already beginning to feel like another world, it was early afternoon; Polyi claimed to be tired, and so lay down among her furs, and soon began to breathe evenly. Savn lit fresh torches and tidied up the area. Was it Endweek again? If he were at home, would he be cleaning? What would Mae and Pae say when they saw him again? Were they really worried?

Could he trust anything Vlad said?

While Vlad and Polyi slept, Savn thought over all that Vlad had told him. What if the herbs were unnecessary to combat fever, and they'd just been used from the custom of years uncounted? What if *any* custom could be wrong? What if His Lordship was undead?

He considered truth and knowledge and trust, and responsibility, until they whirled around in his head empty of meanings, only occasionally coming to light on some real example of deceit, ignorance, betrayal, or neglect, which would give him some hint of understanding before vanishing once more into the whirlpool of half-understood platitudes and questionable wisdom.

He kept returning to one phrase the Easterner had let fall: "Don't assume, find out."

He thought about this very carefully, feeling the truth in the phrase, and asking himself if he was trusting the Easterner, or logic.

Even after he'd decided, he hesitated for some time before taking the obvious next step.

Savn stood at the Curving Stone for a long time, staring down the road that led to the door of His Lordship's manor house, which was itself out of sight behind a curve in the road. A score of years before, he and his friends had played on the grounds, hidden from all the glass windows except the one in the highest dormer, enjoying the feeling of danger, though safe in the knowledge that the manor house was empty.

Now His Lordship was in residence, and now Savn, though he wasn't certain what he was doing, was not playing. He walked on the road as if he belonged there, step by step, as if he were himself a visiting noble, although he had heard that these people teleported instead of walking, even when they only needed to go ten or twenty miles.

The manor house came in sight—a wide, tall building, full of sharp angles. In the years since he had seen it up close, he'd forgotten how big it was, or else decided it was only the exaggeration of a child's memory. Now he stared, remembering, taken again with the feeling that the magnificence of the house must reflect the power of he who dwelled within.

The roof looked like the edge of a scythe, with dormers on either side like wisps of straw. The brick of the house itself was pale green, and high on the front wall were wide windows made of glass—Savn could even see light creeping around the edges of the curtains inside. He strained his eyes, looking for movement. He looked for and eventually found the gully he had daringly played in so many years ago, as close to the house as one could get without being seen. There were glass windows on that side, too, but he remembered quite clearly that if you kept your head down you were only visible from the one lonely window high on the side.

Oddly enough, it was only then, looking at all the windows, that he realized it was becoming dark, and was surprised once more by how fast time went by in the cave. At that moment, more light began to glow around the far side of the house. He stopped where he was, and soon a servant appeared from around that side. Savn watched as the servant walked around the house using a long match to light lamps that were stuck onto the house at various points. When he was finished, the entire house was lit up as if it were burning.

When the servant was gone, Savn watched the house a little longer, then resumed his walk along the road, directly toward the house, and up to the large front door. He felt very much as he imagined a soldier would feel marching into battle, but this was another thought he didn't care to examine closely.

He stood before the door and stared at it. It seemed like such a plain door to be part of His Lordship's manor house—just wood, and it opened and closed like any other door, although, to be sure, it had a brass handle that looked too complicated for Savn to operate. He took a deep breath, closed his eyes, opened them, and clapped.

Nothing happened.

He waited for what seemed like several hours, although in fact it was hardly more than a minute. Still, he felt his courage slipping away. He tapped his foot, then stopped, afraid someone would see.

Why didn't someone come to the door?

Because he couldn't be heard, of course; the door was too thick.

Well, then, how was someone supposed to get the attention of His Lordship's servants?

He looked around, and eventually saw a long rope hanging down in front of the door. Without giving himself time to think, he gave it one long, hard pull, and almost screeched when he heard, from inside, a rattling sound as if several sticks or logs were rolling against each other.

His heart, which had been beating fast for some time, began to pound in earnest. He was, in fact, on the point of turning and bolting, when the door opened and he found himself looking up at a slight, sharp-featured man in the livery of Baron Smallcliff. After a moment, Savn recognized him as someone called Turi, one of His Lordship's servants who occasionally came into town for supplies. Come to think of it, Turi had been doing so ever since Reins had quit—

He broke off the thought, and at the same time realized he was staring. He started to speak but had to clear his throat.

"Well?" said the servant, frowning sternly.

Savn managed to squeak out, "Your pardon, sir."

"Mmmmph."

Savn took a breath. "May I request an audience with His Lordship? My name is Savn, and I'm the son of Cwelli and Olani, and I—"

"What do you want to see His Lordship about, boy?" said Turi, now looking impassive and impenetrable.

"If it please His Lordship, about the Easterner."

Turi slowly tilted his head like a confused dog, and simultaneously raised his eyebrows. "Indeed?"

"Yes, sir."

"You have information for His Lordship?"

"I . . . that is—"

"Well, come in and I will see if His Lordship is available. Your name, you said, is Savn?"

"Yes, sir."

"And you are a peasant?"

"I'm apprenticed," he said.

"To whom?"

"To Master Wag, the physicker."

At this Turi's eyes grew very wide, and for a moment he seemed at a loss for words. Then he said, "Come in, come in, by all means."

The inside of the house was even more magnificent than the outside, especially when it became clear to Savn that the room he stood in—which contained nothing but some hooks on the wall and another door opposite the one he'd come in—existed for no other purpose than as a place for people to wait and to hang up their cloaks.

"Wait here," said the servant.

"Yes, sir," said Savn as Turi went through the inner door, closing it behind him.

He stared awestruck at the fine, dark, polished wood, realizing that this one, unfurnished room must have cost His Lordship more than Savn's entire house was worth. He was studying the elaborate carved brass handle on the inner door, trying to decide if there was a recognizable shape to it, when it turned and the door opened. He braced himself to face His Lordship, then relaxed when he saw it was Turi again.

"This way, boy," said the servant.

"Yes, sir," said Savn, and, though his knees felt weak, he followed Turi into a place of splendor greater than his mind could grasp. The walls seemed to shimmer, and were adorned with richly colored paintings. The furniture was huge and came in amazing variations, and Savn couldn't imagine sitting on any of it. Bright light filled every corner of the room, glittering against objects of incomprehensible purpose, made of crystal, shiny metal, and ceramics that had been glazed with some unfathomable technique that made the blues and reds as deep and rich as the soil.

"Watch your step," said Turi sharply.

Savn caught himself just before walking into a low table that seemed made entirely of glass. He continued more carefully, while still looking around, and it suddenly came to him that some of the crystal and metal objects were drinking vessels. He didn't think he'd be able to drink from such objects—his hand would be shaking too much.

The shape and color of his surroundings changed. He had somehow entered another room, which might as well have been another world for all the sense he could make of anything around him, until he realized that every one of the objects that filled the room were books—different books—more books than a man could read in his entire lifetime—more books than Savn had thought had ever been written. There were hundreds and hundreds of them. These were cases that had obviously been made just to hold them. There were tables on which they lay, carelessly flung open to—

His gaze suddenly fell on a figure standing before him, dressed in a gleaming white shirt, which set off a bright red jewel suspended from a chain around his neck. The pants were also perfectly white, and baggy, falling all the way to the floor so that the figure's feet were invisible. Savn looked at his face, then looked away, terrified. On the one hand, though he was big, it seemed odd to Savn how human he looked; the thought, *He's just a man, after all,* came unbidden to his mind. But even as Savn was thinking this, he discovered that he had fallen to his knees and was touching his head to the floor, as if in response to something so deeply buried within him that it went beyond awareness or decision. As Savn knelt there, confounded and humbled, with the image of the Athyra nobleman burned into his mind, it struck him that His Lordship had seemed very pale.

Unnaturally pale.

Savn tried not to think about what this might mean.

When His Lordship spoke, it was with an assurance that made Savn realize that Speaker, with all his shouting, raving, and fits of temper, had only pretended to have authority—that real authority was something stamped into someone from birth or not at all. He wondered what Vlad would say about that.

"What is it, lad?" said His Lordship. "My man tells me you have something to say about the Easterner. If you want to tell me where he is, don't bother. I know already. If you are here asking about your Master, I'm not finished with him yet. If you want to tell me what sort of condition the Easterner is in, and what his defenses are like, that is another matter; I will listen and reward you well."

Savn's head spun as he tried to make sense out of this strange collection of ideas.

Your Master.

Master Wag?

Not finished with him yet.

Savn managed to find his voice, and croaked out, "I don't understand, Your Lordship."

"Well, what are you here for? Speak up?"

"Your Lordship, I—" Savn searched for the words, hindered in part by no longer being certain what he wanted to find out, or if he dared ask any of it. He looked up, and his eye fell on someone who had apparently been there all along, though Savn hadn't noticed him. The man, who Savn was certain he'd never seen before, stood behind His Lordship, absolutely motionless, his face devoid of the least hint of expression or of feeling, dressed in grey from head to foot, save for a bit of black lace on the ruffles of his shirt, and his high black boots. In some indefinable yet definite way, he reminded Savn of Vlad.

Below the collar of his cloak was the insignia of the House of the Jhereg, as if Savn needed that, or even his colors, to know that this was the assassin Vlad had spoken of.

Savn couldn't take his eyes off him, and, for his part, the stranger stared back with the curiosity of one looking at an interesting weed that, though it didn't belong in one's garden, had some unusual features that made it worth a moment's study before being pulled and discarded.

"Speak up, boy," snapped His Lordship, but Savn could only stare. Speech was so far from him that he couldn't imagine ever being able to talk again—the command of His Lordship, compelling though it was, belonged to another world entirely; surely His Lordship couldn't imagine that he, Savn, would be able to form words, much less sentences.

"What do you have to tell me?" said His Lordship. "I won't ask again."

Savn heard this last with relief; at this moment, all he wanted from life was for His Lordship not to ask him to speak anymore. He thought about getting up and bowing his way out of the room, but he wasn't certain his legs would support him, and if it wasn't the proper thing to do, he might never get out of the house alive. The complete folly of coming here hit him fully, rendering action or speech even more impossible.

His Lordship made a sound of derision or impatience and said, "Get him out of here. Put him with the other one. We don't have time now, anyway."

Another voice spoke, very softly, with a bite to the consonants that made Savn sure it was from the Jhereg: "You're an idiot, Loraan. We could find out—"

"Shut up," said His Lordship. "I need your advice now less than—"

"Indeed," interrupted the other. "Less than when? Less than the last time you ignored me and—"

"I said, shut up," repeated His Lordship. "We don't have time for this; we've got an Easterner to kill, and the troops should be in position by now."

"And if they find him before morning I'll eat my fee."

"I'll bring you salt," said His Lordship. "We know where to begin looking, and we have enough manpower that it won't take more than two or three hours."

At that moment, rough hands grabbed Savn's shoulders. The Jhereg and the Athyra did not seem to notice.

"He'll be gone before you find him," the Jhereg said.

Savn was pulled to his feet, but his knees wouldn't support him and he fell back down.

"Unlikely, I've put a block up."

"Around three square miles of caves?"

"Yes."

Savn was grabbed once more, held under his armpits by very strong hands.

"Then he's already alerted," said the Jhereg.

Savn was dragged away. He got a last glimpse of His Lordship, hands balled up in fists, staring at the Jhereg, who wore a mocking smile that seemed the twin of the one Vlad had put on from time to time. His Lordship said, "Let him be alerted. I have confidence in your . . ." and His Lordship's voice was drowned out by a sound that Savn realized was his own boots scraping along the floor as he was taken off.

He was completely unaware of the places he passed through, and wasn't even aware of who was dragging him, despite the fact that he heard a man's voice and a woman's, as if from a distance, telling him to walk on his own if he didn't want to be beaten flat. The voices seemed disconnected from the hands pulling him along, which felt like forces of nature rather than the work of human beings.

They came to the top of a stairway, and the woman,

laughing, suggested they throw him down. He thought, *I hope they don't,* but knew he couldn't do anything about it in any case.

However, they continued to drag him down the stairs, and then through a dimly lit corridor, until at last they arrived at a large wooden door, bound with iron strips, with a thick bar across it as well as a locking mechanism. They leaned Savn against a wall, where he promptly sagged to the floor. He heard sobbing and realized it was his own. He looked up for the first time, and saw who had been dragging him—two people in the livery of the Athyra, both armed with large swords. The woman had a heavy-looking iron key. She unlocked the door and removed the bar. They opened the door, picked up Savn, and pushed him inside, where he lay face down.

The door was closed behind him, and he could hear the lock turning and the bar falling. At first it seemed dark inside, since there were no lanterns such as there had been along the corridor, but then he realized there was some light, which came from a faintly glowing lightstone—a device Savn had heard about but never seen. It was high up in the middle of the ceiling, which was a good twelve feet overhead. In other circumstances Savn would have been delighted to have seen it, and studied it as best he could, but for now he was too stunned.

He saw now that what he'd at first taken to be a bundle of rags was actually a person, and he remembered His Lordship saying something like *Put him with the other.* He looked closer, and as his eyes adjusted to the dimness of the room, he recognized Master Wag. He approached, and realized there was something wrong with the way the Master's arm was lying above his head. He stared, hesitating to touch him, and was gradually able to see some of what had been done to him.

The room spun, the light faded in and out. Savn could never remember the next few minutes clearly; he spoke to the Master, and he shouted something at the closed door, and looked around the room for he knew not what, and, after a while, he sat down on the floor and shook.

* * *

She flew low, well below the overcast, starting out near to her lover, then gradually getting further away as their search took them apart.

The Provider had told them to be careful, to be certain to miss nothing, so they covered every inch of ground below them, starting in a small circle above the cave-mouth and only widening it a bit at a time.

She was in no hurry. Her lover had relaxed, now that the Provider seemed to be out of danger, and it was a fine, cool day. She never forgot what she was doing—she kept her eyes and her attention on the ground below—but this didn't prevent her from enjoying the pleasures of flight. Besides, her feet had started hurting.

She recognized the large rock, the nearby house, and the winding, twisting road as things she'd seen before, but they didn't mean a great deal to her. For one thing, there was no meat there, living or dead. At the same time she could feel, in her wings and her breath, the difference in the feel of the air when she flew over fields or over forests, over water or over bare ground where only a stubble of growth was now left. All of these added to the pleasure of flying.

She could always feel where her mate was, and they spoke, mind to mind, as they flew, until at last she looked down and saw one of the soft ones below her. This seemed strange, and after thinking about it for a moment, she realized it was because he could not have been there a moment before, and she ought to have seen him approach. She swept back around, and there was another, and no more explanation of how this one had appeared. She recalled that the Provider could do something like this, and decided that she ought to mention it. She came back around again, and by now an entire herd of the soft ones had appeared, and they were walking along the road that cut through a thin, grassy forest.

She called to her mate, who came at once. He studied them, knowing more about their habits than she; then he told the Provider what they had discovered. They watched *a little longer, until the herd left the road and began to walk down the narrow, curving path that led toward the caves.*

Then they returned to the Provider, to see what he wanted them to do.

Chapter Sixteen

> I will not marry an aristocrat,
> I will not marry an aristocrat,
> He'd treat me like a dog or cat.
> Hi-dee hi-dee ho-la!
>   Step on out . . .

COHERENT THOUGHT GRADUALLY returned, bringing sensations with it like trailing roots behind a plow. Savn lay very still and let the mists of his confused dreams gradually fade away, to be replaced by the vapors of true memory. He looked to see if Master Wag was really there; when he saw him, he squeezed his eyes tightly shut, as if he could shut out the sympathetic pain. Then he looked around, staring at anything and everything that wasn't his Master and wasn't so terribly hurt.

The room was about ten feet on a side, and smelled slightly dank, but not horribly so. He listened for the sounds of scurrying rodents and was relieved not to hear any. There was a chamber pot in a far corner; judging from the lack of odor, it had not been used. Things could, Savn decided, be much worse.

The light hadn't changed; he could still see Master Wag huddled against a wall; the Master was breathing, and his eyes were open. Both of his arms seemed to be broken or dislocated, and probably his left leg, too. There were red marks on his face, as from slaps, but no bruises; he hadn't been in a fight, he had been tortured.

On seeing that Savn was looking at him, the Master spoke, his voice only the barest whisper, as Vlad's had been after the first fever had broken, but he spoke very clearly, as if he was taking great care with each word. "Have you any dreamgrass?"

Savn had to think for a moment before replying. "Yes, Master. It's in my pouch."

"Fetch some out. We have no food, but they've left us water and a mug, over in the corner. I haven't been able to move to get it."

Savn got the mug of water and brought it back to the Master. He gave him a drink of plain water first, then mixed the dreamgrass into it as best he could without a mortar and pestle. "That's good enough," whispered the Master. "I'll swallow it whole. You'll have to help me, though. My arms—"

"Yes, Master." Savn helped him to drink again and to swallow the dreamgrass.

The Master nodded, took a deep breath, and shuddered with his whole body. He said, "You're going to have to straighten out my legs and arms. Can you do it?"

"What's broken, Master?"

"Both legs, both arms. My left arm both above and below the elbow. Can you straighten them?"

"I remember the Nine Bracings, Master, but what can we splint them with?"

"Never mind that, just get them straightened. One thing at a time. I don't wish to go through life a cripple. Am I feverish?"

Savn felt his forehead. "No."

"Good. When the pain dulls a bit, you can begin."

"I . . . very well, Master. I can do it, I think."

"You think?"

"Have some more water, Master. How does the room look? Does your face feel heavy?"

The Master snorted and whispered, "I know how to tell when the dreamgrass takes effect. For one thing, there will be less pain. Oh, and have you any eddiberries?"

Savn looked in his pouch, but had none and said so.

"Very well, I'll get by without them. Now . . . hmmm. I'm starting to feel distant. Good. The pain is receding. Are you certain you know what to do?"

"Yes, Master," said Savn. "Who did this to you?"

His eyes flickered, and he spoke even more softly. "His Lordship had it done by a couple of his warriors, with help from . . . There is a Jhereg here—"

"I saw him."

"Yes. They tied me into a chair and . . . they wanted me to tell them where the Easterner was."

"Oh. Did you tell them?"

The Master's eyes squeezed tightly shut. "Eventually," he said.

"Oh," said Savn. The importance of this sank in gradually. He imagined Vlad, lying quietly in the cave with no way of knowing he'd been betrayed. "I wish there was some way to warn him."

"There isn't."

"I know." But the Easterner had means of receiving a warning. Maybe he'd escape after all. But he'd think that Savn, who had vanished, had been the betrayer. Savn shook his head. It was petty of him to worry about that when Vlad's life was in danger, and pointless to worry about Vlad's life when Master Wag was in pain that Savn could do something about. "Can we get more light in here?"

"No."

"All right." Savn took a deep breath. "I'm going to undress you now."

"Of course. Be careful."

"Then I will—"

"I know what you're going to do."

"Do you need more dreamgrass?"

"No." The Master's voice was almost inaudible now. He said, "Carry on, Savn."

"Yes. It is true and it is not true that once there was a village that grew up at a place where two rivers came together. Now, one river was wide, so that one—"

"Shallow and wide."

"Oh, yes. Sorry. Shallow and wide, so that one could walk across the entire length and still be dry from the knees up. The—"

Master Wag winced.

"—other was very fast, and full—I mean, fast and deep, and full of foamy rapids, whirlpools, rocks, and twisting currents, so that it wasn't safe even to boat on. After the rivers came togeth—"

The Master gasped.

"—er, the river, which they called Bigriver, became large, deep, fast, but tame, which allowed them to travel down it to their neighbors, then back up, by means of—"

The Master began moaning steadily.

"—clever poles devised for this purpose. And they could also travel up and down the wide, slow river. But no one could travel on the fast, dangerous river. So, as time went on—"

The moans abruptly turned to screams.

"—the people of the village began to wonder what lay along that length, and talk about—"

The screams grew louder.

"—how they might find a way to travel up the river in spite of the dangerous rapids and the swiftness of the current. Some spoke of using the wind, but . . ."

Soon Savn no longer heard either his own voice or the Master's cries, except as a distant drone. His attention was concentrated on straightening the bones, and remembering everything his Master had taught him about using firm, consistent pressure and an even grip with his hands, being certain that no finger pressed against the bone harder or softer than it should, which would cause the patient unnecessary pain. His fingers felt the bones grinding against one another, and he could hear the sounds they made, even through the drone of his own voice, and his eyes showed him the Master turn grey with the pain, in spite of the dreamgrass, but he neither stopped nor slowed in his work. He thought the Master—the *real* Master, not this wrecked and broken old man he was physicking—would be proud of him.

The story told itself, and he worked against its rhythm, so that the rise in his voice and the most exciting parts of the story came when his hands were busiest, and the patient most needed to be distracted. Master Wag turned out to be a good patient, which was fortunate, because there was no way to render him immobile.

But it seemed to take a very long time.

Savn looked at his Master, who lay back moaning, his ankles cross-bound with strips of his own clothing and his face covered with sweat. Savn's own face felt as damp as the Master's looked. Savn started to take a drink of water, saw how much was left, and offered it to the Master along with more dreamgrass. Master Wag accepted wordlessly.

As Savn helped the Master eat and drink, he noticed that his own hands were shaking. Well, better now than while he'd been working. He hoped he'd done an adequate job. The Master opened his eyes and said, "They were about to start on my fingers. I couldn't let them—"

"I understand, Master. I think I would have told them right away."

"I doubt that very much," said the Master, and closed his eyes. Savn moved back against the wall to relax, and, when he tried to lean against it, found that there was something digging into his back. He felt around behind himself, and discovered a bundle jammed into the back of his pants. It took him a moment to recognize it as the good kitchen knife, all wrapped up in a towel.

He unwrapped it, took it into his hand, and stared at it. He had cleaned it carefully after cutting the norska to make the stew for Vlad, so it gleamed even in the feeble light of the cell. The blade was ten inches long, wide near the handle, narrowing down toward the point, with an edge that was fine enough to slice the tenderest bluefish, but a point that was no better than it had to be to pry kethna muscle from the bone. As he looked, he wondered, and his hands started shaking harder than ever.

He imagined himself holding the knife and fighting his way past all of His Lordship's guards, then rescuing Vlad at the last minute. He knew this was impossible, but the thought wouldn't go away. How would he feel, he wondered, if he allowed the Easterner to be killed, and maybe Master Wag as well, when he had a knife with him and he never tried to use it? What would he say to himself when he was an old man, who claimed to be a physicker, yet he had let two people in his care die without making any effort to stop it? Or, if he left home, he would spend his life thinking he was running away from his own cowardice. It wasn't fair that this decision, which had become so important, should be taken away by something that wasn't his fault.

He turned the knife this way and that in his hand, knowing how futile it would be to challenge a warrior with a sword when he had nothing but a cooking knife, and had, furthermore, never been in a knife fight in his life. He had seen Vlad fighting some of His Lordship's soldiers, and couldn't imagine himself doing that to someone, no matter how much he wanted to.

He shook his head and stared at the knife, as if it could give him answers.

He was still staring at it some half an hour later, when there came a rattling at the door, which he recognized as the opening of the lock and removal of the bar. He stood up and leaned against the wall, the knife down by his side. A guard came into the room and, without a glance at Savn or Master Wag, slopped some water into the mug.

He seemed very big, very strong, very graceful, and very dangerous.

Don't be an idiot, Savn told himself. *He is a warrior. He spends all of his life around weapons. The sword at his belt could slice you into pieces before you took two steps. It is insanity. It is the same as killing yourself.* He had been telling himself these things already, but, now that it came to it, with the guard before him, the mad ideas in his head would neither listen to reason nor bring themselves forward as a definite intention. He hesitated, and watched the guard, and then, while the man's back was turned,

Savn inched his way closer to the door, the knife still held down by his side.

It's crazy, he told himself. *If your knife had a good point, you could strike for his kidneys, but it doesn't. And you aren't tall enough to slit his throat.*

The guard finished and straightened up.

The knife is heavy, and there is some *point on it. And I'm strong.*

Still not deigning to look at Savn or Master Wag, the guard walked to the door.

If I strike so that I can use all of my strength, and I find just the right place, then maybe . . .

Savn was never aware of making a conscious decision, but, for just a moment, he saw an image of His Lordship standing next to the Jhereg as they broke the Master's bones. He took a deep breath and held it.

As the soldier reached the door, Savn stepped up behind him, picked his spot, and struck as hard as he could for a point midway down the guard's back, next to his backbone, driving the knife in, turning it, and pulling toward the spinal cord, all with one motion. The jar of the knife against the warrior's back was hard—shock traveled all the way up Savn's arm, and he would have been unable to complete the stroke if he had attempted anything more complicated. But it was one motion, just as Master Wag had done once in removing a Bur-worm from Lakee's thigh. One motion, curving in and around and out. Removing a Bur-worm, or cutting the spine, what was the difference?

He knew where he was aiming, and exactly what it would do. The guard fell as if his legs were made of water, making only a quiet gasp as he slithered to the floor jerking the knife, which was stuck against the inside of his backbone, out of Savn's hand. The man fell onto his left side, pinning his sword beneath him, yet, with the reflexes of a trained warrior, he reached for it anyway.

Savn started to jump over him, but couldn't bring himself to do it. The guard seemed unable to use his legs, but he pushed himself over to the other side and again reached for his sword. Savn backed into the cell, as far away from the guard as he could get, and watched in horrified fascination as the warrior managed to draw his sword and began to pull himself toward Savn with his free hand. He had eyes only for Savn as he came, and his face was drawn into a grimace that could have been hate or pain or both. Savn tried to squeeze himself as far into the corner as he could.

The distance between them closed terribly slowly, and Savn suddenly had the thought that he would live and grow old in a tiny corner of the cell while the guard crept toward him—an entire lifetime of anticipation, waiting for the inevitable sword thrust—all compacted into seven feet, an inch at a time.

In fact, the warrior was a good four feet away when he gasped and lay still, breathing but unable to pull himself any further, but it seemed much closer. Savn, for his part, didn't move either, but stared at the man whose blood was soaking through his shirt and beginning to stain the floor around him, drip by fascinating drip.

After what was probably only a few minutes, however long it felt, he stopped breathing, but even then Savn was unable to move until his sense of cleanliness around a patient overcame his shock and led his feet across the cell to the chamber pot before his stomach emptied itself.

When there was nothing more for him to throw up, he continued to heave for some time, until at last he stopped, shaking and exhausted. He rinsed his mouth with water the guard had brought, making sure to leave enough for Master Wag when he awoke. He didn't know how the Master was going to drink it, but there was nothing he could do about that now. He moved it next to him, in any case, and checked the Master's breathing and felt his forehead.

Then he stood and gingerly made his way around the corpse. It was funny how a man's body could be so like and yet unlike that of a dead animal. He had butchered hogs and kethna, poultry and even a goat, but he'd never killed a man. He had no idea how many dead animals he had seen, but this was only the second time he'd looked closely at a dead man.

Yes, an animal that was dead often lay in much the same way it would as if resting, with none of its legs at odd angles, and even its head looking just like it should. And that was fine. But there ought to be something different about a dead man—there ought to be something about it that would announce to anyone looking that life, the soul, had departed from this shell. There should be, but there wasn't.

He tried not to look at it, but Paener's best kitchen knife—a knife Savn had handled a thousand times to cut fish and vegetables—caught his eye. He had a sudden image of Paener saying, "You left it in a man's body, Savn? And what am I going to trade for another knife? Do you know how much a knife like that costs in money? How could you be so careless?" Savn almost started giggling, but he knew that once he started he would never stop, so he took a deep breath and jumped past the corpse, then sagged against the wall.

Because it felt like the right thing to do, he shut the door, wondering what Master Wag would think upon waking up with a dead soldier instead of a living apprentice. He swallowed, and started down the corridor, but, before he knew it, he began to trot, and soon to run down the hallway he'd been dragged along only a few scant hours before. Was the man he'd killed the same one who'd helped to push him into the cell? He wasn't sure.

When he reached a place where a stairway went up while the hall sloped down, he stopped, licked his lips, and caught his breath. *Think, Savn. What now? Which way?*

Upwards meant escape, but upwards was also where His Lordship was, as well as the Jhereg. The hallway could lead to almost anywhere—anywhere except back out. There was no point in going on, and he couldn't go up. Neither could he return to his cell, because the corpse was still there, and he thought he'd go mad if he had to see it again.

I'm trying to reason it out, he thought. *What's the point?*

It isn't a reasonable situation, and I might as well admit that I don't have the courage to go back up and risk meeting His Lordship. And they're going to find the body. And they'll kill me, probably in some horrible way. He thought about taking his own life, but the kitchen knife was still in the dead man's body.

Then he remembered the caves.

Yes. The caves that Vlad had said must lead into the manor. If so, where in the manor would they be? Down. They could only be down.

There was no way to go but down the sloping hall, then—perhaps, if he didn't find a way to the caves, he'd find a place to hide, at least for a while, at least until he could think.

Savn realized that he had been standing in darkness for some few minutes. He tried to reconstruct his path, and vaguely remembered going down a long stairway to a door at the bottom, finding it open, walking through it, and, as the door closed behind him, finding there was no light.

He had never before been in darkness so complete, and he wondered why he wasn't panicking—it was more fascinating than frightening, and, oddly enough, peaceful. He wanted to sit right where he was and just rest.

But he couldn't. He had to be doing something, although he had no idea what. They would be searching for Vlad, and if they found him, he would have no choice but to risk teleporting, and he had said himself he might not— He remembered fragments of conversation.

Unlikely, I've put a block up.

Around three square miles of caves?

Yes.

And—

As long as they don't put a teleport block up over the entire area . . .

Understanding seeped into Savn's brain. The one chance Vlad had of escaping was gone, and he was in no condition to fight. Oh, certainly his jhereg would fight for him, but what could they do against all of His Lordship's men?

And, if Vlad had told the truth about the assassin, which now seemed likely, then that assassin was carrying a Morganti weapon.

If only he could reach Vlad. But even if he could, what could he tell him?

The way out, of course.

Suddenly, it was just as it had been when he'd been healing the Easterner. There *was* a solution; there *had* to be a way. If only—

Witchcraft? Speaking to Vlad mind to mind?

But, no, Vlad had that amulet he wore, which prevented such things.

On the other hand, there was the chance that . . .

It was a very ugly thought, and Savn didn't know if he was more afraid of failure or success, but it was the only chance Vlad was going to have.

Savn sat down where he was, lost in the darkness, and took a deep breath. At first he did nothing else, just sat there thinking about breathing, and letting the tension flow out of his body. His mind didn't want to cooperate—it kept showing him what would happen if he failed, or if he was too late. But he looked at each scene of death or torment, viewed it carefully, and set it aside, and as he did so, he told himself to relax, just as Vlad had taught him, starting at the top of his head, and working down.

It took longer than it should have, but he knew when he was there—floating apart from the world, able to move at will, everywhere and nowhere.

He imagined the cave, imagined the Easterner lying there, his eyes closed, the two jhereg around him, unaware of what was happening. Or maybe Vlad was awake, but unable to do anything about it.

He got a picture of the larger of the two jhereg, and concentrated on it, trying to talk. Did it understand? How could he communicate to such a beast; how would he know if he was succeeding?

He tried to imagine what its mind might feel like, but couldn't conceive of it. He imagined it, and imagined himself, calling to it, and imagined it answering him, but as far as he could tell, nothing happened. In desperation, he shouted his message to it, but it was as if he shouted to the air.

After some time—he didn't know how much—he came to himself, feeling shaky and exhausted. He opened his eyes, but was still in darkness, and now the darkness began to terrify him. He forced himself to stand slowly, and reached out with his hands. But wait, which way had he come in? He had sat down without turning, so he should turn now. He did so, reached out again, and again felt nothing.

Don't panic. Don't panic. It can't be far.

He tried taking a step, didn't run into anything, and reached out once more. Still nothing. He risked one more step, and this time he felt the cool, damp stone of a wall. He wanted to kiss it.

He slid forward until he was practically hugging the wall, and reached out in both directions, and so found the door. Now the darkness was becoming even more threatening, so it was with great relief he found that the door opened easily on its leather hinges. Very little light came through it, and as he stuck his head out, he saw that what there was came from a single lantern placed at the top of the stairs. He wondered how often these lanterns were checked, and who filled them, and how long it would be before someone missed it, and, for that matter, how much more kerosene it contained.

But there was no time for that. He went back up the stairs, fetched the lantern down, and went through the door once more. The room turned out to be big, and, except for several wooden tables, empty. He looked at the floor, and was unsurprised to find the remains of faint markings on it—this had been one of the places His Lordship had been accustomed to practice his wizardous work. But, while he didn't know exactly what he was looking for, he knew that wasn't it.

One wall, the one furthest from the door, looked odd. He crossed over to it, being careful to walk around the markings on the floor, and held up the lamp. There were

several—four, in fact—odd, door-like depressions in the
wall, each one about ten feet high and perhaps five feet
wide at the bottom, curving at the top. And carved into the
floor in front of each was a small, straight gutter that ran
the length of the room and ended, as he followed them, in
what looked to be a dry, shallow well.

He returned to the far wall and looked at the doors
again. They looked almost like—

Almost like tunnels.

Or waterways.

Yes, there they were, just where they ought to be. He
stared at them until the lamp flickered, which broke his
reverie and reminded him that if he was going to do something, now would be a good time. He looked around the
room, hoping to see some tool with which to open the
gates, but the room was empty. He remembered Vlad saying something about traps and alarms, but there was no
point in worrying about setting those off if he couldn't figure out a way to get the waterways open in the first place.

He approached one, and struck it with the side of his
fist, and it did, indeed, sound hollow. He studied the wall
around it, the floor below it, the ceiling above it.

And there it was, a chain, hanging down from the ceiling, as if there were a sign on it saying, "Pull me." And,
in case it wasn't obvious enough, there were three more,
one in front of each door. Well, on reflection, why should
His Lordship have made it difficult for himself in his own
work area?

So, Savn asked himself, *what now?* If he pulled the
chain, the waterway would open, and all sorts of alarms
would go off, and, no doubt, His Lordship would appear
as fast as he could teleport. Then what? Could Savn escape, maybe swimming underwater for all he knew, before
His Lordship caught him?

Not a chance.

He thought about trying once more to reach one of the
jhereg, but at that moment he was startled almost out of
his wits by a soft *tap tap* that came from somewhere he
couldn't place.

He looked around, wildly, and it came again.

Could he have reached the jhereg after all?

Tap tap . . . tap tap.

He followed the sound, and discovered that, without doubt, it came from behind one of the waterways.

He hesitated no more. He stood in front of it, straddling the small gutter, then reached up and took the chain. It felt grimy with old rust, but he was able to get a good grip. He pulled.

At first it didn't move, as if rusted from long disuse, but he put his whole weight on it, and all of a sudden it gave.

In the dim light of the lantern, it looked for a moment as if the wall was moving backward, but then the reality of it became clear. The door in front of him creaked open noisily and admitted a small stream of water; a pair of jhereg; Polyi, dripping wet and looking frightened; and one very wet, very pale, very shaken-looking Easterner who stumbled forward and collapsed onto the floor at Savn's feet.

At that moment, as if Vlad's weight were enough to shake the entire manor, the floor began to vibrate. Savn looked around, but, for a moment, nothing happened. And then there was the sudden pop of displaced air, and Savn was looking at His Lordship and the Jhereg assassin, standing not ten feet away from him. His Lordship seemed very tall, with his hands out in front of him as if to touch the air, while the Jhereg crouched on the balls of his feet, holding a long, gleaming knife before him.

And there was a feeling Savn had never had, but could not possibly mistake for anything else: the knife in the Jhereg's hand was certainly Morganti.

Chapter Seventeen

I'm gonna marry me a bandit,
I'm gonna marry me a bandit,
Rich and free is how I've planned it.
Hi-dee hi-dee ho-la!
　　　Step on out . . .

SAVN GRABBED POLYI with his free hand and pulled her back against the wall. Vlad remained where he was, on his hands and knees, looking up at His Lordship and the Jhereg assassin, who stood about ten feet away, motionless. The pair of jhereg took positions on either side of Vlad, and everyone waited.

Then Vlad slowly rose to his feet. He seemed to have some trouble standing, but managed. The jhereg flew up to land on either shoulder. Savn noticed that Vlad held a flask in his right hand.

"Careful," said His Lordship. "He's probably not hurt as badly as—"

"Shut up," said the Jhereg.

"Tsk," said Vlad. "No squabbling, now. It's unseemly. I have something for you, Loraan." He started forward, and there was a flash. Polyi screamed, but the knife didn't strike Vlad; it struck the flask in his hand.

Vlad chuckled and dropped it. "Well, it was a good idea. Nice throw, Ishtvan."

"Thanks, Taltos," said the assassin. "I try to keep my hand in."

"I know," said Vlad. "That's why I hired you."

His Lordship said, "Keep your mouth shut, East—"

"You're right," said the Jhereg. "Pardon us." Then he turned to His Lordship and said, "Immobilize him, and let's get this over with."

There was a tinkling sound from around Vlad's knees, and Savn noticed that Vlad now held in his left hand something that looked like a length of gold chain. His Lordship evidently saw it too, because he cried, "That's mine!"

"Yes," said Vlad. "Come and take it." But his strength wasn't the equal of his words; even as he spoke, his knees seemed to buckle and he stumbled forward. His Lordship took a step toward him and lifted his hands.

Without thinking about it, Savn ripped the top off the lantern and splashed the burning kerosene against the wall behind him. The room became very bright for a moment, then was plunged into total darkness.

Polyi screeched. Savn pulled her away, thinking that no matter what happened, they ought to be somewhere other than where they'd been standing when he put out the light. He took a few steps, found that he was standing in running water, and decided that was just as well with kerosene splashed everywhere. "Are you all right?" he asked in a whisper that sounded much too loud.

"You burned me," she whispered back.

"Sorry."

Why didn't someone make a light? Whole seconds had passed since he'd plunged the room into darkness; you'd think someone would want to see what was going on. And no one was moving, either.

Well, that might not be true; Vlad might still be able to move silently, and the Jhereg almost certainly could. And His Lordship was a sorcerer; for all Savn knew, there was a spell that would allow him to move silently. So maybe they were all moving all over the place, with Savn and Polyi the only ones fooled.

He thought about screaming, but was afraid it would up-set his sister.

He heard a very faint *whsk whsk* that had to be the sound of jhereg wings. Shortly thereafter there was a very, very bright flash, but it showed him nothing; it only hurt his eyes and left blue spots in them. Polyi clung to him tightly; she was trembling, or he was, or maybe they both were—he couldn't tell.

He heard the flapping again, this time closer—he flinched even though he knew what it was. There was more movement, and another flash. This one wasn't as bright and lasted longer; he caught a quick glimpse of the Jhereg, crouched over holding the dagger out in front of him, and Vlad, on his feet once more, leaning against a wall, his sword in one hand, the gold chain swinging steadily in the other.

The flapping came again, even closer, and it seemed the jhereg hovered for a moment next to Savn's ear. He held his breath, half expecting what would come next, and it did—there was a touch on his shoulder, and then a gentle weight settled there. Savn, who had been standing motion-less,.froze—a difference hard to define but impossible to miss. Water soaked through his boots, but he was afraid to move.

"Savn? What happened?"

"Hush, Polyi."

Why had it landed on his shoulder? There must be a reason. Did it want him to do something? What? What could he do? He could panic—in fact, it was hard not to. What else could he do? He could get himself and Polyi out of there, if he had a light. Was the jhereg trying to tell him something?

He felt its head against his neck; then suddenly it jumped down to his right hand, which still held the empty lantern. He almost dropped it, but held on, and the jhereg hopped back up to his shoulder.

How had Vlad known to escape the searchers by enter-ing the manor house through the cave? Was it desperation and lack of any other way, or had he, Savn, actually man-aged to get through to Vlad? If he had, then . . .

He tried to recapture the feeling he'd had before, of

emptiness, of reaching out. He discovered that standing frozen in place with unknown but murderous actions going on all around was not conducive to the frame of mind he associated with witchcraft.

He had just reached this conclusion when Vlad began speaking. "I have to thank you for the loan of your device, Loraan. It's proven useful over the years. Have you missed it?"

"Don't speak," said the Jhereg. "He's trying to distract you. Ignore him."

"He's right," said Vlad. "Ignore me. But, just for something to think about, consider that your partner has a Morganti weapon, one of the few things that can destroy you, and consider that he's an assassin, and that assassins are very uncomfortable leaving witnesses alive. Any witnesses. Think about it. How have you two been getting along, by the way? Just curious—you don't have to answer."

Savn heard a chuckle from the vicinity of the Jhereg. "Give it up, Taltos. We have a deal."

"I'm certain he knows what a deal with you is worth."

"What's your game, Taltos?"

"Use your imagination, assassin."

Polyi whispered, "Savn, when he said witnesses, could that mean us?"

Savn swallowed. He hadn't thought of that.

If he had light, he'd be able to sneak out through the manor house, or maybe even the caves. Putting out the light, it seemed, hadn't helped anyone.

The jhereg bumped Savn's neck with its head again, and, once more, landed on the hand that held the lantern. It stayed there for a moment, flapping its wings for balance, then returned to Savn's shoulder.

It was, without doubt, trying to tell him something—something about the lantern, maybe. That he should light it? If so, it was too late, the oil was gone, although perhaps that was too complex an idea for a jhereg.

He started to say, "Are you trying to tell me something?" but stopped himself, realizing that it could be very dangerous to speak aloud. The jhereg bumped his neck again, as if in answer to his unspoken question.

He formed the sentence, "Was that an answer?" but didn't speak it.

Bump. At the same time, he imagined he heard a very tiny voice, located somewhere inside the very base of his head, voicelessly saying, *"Yes, idiot."*

"Who are you?" he thought back.

"Vlad, idiot," it told him.

"How can we be talking like this?"

"I've removed the amulet, and that's really what's important right now, isn't it?"

"Sorry. What should I do?"

"Take your sister and get out of here. Loiosh will guide you."

"I—"

"Damn it!"

"What?"

"Loiosh says he won't guide you. I'll—"

"It doesn't matter, Vlad. I want to help you."

"You've already helped me. From here on out—"

There was another bright flash of light. This time, Savn got a glimpse of His Lordship, both hands stretched out in front of him, just a few feet from the Jhereg.

"Almost got me, that time," said Vlad. *"Look, I can't hold them off much longer, and I'm finished anyway. Take your sister and—"*

"What's going on?"

"About as much sorcery as I've seen in one place at one time. They've got some sort of spell that keeps the jhereg from getting to them, and Loraan keeps shooting things at me, and the assassin is trying to maneuver into a position to nail me—the idiot thinks I'm faking or he'd just move in and have done with it—and Loraan's personal cutthroats are going to be here any minute. So, would you please—"

There was more scuffling, then Vlad said, *"That was close."*

Then he spoke aloud, "Careful, Loraan. You're getting too near our assassin friend. He's quick."

"Shut up," growled His Lordship.

"Oh, you're safe until he's gotten me, I'm sure. But you'd better think about what happens after that. Or have you? Maybe I've got it backwards. Maybe you're already planning to do him. I'm sorry I won't be around to watch it."

"It's not working, Easterner," said His Lordship. "Ishtvan, he's getting desperate. Maybe he really is hurt. Why don't you just finish him? I've got all the protections up; I don't think he can do anything about it."

"Yes," said Vlad. "Why don't you, Ishtvan? Finish me, then he'll finish you. Why don't you ask *him* to finish me? Afraid you will lose the wages, my lord? Of course not, because you've already been paid, and you know very well you're going to have to kill him any—"

There was still another flash, and Savn saw His Lordship, hands now raised high above his head. At the same time, Vlad gasped.

"Vlad, are you all right?"

"Barely."

"Isn't there something you can do?"

"I don't carry poison darts anymore, and I don't have the strength to throw a knife. You have any ideas?"

Another flash of light illuminated the scene. The assassin had moved around to Vlad's right, but was still keeping his distance. Vlad had moved a foot or so to his left, and was still swinging the gold chain. Loiosh gripped Savn's shoulder, and occasionally squeezed with his talons. Savn wished he knew what Loiosh was trying to tell him. It would almost be funny if some brilliant idea for escaping were locked up in that reptilian brain but the poor thing couldn't communicate it. But of course that couldn't be the case, or Loiosh would have told Vlad. Unless, perhaps, it was something Vlad wouldn't approve of. But what wouldn't Vlad approve of if it would get him out of this?

Well, Vlad apparently wouldn't approve of Savn doing

anything risky, whereas Loiosh probably wouldn't care.
But what could he, Savn, do, anyway? He could hardly attack an assassin, barehanded, in the dark. And to do anything to His Lordship was both impossible and
unthinkable.

*You're so convinced that your Baron Smallcliff is invin-
cible and perfect that you'd stand there and let him kill
you rather than raising a finger to defend yourself.*

Vlad had been right about that, just as he'd been right
about the assassin, and the Morganti weapon, and even
about His Lordship being . . .

He could imagine the jhereg saying, "You've finally figured it out, fool." Because he *had* figured it out, only now
he didn't know if he had the courage to do anything about
it.

*You're so convinced that your Baron Smallcliff is invin-
cible and perfect that you'd stand there and let him kill
you rather than raising a finger to defend yourself.*

It had rankled because it was true, and now, when he
thought he knew what he could do about it, it rankled even
more.

"Savn, don't," said Vlad. *"Just get out of here."*

Savn ignored him. He knelt down into the slowly flowing water and filled up the lamp.

"Savn!"

His sister whispered, "What are you doing?"

"Wait," he whispered back. "Don't move."

He stood up, and as best he could, walked quickly and
firmly toward where he had last seen His Lordship, holding before him the lamp filled with Dark Water, stagnant
and contained. *When stagnant and contained, it can be
used to weaken and repel the undead. . . .*

His Lordship's voice came from directly in front of him.
"What are— Ishtvan! Kill this Teckla brat for me."

Savn felt his hand shaking, but he continued walking
forward.

The Jhereg answered, "I can't see anymore."

"Then make a light. Hurry! I can't do anything
while—"

"The Easterner—"

His Lordship made an obscene suggestion concerning
the Easterner, which Savn noticed indifferently as he continued to walk forward. He hardly blinked when a soft
light filled the room, and, oddly enough, it hardly mattered
that he could now see His Lordship, about five feet away,
walking slowly backward, and glaring.

Savn wondered, in a familiar, detached way, how he
could survive an attack by a Jhereg assassin. But the attack
didn't come, because at that instant, Loiosh left Savn's
shoulder.

Savn couldn't help it—he turned and watched as Loiosh
and his mate simultaneously attacked. Evidently, His Lordship's spells that had kept them away were now gone.
Ishtvan snarled and cut at the jhereg with the Morganti
dagger. He turned, and apparently realized, at the same
time as Savn did, that he was offering his back to Vlad,
and that he was within range of the Easterner's sword.

He tried to spin back, but it was already too late. It
made Savn wince to see Vlad, in his condition, execute a
maneuver so demanding, but the Easterner managed it—
the point of his sword penetrated deeply into the assassin's
back right over his heart. At the same time, Polyi was
shrieking—"Savn!" and Vlad continued forward, falling
limply onto his face as the assassin screamed and the
Morganti dagger went flying into the air—

—and the lamp was struck from Savn's hand to land
and shatter on the floor. He turned in time to see His Lordship recovering from delivering a kick that must have been
very difficult for him, judging by the look of concentration
and effort on his face, and Savn felt an impossible combi-
nation of pride and shame in having caused His Lordship
such distress. He wondered what His Lordship would do
now, but—

—he didn't know, because the assassin's light-spell
faded, and the room was suddenly pitched into darkness. It
seemed that proximity to the Dark Water had taken His
Lordship's magical powers, but hadn't actually hurt
him—he could still kick. Which meant he might also be

able to simply grab Savn and throttle him. Savn started to back away, but he was struck a blow that knocked him onto his back and caused him to crack his head sharply on the floor.

He decided he was glad he hadn't hit his head harder, when he realized that he *had* hit his head harder, that he was sick and dizzy and was almost certainly about to die, and, worst of all, he wasn't certain that he didn't deserve to.

It came to him that he had once again achieved the state of witchcraft, this time by the accident of bumping his head. He didn't have anything to do, but it was much more pleasant here, flying over walls, and cavorting in the air like a disembodied jhereg. There were terrible things happening to his body, and he had done terrible things himself, but they didn't matter anymore. He could—

There, before him, was His Lordship, grinning a terrible grin, his hand looming large, ready to smash him down as Savn would swat an insect.

I am not an insect, cried Savn in a voice no one could hear as, in helpless rage, he flew right into His Lordship's face, defying him, and waiting for his consciousness to end, for the sleep from which there is no waking.

He felt something break, but it didn't seem to matter, even though it was himself. He hoped somehow Vlad would survive, but he didn't see—

—he didn't see anything, because the room was dark, and his thoughts, all that remained, were becoming scattered, misty, and going away.

What he asked was impossible.

Not physically impossible; the evil thing spun and twirled right in front of her, and plucking it out of the air would be no problem at all, even in the total darkness. She could feel exactly where it was all along its path through the air. But it was still impossible. To touch such a thing was—

But her mate was insistent. Her lover was saying that if she didn't, the Provider would die. She didn't understand

*how this could be, or why it would be too late if she didn't
do it now, as the evil thing reached the top of its arc and
began to fall to the ground.*

*She didn't understand what it was, but she hated the
idea of coming near it more than she had ever hated anything in her life. Did he understand that—*

*And her mate told her that there was no more time, she
must get it now, because the undead soft one was going to
kill the Provider, and, even if he didn't, couldn't she hear
the footsteps of more of the soft ones coming? She should
trust him, he said—these were not friends.*

*And what was she supposed to do when she had it? she
wondered, but she nevertheless did as she was asked—she
took it from the air, wrapping her feet around the bone
part, trying to keep as far from the metal part as she could
and—*

Is that what she was supposed to do? How?

*The other soft one, the one the Provider had been
spending so much time with, the one who had saved him,
was somewhere near here, but she couldn't see him.*

*Her mate could feel him? Well enough to know where
his hand was? To direct her to . . . Oh, very well, then.*

*And so he guided her, and she went where he said, and,
at the right time, she let the evil thing fall into the hand
of the soft one who had saved the Provider—although it
seemed odd to her that someone who would do that would
have a use for such a thing. What would he do with it?*

*Although she couldn't see, she was able to tell what use
he had for it—he plunged it into the side of the other soft
one, the undead, who was on top of him, strangling the life
out of him.*

*The odd thing was that both of them screamed—first the
one who had been stabbed, then the one who did the stabbing, and they both screamed where she could hear it
more within her mind than in the room, and both screams
went on for a long time.*

*In fact, the one who was still alive didn't stop screaming
with his mind at all, even after he had stopped screaming*

with his voice. He kept screaming and screaming, even after the Provider managed to make a small amount of light appear, and to gather them all together, and to take them all far, far away from the place where the evil thing lay with the two bodies in the dark cavern.

EPILOGUE

THE MINSTREL SENT the Easterner a look containing equal portions of disgust and contempt. It didn't seem to bother him; he was used to such things. But he avoided looking at the girl who sat by the fire, holding her brother's hand. The two jhereg sat complacently on the Easterner's shoulders, not terribly bothered by anything now that—in their reptilian opinions—the crisis was past. They finished up the scraps of the roasted athyra.

"Well?" said Sara.

"I'm glad you made it here."

"Your jhereg are good guides," said Sara. "I had a pretty good idea what they wanted."

"I thought you might. Thanks for coming."

"You're welcome," she said. And repeated, "Well?"

"Well what? If you're asking after my health, breathing doesn't hurt as much as it did a couple of days ago."

"I'm not asking after your health, I'm asking after *his*."

Vlad apparently didn't need to follow her glance to know of whom she was speaking—Savn sat staring into the fire, oblivious of the conversation, and of everything else going on around him.

"His health is fine. But, as you can see—"

"Yes. As I can see."

"I suppose I'm being hunted as a kidnapper."

"Among other things, yes. The village Speaker has appealed to the Empire, and he's been ranting about gathering the entire region to hunt for you tree by tree and stone by stone. And their parents are in agony, wondering where they are, imagining you've killed them or used them for some Eastern ritual or something. I don't know why I don't summon—"

"Summon who? The Jhereg? That's been tried."

"Yes, I suppose it has. They found the body next to His Lordship's. And they found the village physicker there, too."

"Wag? Really? Was he dead?"

"No, barely alive. Did you do that to him?"

"Do what?"

She searched his eyes, trying to see if he was lying. Then she shrugged. "He'd been tortured."

"Oh. No, I imagine that Loraan and the assassin did that. It makes sense, at any rate; that's probably how they found me."

"Well, he's going to live. He says Savn physicked him. The child will be a good physicker, if he ever comes out of it."

"Yes. If."

Polyi glared at him. Sara guessed that there hadn't been much small talk between Vlad and the girl in the two days since the death of Baron Smallcliff.

Sara said, "So Loraan and the Jhereg found you. How did you beat them?"

"I didn't. He did."

Sara's eyes turned to the Teckla boy, and widened. "*He* did?"

"Yes. He nullified Loraan's magic, helped distract the assassin, and, in the end, killed Loraan."

"I don't believe you."

"I couldn't care less."

Sara chewed her lip. "Exactly what happened to him, anyway?"

"I don't know for certain. My guess is that the shock of even holding, much less using, a Morganti dagger was pretty severe, and I think he hit his head and was dazed before that happened, and then he killed his own lord. He woke up after I teleported us out of there, stared at his hand, bit it, screamed, and hasn't said a word since."

"Oh," said the minstrel.

"He'll do what he's told, and he'll eat, and he keeps himself clean."

"And that's all."

"Yes."

"What are you going to do?"

"I'm going to keep moving. It would be a shame to let the townsfolk kill me after escaping Loraan and the Jhereg."

"And you want me to see to it the boy and his sister are returned home?"

"No, only the sister."

"What do you mean?"

"Think about it. The boy was seen with me, his friends tried to beat him up, and everyone's going to figure out that he at least helped kill His Lordship, who was a pretty well-liked bastard, for an undead. What sort of life is the kid going to have around here?"

"What are you talking about?"

"I'm talking about the fact that he saved my life, several times, and his only reward was being given such a shock that he has gone mad."

"What can you do about it?"

"I can try to cure him, and keep him safe in the meantime."

"You're going to wander around, running from the Jhereg, and keep a child with you?"

"Yes. At least until he's cured. After that, I don't think he'll be a child anymore, and he can make up his own mind."

"What makes you think he won't hate you?"

"He probably will."

"What makes you think you can cure him?"

Vlad shrugged. "I have some ideas. I'll try them. And I know people, if I get desperate."

"So you're going to take him away from his family—"

"That's right. Until he's cured. Then it's up to him."

Sara stared at him for a long moment, then burst out, "You're crazy!"

"No, just in debt. And intending to discharge the debt."

"I—"

"You can take the girl back to her family, and explain what I'm doing."

"They'll never let you do this. They'll hunt you down and kill you."

"How? I've avoided the Jhereg for more than two years, I can certainly avoid a few peasants long enough to see the boy cured."

Sara turned and looked at Savn, who continued to stare into the fire, and Polyi, who looked at her brother with red eyes. Sara said, "Polyi, what do you think of all this?"

"I don't know," she said in a small voice. "But he did this to Savn, so he ought to cure him, and then bring him back."

"That's my opinion," said Vlad.

"Don't you realize," said Sara slowly, "that traveling with the boy is going to make you ten times—a *hundred* times as easy a target for the Jhereg?"

"Yes."

"Work fast," said Sara.

"I intend to," said Vlad.

"Do you even have supplies for the journey?"

"I have gold, and I can teleport, and I can steal."

Sara shook her head.

Vlad stood up and reached a hand out. "Savn, come on."

The boy obediently stood, and Sara glanced at his eyes; they seemed empty. "Can you really heal his mind?" she asked.

"One way or another," said Vlad. "I will."

Polyi stood and hugged her brother, who seemed not to notice. She stepped back, gave Vlad a look impossible to describe, went over to Sara, and nodded.

"I don't know what to tell you, Easterner," said Sara.

"You could wish me luck."

"Yes. Good luck."

"Thanks."

He took the boy's arm, and led him off into the woods, walking slowly as if his wounds still bothered him. Sara put her arm around the girl, who didn't resist, and they watched the Easterner, the human, and the two jhereg until they disappeared. "Good luck," Sara repeated softly to their backs.

Then she turned to the girl and took her hand. "Come on," she said. "Let's get you home. Your Harvest Festival is beginning, and the gods alone know what sort of animals live out here."

The girl said nothing, but held onto Sara's hand, tightly.

STEVEN BRUST

__*ATHYRA*__   0-441-03342-3/$5.50

Vlad Taltos has a talent for killing people. But lately, his heart just hasn't been in his work. So he retires. Unfortunately, the House of the Jhereg still has a score to settle with Vlad. So much for peaceful retirement.

__*PHOENIX*__   0-441-66225-0/$4.99

Strangely, the Demon Goddess comes to assassin Vlad Taltos's rescue, answering his most heartfelt prayer. But when a patron deity saves your skin, it's always in your best interest to do whatever she wants . . .

__*JHEREG*__   0-441-38554-0/$4.99

There are many ways for a young man with quick wits and a quick sword to advance in the world. Vlad Taltos chose the route of the assassin and the constant companionship of a young jhereg.

__*YENDI*__   0-441-94460-4/$4.99

Vlad Taltos and his jhereg companion learn how the love of a good woman can turn a cold-blooded killer into a <u>real</u> mean S.O.B....

__*TECKLA*__   0-441-79977-9/$4.99

The Teckla were revolting. Vlad Taltos always knew they were lazy, stupid, cowardly peasants...revolting. But now they were revolting against the empire. No joke.

__*TALTOS*__   0-441-18200/$4.99

Journey to the land of the dead. All expenses paid! Not Vlad Taltos's idea of an ideal vacation, but this was work. Even an assassin has to earn a living.

__*COWBOY FENG'S SPACE BAR AND GRILLE*__

__*0-441-11816-X/$3.95*__

Cowboy Feng's is a great place to visit, but it tends to move around a bit— from Earth to the Moon to Mars to another solar system—always just one step ahead of the mysterious conspiracy reducing whole worlds to ash.

Payable in U.S. funds. No cash orders accepted. Postage & handling: $1.75 for one book, 75¢ for each additional. Maximum postage $5.50. Prices, postage and handling charges may change without notice. Visa, Amex, MasterCard call 1-800-788-6262, ext. 1, refer to ad # 315

Or, check above books and send this order form to: The Berkley Publishing Group 390 Murray Hill Pkwy., Dept. B East Rutherford, NJ 07073	Bill my: ☐ Visa ☐ MasterCard ☐ Amex _____ (expires) Card#_____ ($15 minimum) Signature_____
Please allow 6 weeks for delivery.	Or enclosed is my: ☐ check ☐ money order
Name_____	Book Total $_____
Address_____	Postage & Handling $_____
City_____	Applicable Sales Tax $_____ (NY, NJ, PA, CA, GST Can.)
State/ZIP_____	Total Amount Due $_____

Somewhere beyond the stars, the age of dinosaurs never ended...

ROBERT J. SAWYER

"He's already being compared to Heinlein, Clarke, and Pohl."–Quill and Quire

"Thoughtful and compelling!"–Library Journal

__FAR-SEER   0-441-22551-9/$4.99

Young Afsan the saurian is privileged, called to the distant Capital City to apprentice with Saleed the court astrologer. But Afsan's knowledge of his dinosaur nation's heavens will test his faith...and also may save his world from disaster.

__FOSSIL HUNTER
0-441-24884-5/$4.99

Toroca, son of Afsan the Far-Seer, is a geologist searching for the rare metals needed to take his species to the stars. But what he's discovered instead is an artifact that may reveal at last the true origin of a world of dinosaurs.

__FOREIGNER   0-441-00017-7/$4.99

A new age of discovery is being ushered into the saurian world. Novato, mate of Afsan, is mastering the technology of space travel, while Afsan, to overcome his blindness, is seeking the help of a new kind of doctor–one whose treatment does not center on the body...but the mind.

Payable in U.S. funds. No cash orders accepted. Postage & handling: $1.75 for one book, 75¢ for each additional. Maximum postage $5.50. Prices, postage and handling charges may change without notice. Visa, Amex, MasterCard call 1-800-788-6262, ext. 1, refer to ad # 483

Or, check above books and send this order form to: The Berkley Publishing Group 390 Murray Hill Pkwy., Dept. B East Rutherford, NJ 07073	Bill my: ☐ Visa ☐ MasterCard ☐ Amex (expires) Card#_____ ($15 minimum) Signature_____
Please allow 6 weeks for delivery.	Or enclosed is my: ☐ check ☐ money order
Name_____	Book Total $_____
Address_____	Postage & Handling $_____
City_____	Applicable Sales Tax $_____ (NY, NJ, PA, CA, GST Can.)
State/ZIP_____	Total Amount Due $_____

NEW YORK TIMES BESTSELLING AUTHOR

⎯⎯ ANNE McCAFFREY ⎯⎯

__LYON'S PRIDE   0-441-00141-6/$5.99
The children of Damia and Afra Lyon stand ready to face their
most difficult challenge yet against a relentless alien race that is
destroying life on entire planets.

__THE ROWAN   0-441-73576-2/$5.99
"A reason for rejoicing!" —WASHINGTON TIMES
As a little girl, the Rowan was one of the strongest Talents ever
born. When she lost her family, her power alone could not bring
her happiness. But things change when she hears strange
telepathic messages from an unknown Talent named Jeff
Raven.

__DAMIA   0-441-13556-0/$5.99
Damia, the most brilliant and powerful of the Rowan's children,
is stung by a vision of an impending disaster of such magnitude
that even the Rowan can't prevent it. Now, Damia must
somehow use her powers to save a planet under siege.

__DAMIA'S CHILDREN 0-441-00007-X/$5.99
They inherited remarkable powers of telepathy, and their
combined abilities are even greater than those of their legendary
mother. And Damia's children will learn just how powerful they
are when faced with another attack by the mysterious enemy
that Damia drove away... but did not destroy.

Payable in U.S. funds. No cash orders accepted. Postage & handling: $1.75 for one book, 75¢
for each additional. Maximum postage $5.50. Prices, postage and handling charges may
change without notice. Visa, Amex, MasterCard call 1-800-788-6262, ext. 1, refer to ad # 363

Or, check above books Bill my: ☐ Visa ☐ MasterCard ☐ Amex	
and send this order form to:	(expires)
The Berkley Publishing Group Card#_____	
390 Murray Hill Pkwy., Dept. B	($15 minimum)
East Rutherford, NJ 07073 Signature_____	
Please allow 6 weeks for delivery. Or enclosed is my: ☐ check ☐ money order	
Name_____	Book Total $_____
Address_____	Postage & Handling $_____
City_____	Applicable Sales Tax $_____
	(NY, NJ, PA, CA, GST Can.)
State/ZIP_____	Total Amount Due $_____